ALL THAT FOLLOWED

ALL THAT FOLLOWED

A NOVEL

WITHDRAWN

GABRIEL URZA

HENRY HOLT AND COMPANY
NEW YORK

Henry Holt and Company, LLC
Publishers since 1866
175 Fifth Avenue
New York, New York 10010
www.henryholt.com

Henry Holt® and 🏛® are registered trademarks of Henry Holt and Company, LLC.

Library of Congress Cataloging-in-Publication Data

Urza, Gabriel.
  All that followed : a novel / Gabriel Urza.
     pages cm
  ISBN 978-1-62779-243-1 (hardback)—ISBN 978-1-62779-244-8 (electronic book)
  1. Basques—Spain—Fiction. 2. Murder—Investigation—Fiction. I. Title.
  PS3621.R93A55 2015
  813'.6—dc23   2014041150

Henry Holt books are available for special promotions and premiums.
For details contact: Director, Special Markets.

First Edition 2015

Designed by Meryl Sussman Levavi

Printed in the United States of America

10 9 8 7 6 5 4 3 2

This is a work of fiction. All of the characters, organizations, and events portrayed
in this novel either are products of the author's imagination or are used fictitiously.

For my family

Gezurra esan nuen etxean; ni baino lehenago kalean.

I told a lie at home and it was in the street before me.

—BASQUE PROVERB

ALL THAT FOLLOWED

I. JONI

THIS MORNING THE FRONT PAGE OF THE *DIARIO VASCO*— for once—shares the same headline as the other Spanish newspapers. Sabino Garamendi's newsstand is wallpapered with photographs of the Atocha train station in Madrid, each cover depicting train carriages that had burst from the inside as if they were overshaken cans of soda, the aluminum paneling peeled back, revealing their contents: strips of dark fabric, handfuls of foam cushioning, bits of bone, women's shoes, the pages of a child's notebook. It is the twelfth day of March 2004.

I slide money across the counter to Sabino and fold the *Diario* under my arm before crossing the street to the Boliña. Estefana is just inside the kitchen at the end of the bar, a deep-burgundy skirt beneath her stained white apron, and the briny smell of anchovies cooking in a heavy frying pan fills the room. I knock on the wooden bar; when she looks up I give a small wave to let her know that I have arrived and am ready for coffee, and then I return to the patio outside the bar.

On television last night it was reported by every national news station that although Prime Minister Aznar, as well as the king himself, had refused to directly implicate the group responsible for the attacks, all available evidence pointed to the Basque separatist group Euskadi Ta Askatasuna, the ETA. And though the residents of Muriga collectively denied this suggestion, spat on the sawdust-covered floors of the bars each time a news anchor used the word "separatist," there was also an underlying air of shared guilt, of collusion in the bombings that had left, as of last night, 191 victims dead. People lingered quietly in the bars, whole families with their children sitting at long, stout oak tables around half-empty bottles of red wine, Coke cans filled with cigarette filters, uneaten plates of potato omelet or grilled prawns. I had lingered a bit.

The Fernandez de Larrea family sent their youngest over to invite me, the old American, to a table crowded with small plates of food, and when the parents of the youngest children began to filter out I joined the old men lined up against the wooden bar. It's in these moments of acute community that the delusions I live by—that I am a part of this town, that I have earned my way into the life of Muriga and its people—are quickly and easily unraveled.

By eleven last night, early for Muriga, most of the bars in the old part had emptied. Santi Etxeberria refused my offer of a second glass of *patxaran*, but I agreed when he asked if I'd like to join him on the walk up the Ubera River. The evenings were still cool, and a fine mist began before we had reached the cathedral.

"*Txirimiri*," Santi said forlornly. It's a word used to describe a type of rain that they say exists only here in the foothills of the Pyrenees. A rain so fine that an umbrella is useless against it, wisps of water blowing under the umbrella's cuff to cling to the rough whiskers of your cheeks at the end of the day. It's a poetic word, one of the first words of Basque I learned, and hearing it never ceases to conjure the image of the woman who explained its meaning my first week in Muriga, more than fifty years ago.

The woman and I had been leaning against the stone wall of San Telmo Cathedral—the same cathedral that Santi and I now passed.

"*Txi . . . rri . . . mi . . . rri*," she had said. The knees of my slacks darkened from the rain as she deconstructed the word, laying out its component parts for me to examine. "*Txi . . . rri . . . mi . . . rri.* Now you."

It had felt small and thin in my clumsy American mouth. I was accustomed to deep, round sounds, not these diminutive *tsk*'s against the front teeth. I'd expected her to laugh, but instead she took my hand up in hers. Her fingers were cold and thin and they vibrated lightly around mine.

"*Txirimiri,*" she repeated slowly, holding my palm up to her mouth so that I could feel how little air came out. She leaned off the wall of the cathedral, closer to me so that now our knees were touching, and she said again the word, that wonderful word. "*Tsk . . . tsk . . . txirimiri.*"

"PRIMARY INVESTIGATION POINTS TO ETA," the front page now announces as I unfold my paper against a patio table at the Boliña. It's still early spring, and it's unusual to be able to enjoy a morning coffee outside like this. And yet the last two days have brought a warm current up from the Canary Islands that has pushed back against the arctic current. I roll up the sleeves of my sweater, wipe my hands over constellations of sun spots spread across my pale forearms.

I read the first few lines of the cover article, then turn to the sports section on the second-to-last page of the paper before placing it back down on the table. What can such an article convey, really? How many words are needed to announce an inexplicably horrible thing, to tell us that there will be no recovery from this? But Muriga has experience with these acts that erode the soul of a people.

The bombing of Atocha, inevitably, has torn the stitches from a wound nearly six years healed, and this morning's stillness is evidence of the effort required to convince ourselves that our lives are still intact after the death of José Antonio Torres. I watch Mariana, his widow, crossing Zabaleta holding their daughter, Elena, by the wrist. The girl is now eight years old, nearly nine. She has her mother's features but the large, startlingly blue eyes of José Antonio. Behind her, Martín mops the walk in front of his small grocery at the corner of Atxiaga and Zabaleta, stopping after every few passes to pull from a cigarette pinched between two fingers. A pair of boys I recognize from Colegio San Jorge speed along Calle Zabaleta on their motor scooter, their light-blue oxfords untucked, flicking behind them. They are seventeen or eighteen, the same age Iker was the year that he was arrested for José Antonio's abduction and murder.

As Mariana approaches, I glance back into the bar to where Estefana shuffles across the worn stone floor, the cup of espresso and milk in her hand resting on a thin brown saucer. She brings me this same cup of coffee nearly every morning, and yet today I am surprised by the sight of her—this sturdy, strong woman. For the first time, I notice the ribbons of white that have wound their way through the thick black brambles of her hair. I hear the scrape of her right shoe, which doesn't rise quite as high as the left, as it drags across the stone. *She's become an old woman*, I think, and as if on cue, the dragging right foot catches momentarily on the threshold of the door, and the white cup slides from the saucer with a scraping sound, a sound not unlike the diminutive first syllable of *txirimiri*. There is silence, and then the cup explodes in a crest of ceramic shards and deep-brown coffee.

Estefana curses loudly, waves the back of her hand dismissively at the nearly unbroken sky above her, and turns back to the bar to begin another coffee. Mariana and Elena are just at the end of the block now, and both mother and daughter turn in my direction at the sound of the shattering cup. There is a moment, a fraction of a second, in which recognition outweighs history—when Mariana sees only an old friend, before anger and disgust take over and she pulls the girl in the other direction, back across Zabaleta.

When they've turned the corner, out of sight, I watch Estefana moving busily about the coffee machine. I study the splinters of enamel and the spreading puddle of coffee as it grows bigger on the patio's white tile. My mind drifts to the exploding trains at Atocha, and I begin to imagine time slowing to a pause, the black rush of smoke stopping its ascent from the train platform, then churning slowly backward. I imagine the heat of the explosion, the women's shoes, the bits of dark fabric, all flying back into the hull of the carriage, the peeled strips of aluminum being folded back around its passengers, ironed smooth again.

I allow time to continue flowing in reverse, the world to continue this process of reconstruction. The morning's unseasonably warm winds begin to reverse, to flow back toward the Canary Islands; the white streaks in Estefana's black mane retreat back into her scalp. Elena's spring jacket becomes unstitched, the small pieces of cloth are mended back into long bolts of fabric. The fabric is reconstituted into a row of cotton plants, and then into a handful of shrinking seeds, until finally the seeds are distilled into only sunlight.

I allow myself more. I imagine a bullet spinning back into the rifled barrel of a stolen pistol, a blue Peugeot lifting from an ocean cliffside back onto a ribbon of asphalt. I imagine the world undone back to a spring day six years in the past, when I had not yet been set upon by the ghost of José Antonio Torres.

2. MARIANA

WHEN I WAS A GIRL, MY GRANDMOTHER TOLD US THE STORY
of María de Aulesti, a witch tried in Muriga during the Inquisition in
1610. It's a ghost story that old women use to remind kids to go to
mass on Sundays or to say the Lord's Prayer before they climb
under the covers at night, a story that my own daughter, Elena,
learned not from me or from her grandmother as she should have
but instead from Celia Presona's daughter, who told her at school.

The way my grandmother would tell it, Aulesti, who everyone
called La Cerda—the hog—was born into a family that had secretly
practiced sorcery for generations. She was the unmarried daughter of a charcoal burner and was only twenty-three when the king's
inquisitor, Albert de Gálvez Cortázar, brought the formal charge of
witchcraft against her. He made several allegations: that La Cerda
had caused damage to a farmer's crops, that she had murdered
infants in their sleep by sucking the breath from their lungs, that
she could take the shape of dogs and cats and pigs. My grandmother
would pinch her gold pendant of the Virgin each time she told my
cousins and me about the *akelarres*—the witches' gatherings—where
La Cerda brought young girls to feast on roasted bodies dug up from
the churchyard near where the football fields are now. She described

the girls' nightly orgies with the Devil and La Cerda, consummated in a sulfurous yellow firelight.

When La Cerda had been tried and sentenced by de Gálvez she was given a last opportunity to confess and save her life, but she refused. At dawn, on the Thursday before the start of the Holy Week, the townspeople pulled La Cerda from her cell in the basement of the church. With de Gálvez presiding, they burned her to death in her father's charcoal ovens along the river. According to the story that the old women in Muriga tell, as they forced her into the small iron chamber of the furnace La Cerda began to vomit a black-and-green, evil-smelling liquid. This smell, this excretion finally offered proof to the town that she was, in fact, in league with the Devil. I always remember that phrase. Evil-smelling. *What did evil smell like*? I wondered.

MY FRIENDS and I grew up in Muriga with the ghost of La Cerda, who was said to come to children who were bad Christians or didn't obey their parents. And it worked for a while. Each time I ignored my prayers before bed, I would imagine La Cerda's smell, the smell of evil that her ghost carried with her, then rush out from under the covers to mouth the "Our Father." But as I grew older, I began to skip prayers. I smoked cigarettes and let boys put their hands under my clothes. I did these things and waited for La Cerda, but she never came.

It wasn't until my first year at the university in Bilbao, in a class on Basque anthropology, that I learned the real story of La Cerda. The professor, a feminist scholar from the University of Deusto, projected images of old Church documents onto a screen. The documents were frayed at the edges, written in an old, slanted script. One of the charges made against María de Aulesti was that she had tricked a local priest into her bedroom. The priest testified that she had poured a yellow powder down his throat while he slept, that the Devil had led him into her bedroom with a resin torch, where he was discovered by La Cerda's father in the middle of the night. The professor pointed out that the documents we were reading had been recorded several years after La Cerda's death. They were excerpts from an old court transcript, showing that the same priest who had accused the young woman of witchcraft had later made similar charges against two other girls in nearby villages. The final image was of an order bearing the seal of the archbishop, which excommunicated the priest in 1612 for "acts against the Church."

The professor had used the story of La Cerda to illustrate her own point about the subordinate position of women relative to the Church, but I'd always thought that it said something more. I wasn't interested in de Gálvez—had the professor really expected better from the Church? Instead, I became preoccupied with the execution itself. *It was the townspeople that had dragged La Cerda from the cell in the basement of the church*, I kept thinking. The people among whom she had grown up, who had known her her entire life. I imagined those familiar hands tearing at her clothes, scratching her skin, pulling at her hair. *How bizarre*, I thought, *that she must have known the women who locked the iron door, the man who set flame to the wood.*

"Sometimes I feel like a new version of La Cerda," I told my mother, a couple years after José Antonio's death.

"Why would you say something like that?" she asked, setting her glass abruptly down on the kitchen counter.

"Don't act as if you don't see it," I said. "The way conversation stops when we go to the Boliña, how people look at me at the Eroski when I'm buying milk and eggs with Elena. Even after two years."

"You can't think of it that way, my love," she said, scratching the back of my neck lightly. "Nobody thinks of you as La Cerda."

But still, once Elena had reminded me of the story I couldn't shake it. I remembered all the old tricks my grandmother had used to repel ghosts from her old *baserri* at the edge of town, up against the ash forest below the fortress at San Jorge. An ox tooth placed on either side of a doorway. Ashes made from fingernail clippings burned with sage and saffron, smudged around any window facing north and east.

"What is this?" Elena asked after school last week, holding up the ox tooth that I'd bought at a bazaar in Bermeo the week before.

"It's nothing," I said, taking the bleached white tooth from her hand.

"Why is it here?" she asked.

"It was your father's," I lied. "It's a good luck charm. I like to be reminded of him whenever we come home."

She nodded, watching me curiously.

I wonder how much she knows. If Celia Presona's daughter has told her the story of La Cerda, has she also told Elena the story of her own mother? Of her father, killed six years earlier?

I put the jagged white tooth back at the foot of the apartment door, then smoothed back Elena's hair behind her ear.

"Just leave it alone, love."

3. IKER

THE LETTERS BEGAN IN EARLY FEBRUARY.

I hope you don't mind, the Councilman's wife said at the close of the first letter. *My daughter started school today, and the apartment suddenly feels empty.*

"She's trying to punish you," my cell mate Andreas warned. He was working on a drawing for his sister, a view of the courtyard from the Salto del Negro's cafeteria. "She wants you to know that you've taken everything from her. She wants you not only to rot your life away in here but to feel guilty while you do it."

"No," I said. "I think I believe her."

"Fuck that," Andreas said, blowing carefully at an area of the paper that he'd finished shading.

✳ ✳ ✳

A FEW LETTERS LATER, she asked if the Councilman had begged for his life. If he knew he was going to die or if he thought, up until the very end, that he might escape from all of it.

It's not like that, I had written back. *It wasn't either one, really.*

It has to be one or the other, she said in the next letter, which arrived the day of the explosions in Madrid. *You're just not saying.*

No, I answered. *It doesn't have to be true. Just because you don't beg, this doesn't mean that you have a hope of surviving.*

You're just not saying, she said again. *You don't think I should be asking this question, or you think you have a duty to protect him.*

I waited a long time before responding to this last letter. I scratched the tip of my pen against the concrete walls of the prison for hours at a time, trying to decide if she was right or if in reality I was only interested in protecting myself.

4. JONI

"IT'S THE STRANGEST THING," MARIANA TOLD ME. IT WAS early September 1997, the year before the kidnapping and murder of José Antonio Torres. We were sitting on a white bench along the Paseo de los Robles, overlooking the Bay of Biscay. A late-summer wind swept along the walkway, carrying a bite that reminded you that cider season was nearly here. Mariana's two-year-old, Elena, knelt close to a cement planter box, prodding gently at the recoiling eye of a snail. "I calculated that I have been tying my shoelaces an average of three times a day for thirty-two years. Thirty-five thousand and forty times, always in the same manner: the squirrel runs around the tree, then through the hole and out the other side."

"I think we used a different method in California," I said. "I remember my mother teaching me the 'bunny ears' technique. A knot for the head, and then we add on the rabbit's ears."

"Yes!" she said. "The rabbit's ears! Suddenly, after the squirrel has run around the tree thirty-five thousand and forty times, I begin to use the rabbit ears. Can you explain it?"

"It's not so unusual, is it?" I asked, though it did strike me as odd. I'd known Mariana since she was a child, since before she left

Muriga in her early twenties for design school in Sevilla. She'd always been a little anxious, ruminative; she liked to pick her cuticles until they bled and had a strange habit of underlining sections of the *Diario Vasco* as if she were studying for an exam. But she had never been prone to melodrama. I picked up the small metal spoon from my saucer, placed it facedown against my tongue for the last taste of coffee and sweet cream.

"How are you feeling?" I asked, trying to steer her away. There was, after all, no satisfying answer here.

Mariana placed her hand reflexively at her side and looked over to where Elena now quietly played with a discarded bar napkin.

"Elena, *utzi hori*," she said sharply in Basque. The girl looked to her mother and dropped the napkin to the damp, moss-tinged tiles of the paseo. Mariana held her hand out to the girl, and when she had pulled Elena onto her lap she continued on in Spanish.

"Is it too early for ice cream?" I asked, loud enough for Elena to hear. The girl turned to me, nearly incredulous. Even then, there was a strange wrenching that Elena provoked in me each time the girl was near, a reminder of something I worked hard to tamp down. I smiled weakly at Mariana, shrugging.

"*Mesedez, Ama?*" Elena implored her mother in her voice that seemed improbably high, almost an imitation of a child's voice.

"Well, I can't say 'no' now, can I?" she said, pushing the girl gently from her lap. I reached a hand down and the girl took it, shyly, and let me guide her to the freezer next to the cashier.

When the girl and I returned from the bar, Elena with chocolate ice cream already dripping over the paper wrapper, Mariana was shaking her head, barely trying to hide a smile.

"How is the term, Joni?" she asked.

"They're bringing a new teacher to replace me. An American, Anselmo tells me."

"You're not leaving us, are you?"

By then I'd been living in the village for five decades, most of my life. I had known her father, Iñigo, when he was her age now. And yet her question reminded me that I would always be considered a foreigner here, a visitor passing through. Even Mariana took for granted that one day I'd pack up my apartment, that I would sell my old Volkswagen, walk Rimbaud over to a neighbor's house, and leave for California.

"No," I answered. "Of course not. But they think that I'm too old, that I'm from the past generation. They need a young American, they say. Goikoetxea tells me that the parents prefer their children to learn modern English, whatever that means."

Mariana shook her head and issued that light clucking sound of disapproval that Basque women employ to such great effect, but didn't say anything more. We'd spent a great deal of time together since Elena's birth, Mariana and I, and we were past consolations.

"So who is this American?" she asked. She was still staring at her feet, the bow formed by the two rabbit ears rather than the squirrel around the tree.

"He's a Basque, actually."

Mariana raised the arch of her dark eyebrows a touch, as if skeptical.

"Or at least he is of Basque descent. Anselmo says that his father is from Nabarniz."

"Nabarniz?" Mariana said, smiling. Muriga is a town of only twenty thousand, but its inhabitants never pass over a chance to disparage a town more provincial than itself.

"The usual story. The parents of the father worked the sheep ranches in Idaho for a hundred years, until they had put their children through college, and then both died the day after they retired. In forty years, the parents never returned to the Basque Country."

I used the phrase "Euskal Herria," the indigenous term for the Basque Country; in Muriga, it is virtually unheard of to use the Spanish term, *País Vasco*.

"In a way, then, your story is the usual Basque story, but in reverse, isn't it?"

I hadn't thought about my own life in these terms before. It was unsettling. I recalled the stories I had heard the older generation of Muriga tell, of young men who set off to work as sheepherders in the most remote areas of the American West: the Ruby Mountains of eastern Nevada, the high deserts of southern Idaho. There were the success stories, the boys from the village who would return five years later wearing audaciously cut suits purchased in San Francisco, their pockets jammed with five-thousand-peseta bills. But there were other stories, of young men who had gone mad out in the hills, who had been broken by the absolute solitude of the work. These men didn't return to the Basque Country. Instead, they were found destitute on the streets of Boise or Reno or slumped against the wheel of a camp wagon in the middle of the desert, a thirty-thirty draped across their legs.

"Yes," I said to Mariana after pausing to consider the comparison. "I suppose you could say that."

I remembered my final afternoon in California before taking the bus to the airport in San Francisco in the summer of 1948. It was four years, almost to the day, after my parents had received news of my brother's death, a brief typewritten letter signed by a colonel from the Pacific Theater. A high school basketball injury had kept me out of the war, and my father never let me forget it. He'd found a job for me with the Union Pacific, where he worked as a signalman, though it had seemed more like a punishment than a favor. But the work allowed time to study between shifts. I'd been good with language and became infatuated by Spanish culture after reading *For Whom the Bell Tolls* in my last year of high school. I graduated from Sacramento State a semester early with a degree in Spanish literature—an accomplishment that just drew another shake of my father's head—and had set aside enough of my salary to buy a one-way ticket to Madrid and still have money to travel for a few months before I'd need to find a job. I'd barely left the Central Valley, let alone the United States, but I was certain that the life I'd imagined for myself existed only in my hazy, romantic vision of Spain.

Mariana bounced the young girl on her knee and looked out onto the green expanse of the bay. Across the harbor, the first of the morning fishing boats were returning to the marina.

"You never answered my question earlier," I reminded her. "How are you feeling? You look stronger. What have the doctors told you?"

She lowered Elena down to the sidewalk and gave her a brief pat on the bottom, setting the girl tottering down the paseo.

"The truth, Joni?"

"Of course the truth."

Again, she placed her hand reflexively to her side. I pictured the incision hidden under her blouse. How it must angle down from her ribs against her thin stomach, the way the black stitching pulled her light-brown skin together into an angry line. I stopped myself there, not knowing how far my imagination might go.

I had asked a doctor friend of mine about the operation, and he said, not surprisingly, that any time an organ was transplanted it was a very serious thing. That for the rest of the patient's life there would be the risk of rejection; the body working against itself, always struggling to keep out the foreign object. But Mariana was young and fit, and the prognosis was good. The doctors had been surprised by how well the operation had gone and had, in fact, discharged her from the hospital a day early.

"The truth is that it's fine. I do feel stronger." But she said this without conviction or, rather, with a conviction that ran contrary to her words. I sat quietly, and we both watched Elena in the middle of the walkway, her short legs set apart in a sturdy stance. Nekane Basagoiti said "*Agur*" to us as she passed by pulling a wheeled tote filled with groceries from Martín's store. She stopped to pick up Elena and kiss her on the cheek before continuing on her way.

I knew that Mariana wanted to say more, so I waited. "But the truth, also, is that I don't feel fine. The stronger I feel, the more I think about the organ. It occurs to me, each time I can do something new, that it's only because another person died. Today I showered, and for the first time since the surgery, it didn't hurt. And do you know what I felt?"

I shook my head no.

"*Guilt.*" She stopped herself again, and then asked, "Do you know who the 'ideal donor' is, Joni?"

"No."

"A boy between the ages of twelve and fifteen who has been rendered brain-dead by a traumatic injury. Can you imagine? The 'ideal donor,' a thirteen-year-old boy."

I pictured the incision under her blouse again, and with it came images of a young boy stretched out on the clean white sheets of an operating table, a team of anonymous doctors working around him as if he were a field to be harvested.

"I look at Elena," she continued, "and I can't help but think that in another ten years she'll be nearly an ideal donor. I've become some sort of cannibal, Joni."

We sat together in silence, watching the girl as she stood alone on the paseo.

"Have you talked to José Antonio about this?" I finally said. It was a meaningless question, my way of saying, *I have nothing to offer here. This should be your husband's problem.*

"Not about this," she said. "He asks how I'm doing. He asks if I am feeling any of the side effects of the drugs. He examines the incision for infection, tells me that he has grown to like my new *hozka*, my new bite. But no, I haven't told him about this. About the boy."

"There isn't a boy. You know this, don't you?"

"Of course. But there *is* someone. Maybe it's an old man. Maybe it's a girl, like Elena. I can't pretend that there isn't someone."

"Does it matter, really?" I asked. "You act as if they've been killed just for your purposes. But these people were dead already. There's no connection between you and their death, is there?"

She ran her hand over the space of her stomach, as if she were pregnant. "And would it really not make a difference to you, Joni? Would it not matter?"

She asked this question with a genuine curiosity. It was as if she'd never considered the possibility, or as if she'd never considered that someone might think differently than she had. I couldn't bring myself to lie. "You should talk to José Antonio about this. He would understand, I think."

She shook her head, as if she finally understood I was incapable of helping her. I suppose she had thought of me as an old man who had gathered some amount of wisdom along the journey, and I'd disappointed her.

"No, it's fine," she said. "Besides, José Antonio is in Burgos three days out of the week, and when he is not in Burgos he's working at the Party headquarters. He used all his free days when he was at the hospital with me in Bilbao."

For a moment neither of us spoke. A late-morning breeze carried the first brown oak leaves across the walk, out onto the sand with a scraping sound so soft that it would be lost entirely if you didn't see the leaves creating the sound.

"Anyway, enough talk of kidneys," she said. "Sometimes I feel as if the word 'kidney' is the only one I use anymore." She laughed, and it was, strangely, the most untroubled laugh I had heard from her in a long while. "So, old man, when does your replacement arrive—this new American?"

"He has already arrived, I'm told. Goikoetxea himself is putting him and his wife up for a few days until they find a house."

Elena had returned to where we sat on the chipped white bench. Her small foot flopped loosely in her shoe, and Mariana bent down to retie the hanging laces. I watched the back of Mariana's head, the way her dark hair mingled with Elena's lighter-brown curls, the lightness she had inherited from José Antonio's family from the south.

"So," I said, "can I ask what technique you are using?"

"The rabbit and his ears, of course. Thirty-two years of the squirrel running around the tree, and now it is always the rabbit and his ears."

5. MARIANA

THIS IS WHAT HE SAID WHEN HE ACCEPTED THE JOB AS deputy campaign manager in Bilbao: that he'd always wanted to work in politics, and besides, it was better money than he could earn in Muriga. This town didn't have room for a man of ambition, unless his idea of ambition was leaving at 3:30 each morning on the sardine boats, or working in a video store, or depositing pension checks for ninety-year-old widowers.

"You knew all this," I said. "You knew it before you agreed to move."

"We came here because you insisted on it. And because of her," he said, nodding his head in the direction of Elena's room. "That's hardly agreeing."

We had been living with my mother for two months, the three of us packed into a spare bedroom in an apartment just at the foot of the mountains, where the forest begins. My mother was out with her *mus* group as she was every Friday afternoon, and José Antonio and I were in the kitchen, where we seemed to conduct all of our arguments now. I was unloading the clothes washer, leaning into the breezeway to hang his undershirts and my mother's elastic underpants and the handful of small cloths that we draped over our shoulders after Elena had eaten. José Antonio repetitively reached up to remove the dark sunflower shells from between his teeth, flicking them into the sink. It was a new habit of his, one that he knew I found disgusting.

"You said you wanted to be in the Basque Country," I said evenly.

"Yes," he answered immediately. "I said I wanted to *live* in the Basque Country. I didn't say I wanted to *be* Basque."

"*Joder*," I said. "No one is asking you to be Basque. But this is something else entirely."

Politics hadn't mattered in Sevilla. In Sevilla, all that mattered was the next weekend trip to Benidorm, the next bar for *cañas*. So when José Antonio had voted for the Partido Popular in the '93 elections, it was easy enough to ignore. In that time, to live in Sevilla was to be an amnesiac, something we Spaniards are so accustomed to becoming. Franco had died nearly two decades earlier; the Socialists had been running things in Madrid, and people in Sevilla thought that the transition to democracy was over. The fifty years since the Civil War had seemed forgotten to history already, absorbed back into the city along with ghosts of Sevilla's past like the old Islamic minaret converted into a bell tower for the Saint Mary of the See Cathedral five hundred years earlier.

But it was different in Muriga, where our parents and grandparents had been forbidden to speak their native language for nearly half a century and had lost so many of their artists and politicians and intellectuals forever in Franco's prisons and graveyards. Working for the PP in Muriga would only guarantee that José Antonio would be treated as an outsider, something he had complained about since we'd arrived in August.

"Your people," he said, leaning over the sink to spit another of the black shells. "The persecution complex you have . . ."

IT WAS this conversation. This and a hundred like it that I began to remember only after José Antonio had been buried for a year.

6. IKER

DURING OUR SECOND-TO-LAST YEAR AT SAN JORGE, THE year before the Councilman was killed, Asier and I made a habit of ditching school during the noon breaks. We'd begun to hang around with Ramón Luna's group, kids a few years older than us who liked to think of themselves as political. For me at sixteen years old, the idea that drinking wine instead of going to school could be considered "political" was a revelation. We'd grown up walking by posters of young Basque radicals who had been killed or arrested, had seen the strikes organized by university students when we visited cities like Bilbao or San Sebastián with our families. And with Ramón, suddenly we were a part of it.

When I recall these escapes now—as I often do after the fat guard Ricardo calls lights out each night at nine here in the Salto del Negro—one stands out not only because it involved so many of the places and people that would later shape my life, but because it was just one of those rainy autumn days that I associate with home, days that we never seem to get here in the Canaries.

On this afternoon, we made our break out of the cafeteria, our usual escape route—down the west hallway toward the student bathrooms. Asier took the lead, as he always seemed to, while I lagged behind and kept an eye out for teachers. Just before arriving at the boys' room, we ducked into the corridor that runs past the door of the American professor Garrett's classroom, past the old pictures of famous writers like Pío Baroja and Mario Vargas Llosa, as well as a series of cartoon drawings from *Don Quixote de la Mancha* that he had hung on the walls. To us, they were strange caricatures of our literature, and they stood out in a *secundaria* classroom. They reminded everyone at San Jorge that he didn't quite belong. I've often wondered if he was simply ignorant of these little details that set him apart in this way or if he had known about them all along.

When I looked around the corner the hallway was empty, but we slid off our shoes anyway so that the soles didn't pound the tile. We were almost past Garrett's room when Asier tugged at the sleeve of my jacket, then nodded toward the classroom. Inside, the old man was sitting at a student's desk, drinking a Coca-Cola and reading a ratty old book. A napkin was still tucked into the collar of his shirt. He reminded me of one of the little kids you see standing by themselves on the *primaria* playground.

When we reached the end of the hallway, Asier cracked the door and put his eye to the line of daylight that came in from outside. He took a full thirty seconds before turning back to me. He paused to build the tension (as he always did), before giving a thumbs-up. I pressed in closer as he counted to three, *bat*, *bi*, *hiru*, and then he swung open the door, and we were running across the fifty meters of parking lot in the direction of the wooded hillside that slopes down toward Muriga, still carrying our shoes in our hands.

This is my favorite part of the memory: the run. There's the instant when we come through the door and the sun is so bright that we're temporarily blinded, and we're running only downhill, not toward any place in particular, our blazers bunched into our armpits as we swing our arms, and when my eyes adjust I see Asier's brown hair pushed back off his forehead, his crooked tooth flashing as we sprint into the trees.

When we were safe in the protection of the forest that separates San Jorge from Muriga, Asier sat down on the black pine needles and rotting leaves and leaned back against a tree. He reached into his jacket pocket and took out an Athletic Bilbao pencil box. On the pencil box an image of Imanol Etxeberria stretched across the goal as he punched away a shot, and I remembered that Athletic would play Barcelona tonight.

Asier laid out a cigarette, rolling paper, and lighter from the pencil box. I loosened my tie and lay back on the leaves, my hands behind my head. My mind was already wandering to María Larrañaga and her younger sister Laura, who was only in eighth year but whose tits were already bigger than her sister's.

"María or Laura?" I asked Asier, a game we always played. He was holding a small brown lump of hash, which he warmed with a cigarette lighter and carefully flaked into his palm.

"Again with the Larrañagas?" he said. "If you had any balls, you'd do something about it instead of just talking."

"True," I said. "But which one? For me, it's the younger one."

He laughed. "Last week it was the older one, wasn't it?"

Asier crumbled a Lucky in his right hand and mixed it with the brown scrapings in his left palm, then rolled the mix in a Zig-Zag and licked the paper together. It was, among other things, the year in which Asier had gained his reputation as the best joint roller at San Jorge. He could roll one under his desk without looking—I witnessed it once during one of Irala's never-ending lectures. Asier ran the joint quickly under the cigarette lighter before lighting an end and handing it to me. We lay against the forest floor and smoked, and we stared up through the branches of the trees at the clouds gathering in strange shapes and talked about who would win the game tonight, and if Anderson, Barcelona's new striker, would score a goal. When we were done, we gathered our jackets and ties and walked the two kilometers down to the cliffs just past my grandmother's old house on the east end of town.

By the time we hiked far enough to see the ocean, it had started to rain. A small bit of smoke came out of one of the concrete bunkers dug into the steep cliffside, and when we got closer, we heard Ramón Luna's voice.

The bunker was left over from the Civil War, a history lesson that we had heard both at San Jorge and here on the cliffs. Ramón told us about the Basques' last stand against the dictator's army, about a Basque fishing boat called the *Beau Muriga* that had been recommissioned and outfitted by the Nationalists to battle a Spanish frigate not one kilometer in front of us. But what Ramón never told us, what I learned only years later in an old book I'd found in the library at the Salto del Negro, is that even though Franco later pardoned its captain for bravery in the face of certain destruction, the *Beau Muriga* was sunk after a two-hour fight, and the fascists burned half the town a couple days later. I guess even if I had known the true fate of the *Beau Muriga*, it wouldn't have changed the way I saw the battle Ramón Luna described—not as hopeless but as heroic. As the greatest kind of courage. We were looking for outrage in those days; we were looking for martyrs.

But the Civil War was sixty years ago, and now the walls of the bunker were written over with graffiti and the floor was just old newspapers and cigarette butts, a place where our cuadrilla could meet to smoke and drink and idly listen to Ramón's talk. I never expected anything more to come of these afternoons, though when I trace my journey to the Salto it always begins here. Ramón gave a quick nod as Asier and I entered but didn't break his monologue.

Luken and Daniel leaned against the cracked concrete wall of the bunker, feeding twigs and bits of binder paper into a small fire in the corner. Luken was new to Muriga, but Daniel has been part of our cuadrilla since primary school. His father owned the grocery store at the corner of Zabaleta and Atxiaga, and Daniel had been stealing wine and candies from the old man since we were eleven years old. Between the two of them was a liter box of Don

Pedro, and I sat near the fire and took a drink. In the shelter of the bunker, leaning close to the fire, I felt the wine warm me up from the inside, and as it mixed with the hash I felt tired and happy. I read the graffiti on the low ceiling—*Carlos+Michelle, Fuck Madrid, Marta Sánchez gives good blow jobs*—and listened.

"Did you read the *Diario Vasco* yesterday?" Ramón was asking. We'd known Ramón since before I can remember. He was the best friend of Asier's older brother, Aimar, and it was impossible to look at him and not remember the boy who had pissed himself in his second year as an altar server, even though that was more than ten years ago. It didn't matter. I still saw that same kid. "The Conservatives are planning an expansion of their office in Bilbao. Their goal, according to the article, is to increase their presence in the rural areas and smaller towns."

Ramón was always lecturing like this about our struggle. The struggle of the Basque people. In his own eyes he'd become a leader, a revolutionary, and though we didn't entirely believe this version of him, we didn't try to discredit it either. I felt an elbow in my side, and when I turned toward Daniel, he rolled his eyes as if to say, "This speech again." He pushed a box of cookies toward me. I took one and shoved it in my mouth whole, washing it down with another drink of Don Pedro.

Whenever Asier caught me clowning around during one of these speeches he'd tell me that I should pay attention, believe more in the struggle. I wanted to wave my hands in front of us and say, "What struggle? We live in a small city with a nice beach. They teach Euskera in the public schools, and the street signs are in both Basque and Spanish. Your father is a banker, and you were a Real Madrid fan until Ramón and his lectures." But I knew Ramón spoke in a language that Asier had been learning over the last year—the language of "armed struggle," of Marxism-Leninism, of "wealth condensation" and "anti-imperialism." He was Muriga's sad answer to the Ché poster that Asier had pinned to his bedroom door.

By the time Ramón finished the rain had begun to let up. We passed the box of wine around the fire, and Asier rolled one more before we stood and stretched our legs. Asier and I headed up the hill to San Jorge while Daniel and Luken went back down along the cliffs toward the public school in town.

It wasn't until the fourth day of the trial, two years later, that I realized the significance of those moments when the four of us split ways, Daniel and Luken returning to the dingy school on Atalde Street next to the public health clinic, and Asier and I back to the looming fortress of San Jorge. I never understood the importance of this divide until it was too late.

7. JONI

I WAS STILL CONSIDERING MARIANA'S QUESTION AS I steered the old Volkswagen up the final curves of Monte Zorroztu and turned off into the dark fingers of pines that marked the drive-way to Colegio San Jorge. *Wouldn't it matter to you, Joni?* On the south side of the drive stood a weathered sign bearing the school crest, a red cross over an expanse of peeling white paint. Along the top, in Spanish, read the school motto: "Serve by Teaching, Teach by Serving." Underneath, in English: "International School of Muriga," an addendum that was stenciled onto the sign after I, the lone foreign teacher, accepted the teaching position in 1948.

My window was rolled down to allow in the thin mountain air and to force out the gray smoke from my cigarette. The sounds of the primary school playground came in with the fresh air—high shrieks of pleasure, harshly spoken imperatives, the rattling of chain link from the loners who paced the perimeter of the yard, kicking at the fencing as if testing for a weak spot. As I parked the car I saw the children as Mariana had suggested: not just children but containers of organs playing in the yard, waiting to be har-vested. As David Hermo ran off with Juliana Gorriti's pencil case I imagined a pink liver hidden under his navy V-neck sweater. David sprinted to where a group of boys waited, beckoning him to safety behind the soccer goal. Yes, I admitted, Mariana had been right. It would make a difference where the kidney had come from. It would make all the difference.

Colegio San Jorge was converted to a school from an old Republican army barracks in 1941 after Franco's forces had rooted out the last of the antifascists in Muriga. Before that, it had been a fortress dating back to the sixteenth century. During my first summer in Muriga I would lie in bed with the woman who taught me to say *txirimiri*, naked on top of the sheets in the cold-water flat I had rented from Martín's father above what is now the grocery, and she would tell me what it had been like. She told me how the Guardia Civil had rounded up all of the Republicans, Communists, and Anarchists and shot them against the wall of the barracks. Forty-eight men from a town of two thousand, including her father and uncle. And now the children of Muriga, these grandchildren and great-grandchildren of the Civil War, throw tennis balls against the ramparts, tuck themselves into the mossy alcoves of a five-hundred-year-old doorway to light the tips of their stolen Lucky Strikes. There's some comfort to it, that Muriga still exists among the bones and shell casings of its own people, though whenever I attempt to explain this to my Basque friends they wave their hands and say, "You're an old romantic, Joni. It is only because you are a foreigner. I would say the same, or something similar, if I was with you in California." They always use the Spanish word for foreigner, *extranjero*. Stranger.

By the time I crossed the playground of the primary school, which occupied the western wing of the fortress, the children were no longer lungs or kidneys or livers but were again children. Their black shoes scuffed from kicking at the dirt or at each other, their cheeks flushed with the cool air.

I left my briefcase on the desk in my small office, which overlooked the steep, forested hillside that ran down to Muriga a kilometer below. Rivulets of brown smoke crept up where farmers had begun to burn the chaff from their fields. I heard a knock against the pebbled glass panel on my door, and when I looked up I found Juantxo Goikoetxea's toadlike head wedged into the open space, four or five strands of hair pulled absurdly across the top of his head, thick-rimmed glasses pushed up tight against his face.

"When you are ready, John." He spoke to me in stiff, carefully considered English. "The American waits in my office."

"Are we speaking English today?"

"Yes," Goikoetxea answered gravely, now in Spanish. "The American speaks Basque but does not speak Spanish very well. And his wife not at all. Only English."

"Lucky for you, then, that you hired him to teach English."

Goikoetxea laughed uneasily. He had never been comfortable as an administrator, and I suspected he secretly longed for the days when he only taught geography. He withdrew his toad head from the doorway, saying again, "When you are ready, John."

I had promised Goikoetxea that I would take my replacement to lunch and show him around the town a bit before he observed my afternoon classes. As the only American at Colegio San Jorge (or in Muriga, for that matter), I was often called upon for this sort of duty, to accompany an Australian cousin or British girlfriend on a tour of the city, more for my services as interpreter than for my stellar company. But this was a professional assignment, to situate the new man in Muriga, make sure that he knew how to dial an international number, show him where to take his wife in case of illness.

I took an envelope of graded papers from the briefcase and left them on the desk next to the day's lesson plan. I had used these plans for the better part of thirty years, each one on the same day of each year, so that each time I taught the imperative form of "to leave," I knew that Athletic Bilbao, the nearest football team in the Primera Liga, would open its season that week in San Mamés, and when the children of San Jorge chanted conjugations of "to love" (I love, you love, he loves, she loves, we love, they love . . .), I knew that it would soon be my mother's birthday. I examined the page I had set out for the day, on the use of the imperfect tense. The page of notes, typed decades ago, was lined with handwritten annotations in a half dozen different inks. Within these scrawlings, a more subtle difference came into focus: the earliest notes written in sharp block letters with a youthful crispness, the most recent, scribbled in a sloping, weary script. Hopelessly tattered, its edges torn and dog-eared, the paper itself was yellowed to something resembling parchment, physical evidence of my arrival into old age.

I imagined the American studying this lesson plan, drawing this same conclusion, and so I slid it into a drawer before setting off to Goikoetxea's office, closing the door behind me.

When I entered the office, which awkwardly occupied a turret on the northeastern corner of the school, the American and his wife sat in two chairs opposite Goikoetxea's desk. None of the three were speaking, and I had a feeling that this had been the case for several minutes. Goikoetxea stood up from his desk, relieved, and said in hurried Spanish, "Finally, Joni. We have been waiting."

The new American and his wife stood to greet me. The wife was a classic American beauty, one that stirred an immediate sense of nostalgia after so many years in the Basque Country. Her hair was, of course, blond, cut neatly just above her bare shoulders. She wore a fall dress, dark-brown cotton accented with a colorful red ribbon. It had obviously been picked out from one of the boutiques in Biarritz or San Sebastián on their way to Muriga. But the Europeanness of it was undone by the cream-colored skin, the broom-handle thinness of her arms, the frailty of her features. Here among the women who were, at best, a generation away from the fields, with their dark, solid shoulders, she seemed transported not just from another continent but from another time.

And next to her stood the new American, Duarte. He, too, was undeniably handsome. Broad-shouldered, just enough color mixed into his complexion to betray his Basque ancestry, but with a hint of severity that was absent from his wife. A dark beard encircled his tight mouth, almost concealing the faint scar of a cleft palate.

"John," Goikoetxea said in his stilted English. "I present you to Robert Duarte, and to his woman, Morgan." Neither Robert nor Morgan flinched at the mistranslation.

"*Egun on*, Mr. Garrett," the American said. His voice was softer, of just a higher register than one would expect of a man his size. "Everyone that we have encountered in Muriga has mentioned you. It's great to finally meet."

"Juantxo mentioned that you spoke Basque," I said, Goikoetxea's head perking at the mention of his name.

"Just a bit I learned from my father around the house," he explained.

"I thought you might take them to the Elizondo," Goikoetxea said in Spanish, eager to usher us out of his office so that he could return to his business, his historical maps of medieval Europe, his stacks of biographies on the early cartographers.

"Yes," I said. I caught myself staring at the thin scar running from the top of the American's lip. Jagged, like the sutures running along Mariana's thin abdomen, like the frayed edges of my lesson plan. *I was eating. I used to eat.* "Of course. The Elizondo."

Outside the window of Goikoetxea's office a dark thunderhead was mounting over the harbor; it was just beginning to rain along the Paseo de los Robles, where I had sat to have coffee with Mariana a few hours before.

"There's no use waiting, is there?" I said. "It looks as if a storm is set to arrive."

8. MARIANA

AT FIRST IT WAS EASY ENOUGH TO EXPLAIN AWAY THE SEN-
sations that came to me after the surgery. José Antonio suggested
that the strange smell when I woke in the recovery room might
have only been the anesthesia still lingering in the back of my throat,
and this seemed likely enough. But they continued even after we
returned to Muriga, these amplified sensations of déjà vu. I would
run my fingertips along the underside of the kitchen table, and
suddenly it was as if I were standing on the verge of a memory, at
the edge of an entire life I had forgotten.

Mostly, they would come to me as odd smells, strange appetites
that were easy enough to ignore. Suddenly I would be craving Corn
Flakes, or I'd remember a few words from a song I'd never heard
before, or I'd have the unexpected desire to open the bedroom window during a storm.

"You're getting the floor wet," José Antonio would say. "And
besides, the cold air can't be good for you."

"I'm sure you're right," I'd say, sitting on the floor next to the
open window, tracing designs on the dark hardwood with the water
left by the rain.

TEN DAYS after we returned to Muriga from the hospital, on the first day that José Antonio had returned to work at the Party headquarters in Bilbao, the old American professor Joni Garrett came to visit at the apartment. My mother had left the day before, after I assured her that I could shuffle around well enough to change the girl's diapers and steam vegetables for her lunch. But after a morning alone with Elena I became restless, eager for someone to talk to, and so when I ran into Joni Garrett on the way to the corner bakery I invited the old man up.

"Did they make a large incision?" he asked, and when I lifted my shirt to show him, he knelt down and put a hand lightly up to the clean dressing. It was a strangely personal thing to do; I hadn't expected his touch, only the old man's curiosity. "Does it hurt much?"

"No," I said. "Not as much as you'd think."

He nodded, then asked if I had tea instead of coffee.

As I filled the kettle with cold water he asked, in his usual way (I've never been sure if he's actually poetic or if his way of speaking is just the product of translating his thoughts into Spanish from English), what my first memory was immediately after the operation.

"In the moment that you came back," he began, "before your eyes opened, what did you recollect?"

"*Membrillo*," I said without hesitation. I was surprised by the answer, as if it wasn't me at all that had said it: *membrillo*. Quince jam.

There had been an old woman in the bed next to mine in the recovery room. Unconscious. Chest rising and falling in time with the machinery. A ribbed blue tube down her throat. Wires and bandages holding together every limb. And above the clatter of the room—the sucking and breathing of the woman's respirator, the newscast from Telecinco (a house fire in Burgos; Barça 3–1 over Betis), the burning fumes of alcohol swabs and antiseptics—the undeniable smell of *membrillo*, the sweetness of the caramelized fruit.

"That isn't so unusual," Joni said. "I saw a program once where a woman was having an operation to remove a tumor from her brain. You should consider yourself lucky, Mariana. A new kidney is easy. For brain surgery, they keep the patient awake."

I couldn't help laughing. I'd heard several people in Muriga say that they found Joni Garrett off-putting or eccentric. They mistrusted him for never having married, and they couldn't understand why he'd stayed in Muriga for so long. But he always had a way of cheering me up. "So what does this have to do with *membrillo*?"

"In the program, the doctor performing the surgery is speaking with the patient. The top of the woman's skull is removed completely. The doctor pushes a metal probe against a certain part of her brain and asks her, 'What do you feel?' 'The uncomfortable feeling when you walk on the beach and there is sand between your toes and your sandals,' she says. 'Good,' the doctor says, and then he moves the probe to another part of the patient's brain. 'And now?' 'Cookies,' the woman says. 'I smell the pecan cookies that my aunt made for me when I was eight years old.'"

"So the cookies are like my *membrillo*?"

"Maybe so," Joni said. This was exactly why I liked the old man so much. I could speak freely.

It had never been like this with José Antonio. Everything was intensely personal to him. If I burned the toast in the morning he acted as if I'd slapped him across the face and called his mother a whore. "What's wrong?" he'd say, putting down whatever memorandum he had been reviewing, and when I'd say that it's only the toast left too long in the toaster, he would say, "If there's something bothering you, just say so."

It was easy to complain about then, but to be truthful this is what brought me to José Antonio in the first place. If he had a fault, it was that he cared too much—about me, about his work for the Party, about Elena. It was in my second year at the Institute for Visual Arts in Sevilla that I met him (his cousin was my classmate in Advanced Computer Design), at the tail end of my second consecutive relationship with men who called only in the late hours of the night, dramatic and self-absorbed artist types who insisted on fucking with the lights on. A writer who never seemed to write, and then a sculptor whose sculptures (when he did sculpt, which was rarely) were really crap anyway. And suddenly there was José Antonio, the negative image of these men, who would kiss me awkwardly in the hallway of my apartment building before he went home and I went inside to wait for the call from the sculptor. If I had been interested in the passion and volitility of the two artists, then it was the slow-burning persistence of José Antonio's courtship that drew me to him. The previous two years had left me exhausted, and with José Antonio I felt that I could finally breathe again. There was no threat of destruction, but a somewhat more ominous promise of steadiness and predictability.

Not that any of this was clear to me in the moment, of course. Regardless of how bad his art was, I continued to sleep with the sculptor for the first two months with José Antonio. When I mentioned this to Joni during one of our walks along the paseo he didn't seem surprised. Instead, he took it as he does all things, as a curiosity.

"Did you ever tell José Antonio?" he asked, after a moment.

"Would you have?" I said.

"No," he replied. "Of course not."

"We two are very similar, Joni," I said.

WHEN I finally ended it with the sculptor, he responded as if I had told him that I was cooking up a pork chop for dinner.

"Of course," he had said, scratching at the dried clay smeared conspicuously across the lap of his pants. "We both knew this wouldn't be forever."

But with José Antonio, he *did* seem to know from the beginning that this would be forever.

"I've never been in love with someone like this," he once said as we shared a beer along the Plaza de Galicia. We had only been dating a month, and although I didn't share his certainty, I found myself answering, "I feel the same, José Antonio. I knew, from the first moment, that I would fall in love with you." I've tried to believe it ever since.

We went on like this for two years, until I had finished my degree at the institute. By now José Antonio had been working for the Partido Popular for over a year, as an assistant campaign organizer.

In the July after I finished my studies in Sevilla my period never arrived.

9. JONI

WE CARAVANNED DOWN THE HILL FROM SAN JORGE INTO Muriga, the young American Robert Duarte and his wife following my car down the twisting road overhung by mossy cedars, and by the time we arrived at the Elizondo the rain had started in earnest.

I parked in the alleyway off Goiko Plaza; through the rearview mirror I watched my brake lights illuminate the pelting rain on the Duartes' new Renault. The rain fired sharp, quickly fading shots onto the windshield, and in between the distorted holes I could see the American and his wife. It was a voyeuristic moment there on the side street behind the restaurant, as if I had crept through the dark into their backyard in Idaho, as if I stood just outside the yellow square of light that fell from their kitchen window and watched them clear the table. For longer than I should have, I continued to stare at them through the rearview.

The American craned his neck around to back up into the space directly behind my car, placing his hand on the back of his wife's headrest. As he did so the wipers of the Renault fanned across the glass, and for a moment her face was perfectly visible through the rain. Our eyes met in such a way that I was sure she had caught me spying, but instead of ducking down, I stayed still, watching. Isn't stillness the first camouflage of the cowardly?

She stared straight ahead, until the rain had again mottled the windshield, and then she lowered the vanity mirror to fix the makeup around her eyes. She seemed smaller like that, with Robert's thick hand behind her, as if this single item of scale revealed her true size, not exactly real. When the American had swung the car parallel to the curb he turned the keys to kill the engine, and the two sat not speaking. I opened the door of the Volkswagen and pointed to the awning of the Elizondo at the corner. The cold water ran through my thin cover of hair; I saw the American turn to say something to his wife before catching himself. He pushed open the driver's side door and jogged over to where I stood waiting in the rain.

"She'll be in soon," he said, a little too loudly. Back in the car, his wife peered idly across the square on the other side of Calle Nafarroa. The plaza was surrounded on three sides by apartment buildings, small stores on the ground floor of each. Outside the Arostegui butcher shop fat pigs hung from their back feet, cut lengthwise to reveal the red muscle along their loins, the white fingers of the rib cage. Aitor's dark figure moved silently among the hanging meat, as imposing as he had been the last time we had spoken four decades before, when he had come for his sister at the house we shared by the river. In the window next to the pharmacy, the women of Ogi Berri were placing the first of the afternoon's breads and pastries out on display. Dark-gray water cascaded from the canvas awnings into the small stream that flowed along the gutters, carrying with it a flotilla of toothpicks, leaves, and litter.

"Would you like to wait?" I asked.

"You know how women are," he said. I nodded, thinking, *I have no idea how women are.* "She just needs a minute or so, and then she'll be in."

Patxi's wife, Susana, was behind the bar when we arrived. It was early for lunch, and the restaurant was nearly empty, though it would soon be bustling with customers. It was one of the oldest restaurants in Muriga, known for its seafood dishes and for liberal pours at the bar.

"Susana," I said. "I present you to my successor, Robert Duarte."

Susana looked at me curiously as she wiped her hands on her apron. She walked around the bar to where we stood, a small puddle collecting at our shoes (mine old, scuffed, the counter of the right heel chewed on by Rimbaud; Duarte's pristine oxfords polished, mottled attractively with small beads of rain).

"A pleasure," she said in Spanish. The American bent down to kiss the older woman on each cheek. "Duarte is a Basque name, isn't it?"

"My father is from Nabarniz," Robert said, before adding something in Basque. Susana's face lifted with genuine surprise.

"Nabarniz?" she said. A rush of indecipherable Basque followed before she remembered that I was there and switched back to Spanish. "My cousins live in Aulesti. They have the mechanic's shop there."

"Is it too early for lunch?" I asked.

"No, of course not," Susana said, flicking at me with her dishrag. "For an *euskaldun* like this one," she continued, putting a hand on the American's square shoulder, "my kitchen is always open."

✳ ✳ ✳

SUSANA SAT us at a table just behind the partition between the dining area and the bar. The Elizondo was quiet, except for the rough scrapings of metal on metal as Ainhoa, Susana's youngest daughter, slid an iron skillet back and forth over the gas range. On the television above the bar, as always, was the never-ending game of pelota. As we warmed from the heat of the kitchen, the American and I were mesmerized by the game, the hard *clack* of the handball as it ricocheted off the tall cement wall, the cries of the handball players as they struck the hard resin ball wrapped in worn leather. The boys of San Jorge play their version with old tennis balls. It gives them an idea of pelota technique but not what makes greatness in a *pelotari*. A good *pelotari* is one who possesses an ability to accept pain, to know that he will submit himself to it again and again, the hard slap of the pelota against a palm mutilated with small broken bones and burst capillaries.

"Have you seen a match?" I asked. The pelota cracked against the wall again. The American was leaning forward over the table, his hand on his chin, his forefinger playing absentmindedly with the scar.

"Of course," he said, not taking his eyes from the television. "There is a fronton in Boise, at the social club downtown. On weekends my father would take me down. The old sheepherders would sit around the bar until someone got drunk enough to start up a game."

"If you'd like, I could take you to a match this weekend," I said. Again, the *clack* of the pelota. "Perhaps we could even get Irujo to come. Do you know Irujo yet?"

"No."

Clack.

"He is the history teacher that took over for Goikoetxea when he was moved to administration." *Clack.* "He's a fanatic for pelota."

"I'd like that," he said.

A final *clack*, and the cry of the pelota player as the ball caromed wildly from his hand, missing the wall by several feet. The door to the bar swung open, and Morgan Duarte backed into the bar, shaking an umbrella behind her before leaning it against the wall just below the coat rack. The American straightened, watching his wife's thin, nervous figure at the front of the restaurant.

"I should get her," he said, standing from the table.

"She really doesn't speak any Spanish?" I asked.

"Almost nothing."

Morgan was pointing past Susana toward our table in the dining area. When Robert walked up, he put his hand around his wife's waist and spoke easily to Susana. Susana answered, and the two laughed while Morgan brushed at the left sleeve of her sweater.

I found myself feeling sorry for her. As Robert and Susana spoke in Basque, it occurred to me that Morgan and I were the only ones in the room who were deaf to this language. The two of us alike in this way.

Morgan sidled closer to the American, much the way Elena will tuck herself into the bend behind Mariana's knee when I kneel down (knowing how I must appear to her: a tall, strangely speaking gargoyle) to ask if she has been a good girl today. The American's wife smiled in time with Robert and Susana's laughs; from behind them came the sound of the pelota's *clack clack clack* and outside the faint ticking of rain against the hoods of the cars on the street. I could see the first hints of desperation in Morgan Duarte, as if she had just there in the Elizondo realized that she was marooned in this strange town. She pulled in just a touch to her husband's grasp. Even he was a stranger to her now, speaking to a woman in his nearly extinct language.

AFTER THE second bottle of wine, we began to tell stories. I told them how I had found Rimbaud abandoned at a rest stop outside of Mondragón, nearly dead from malnourishment. Morgan Duarte described meeting Robert four years before, when he was a first-year history teacher at a high school in Boise and she was a sophomore at Boise State.

"On our second date he took me to his parents' house out in Nampa and told his mother, 'I'm going to marry this girl one day, Ama.'"

Robert, taking his cue, chipped in, "That's what I told them about every girl I brought home."

Morgan pretended to take offense, gripping him lightly on the shoulder. She told the story as if she had told it many times before, had revised and whittled it down to the shapely anecdote she shared now over coffee and cheese at the Elizondo. Even so, it was also apparent that she took great pleasure in its telling.

In between platters of breaded lamb chop and *merluza* smothered in tomato sauce, Morgan excused herself for the restroom. By now, the dining area had filled with a local cuadrilla of retired men who made a daily circuit of the few bars and restaurants in downtown Muriga. We both watched her walk among the tables of old Basques, who in turn swiveled to watch this exquisite creature cross the room. Basilio Zabala leaned in to his table and said something in Basque, and the table rocked with a collective laughter. If Robert Duarte had heard the joke, he didn't show that it had bothered him; instead, it seemed to bolster his self-satisfaction, which had become more evident with each cup of wine.

"What will she do while you are at San Jorge?" I asked. His eyes were still on Morgan as she pulled open the door to the restroom.

"You know, we were just married eight months before we left Boise," he said, as if this were an answer to the question. "My father died of an aortic aneurysm in April, two months after the wedding."

He stopped to sip from a glass still half-full of cold table wine. I knocked a cigarette from my pack and struck a match.

"He left us a bit of money, so she won't need to work," he continued. "She's an artist—charcoal sketches, some watercolor—so that will give her something to do. She mentioned enrolling in one of the language schools in Bilbao, but I think Morgan will mostly want to stay at home, get used to being married."

"Of course," I said. Duarte's words were sickeningly familiar. *"Get used to being married.* Of course."

10. IKER

THE FIRST TIME I SAW THE COUNCILMAN IN PERSON WAS IN February of our second-to-last year at San Jorge. It was raining *a cántaros*, like my grandma used to say. And since the crank on Ramón Luna's car window had broken, water was blowing in through the gap and the right shoulder of my blazer was soaked down to the San Jorge crest. Asier was in the passenger seat, and we drove yet again around an apartment building at the corner of Atxiaga and Zabaleta. Ramón's girlfriend, Nere, sat next to me in the back, her leg resting against mine in the dark.

"What're you reading?" she whispered.

I looked at the book sitting in my lap, then handed it to her.

"*Love in the Time of Cholera*," she read, tilting the cover toward the light from the street. I felt Ramón watching us in the rearview mirror.

"It's a political book, actually," I said. Somewhere from the mix of radical histories and anarchist manifestos that Ramón assigned us I'd found writers like García-Márquez and Camus, intellectuals who reinforced our political views but whose books were more than just ideas or slogans. I reached for the book but Nere ignored me, brushing away my hand so that she could read the description on the back. "The author is a socialist."

"Sounds like a love story to me," she said, flipping the book back into my lap.

In the eight months that Asier and I had been with Ramón's cuadrilla, Nere had always dressed in the thin black jeans and tight black military jacket that she was wearing now. I, of course, had fallen in love with her the moment we first saw her, arriving at the *local* behind my mother's art studio to paint banners for a demonstration (just the same ten kids with anti-Madrid slogans painted onto an old bedsheet). A month before, she had shaved off her long, dark hair except for a single thin chunk just behind her left ear. I loved her even more for this. She was cracking sunflower seeds, spitting the shells onto a newspaper clipping. The air in the car was a mixture of salt and saliva and tobacco.

"Let me see the article again," I told her.

She spit the broken husks onto the paper, then leaned past me to brush them out the crack in the window. When she handed me the clipping it was wet with spit and rain, and the black-and-white photograph of the Councilman was darkened in the area above his head as well as at the waist of his suit jacket. Ramón had been talking about the Councilman for weeks—the usual bit about how the man was importing ideas from Madrid into Muriga, about a plan to undermine the Basque independence movement through small-town politics—but this was the first time we'd ever actually looked for him in person. "Know your enemy," Ramón had said when he first proposed tailing him for an afternoon, though it wasn't at all clear what we were supposed to be learning about him. When Ramón again drove the dented Croma past the market on the corner he brushed back the thin hairs from his forehead. "This asshole is just another one of the dictator's men," he said

We referred to him as "the Councilman," even though he was only being mentioned as a possible candidate for the general election the following year. Torres had caught Ramón's attention, I think, because he was so young, something you didn't see from the PP in Muriga. "Deliberate strategy to undermine the younger voting demographic," he'd said. I was used to Ramón's way of speaking, using three long words instead of one short one. When Ramón wasn't around Daniel and I would push our hair off our foreheads to mimic his receding hairline and say, "The social imperative of the Basque revolutionary movement requires that you drink this rum and Coke immediately!" and other nonsense. We believed in Ramón's cause, just not in the words he used to describe it.

But now, in the backseat of the Croma, I didn't make jokes about Ramón. Something real seemed about to happen, and it unsettled us—even Ramón, I think. He was fidgeting nervously with a ciga-rette lighter.

I studied the article from *El Diario Vasco*; in the picture, the Councilman was leaving the Muriga city hall. He didn't look like the demon that Ramón described. He looked a little like a cousin of mine from Irun, actually. His hair was parted in the middle and flopped to each side like a young boy's haircut, and in his left hand he seemed to be carrying a sandwich wrapped in foil. He was just starting to show a gut. In the background of the photo, I could see the Elizondo restaurant, Susana Monreal turned slightly toward the cameraman as she swept a napkin out into the gutter.

The article didn't refer to him as "the Councilman," but rather as "José Antonio Torres." *José Antonio*, I thought, and I tried to remember if I had seen him in town before. He had moved to Muriga after completing his graduate studies in political science in Sevilla, the article said.

It was late afternoon, and the streetlights were just beginning to come on when I felt the start of a headache, the ones that can still drop me where I stand. It started small, just a cold metallic taste at the back of my tongue, as if I had been sucking on a ten-peseta piece. Then a slight smell of burnt hair, and with it an explosion of pain.

The pain started where it always does, just behind my ears, and quickly became so sharp that I leaned over against the back of Asier's seat, and this plunged me underwater—slow and cold and without sound. I held my breath and waited, trying not to be sick.

An endless minute later, as the streetlights slowly came back into focus, I felt Nere's hand at the back of my neck. We rounded the corner, and I saw we had nearly returned to the apartment building where we started.

"Are you OK?" she began to say. But before she could finish, Ramón jammed the brakes of the car, and Asier was pointing across the street to a man and a woman leaving the building. The woman was tall and thin, dressed in dark slacks and a blue rain jacket. Her eyes had dark rings under them. The man with her was pushing a stroller covered by an umbrella. It was the first time I saw José Antonio Torres in person.

The pain continued to ease as we watched, all four of us trying to act casual when the couple made their way past the car.

"She's pretty," Nere said absently, watching the three. She kept her hand on my head, her fingers pushing lightly through the hair at the base of my neck. "He did well for himself, didn't he?"

She was right. The woman was too thin to be entirely healthy, but it was obvious even from a distance that she was beautiful.

"Take a note, Asier," Ramón said, exhaling smoke into the Croma. Asier flipped open his school notebook and held his pen above the page, waiting. "Five twenty-seven. Councilman leaves apartment with wife and child."

II. MARIANA

IN THE MONTHS BEFORE THE DOCTOR IN BILBAO MADE HER diagnosis, the anemia brought on by two barely functioning kidneys had left me lethargic, hardly able to leave the sofa to get Elena dressed. José Antonio had diagnosed it as a mental health issue, a sort of late-onset postpartum depression, and though I never said as much, I tended to agree with him. I was on my own most of the day with Elena and felt suddenly isolated in Muriga, the town that I had spent the greater part of my life in. Occasionally, I'd meet up with Victoria, my oldest friend, at the park on the Paseo de los Robles, and Elena would play on the brightly painted jungle gym with Victoria's son César. Victoria and I would talk for a while about old boyfriends or about our husbands' jobs. But inevitably we ran out of things to talk about, and we would sit in silence and watch our children laughing or screaming as they ran around the little park. I found myself missing Sevilla and the self-centered existence I had there.

But almost immediately after the operation, my energy began to return, and with the new energy came the smells, the cravings, the edges of these new memories. They kept me company, in a way. When they came, I would tap the black stitches on my abdomen and wonder what my new kidney was trying to tell me. When Elena was asleep for her afternoon nap, I would go to the living room mirror and lift up my shirt.

"Who are you?" I'd ask the incision, and as if in response, I would smell a whiff of hashish or feel a humid warmth on the underside of my arm, as if I'd just passed my hand over a boiling pot of stew.

It became a game. On the days that I smelled the hashish, I would speculate that the kidney had belonged to a Moroccan man who had sold cigarettes on the streets of Zaragoza, and on the days that I felt the heat on the underside of my arm, I would picture my kidney pumping away inside a heavyset woman working in the kitchen of an old restaurant.

Soon, though, certain sensations began to crowd out the rest. It was as if the kidney were trying to communicate something to me, something more specific than "I existed before you. I belong to someone else." I found myself craving the smell of burning sulfur, so that I would light a match just to wave it out, then repeat the action. Late at night, I would sit at the kitchen table lighting match after match, touching the pink scar and theorizing that my kidney's original owner had died in a house fire, or perhaps in a burning car.

Eight weeks after the surgery, I began to take Elena to the library in the basement of the Muriga city hall in the afternoons. I would point to Javier Gamboa, a friend of my mother's who had worked as a security guard at city hall for as long as I can remember, and Elena would say, "*Arratsalde on*," in her high child's voice. Javier would lower himself to Elena's height on his brittle knees and say, "*Arratsalde on, Elena. Zer moduz?*" Good afternoon, Elena. How are you today?

While Elena stumbled around the empty aisles of books or slept in her blue stroller, I would scroll through rolls of microfiche, scanning through six weeks of Spanish newspapers for the day of March 4, 1997. When I first told Joni about this new pastime of mine, he had shaken his head in a way that suggested not judgment but real worry. It was a look I had been used to seeing from my mother, or from José Antonio, but never from Joni.

"What do you hope to gain from this new hobby, Mariana?" he had asked during one of our morning coffees at the Boliña. It was his use of my name that did it, that changed it from a question to a warning. The change in tone had annoyed me.

"It's not that I hope to *gain* anything, Joni," I said. "It's interesting, is all. More interesting than staying at home with a two-year-old, anyway."

ON THE first day of my investigations, I learned that there had been no house fires in all of northern Spain the day of my operation, and there had been only two fatal car accidents. According to public record, ninety-eight people died on March 4 in the region of the country that my new organ had come from, though nearly all of these had died of old age and would not have been donors. Of the list of the dead, I found only five viable candidates: an eleven-year-old girl struck down by a car in León; two men in their forties killed in an auto accident between Pamplona and Vitoria; an eighteen-year-old girl who had committed suicide in Pasajes; and one other.

The last death was mentioned on the front page of every newspaper that appeared the day of my surgery. It was accompanied, most often, by a series of three photographs.

The first photograph showed an apartment building like you might have found anywhere in the Basque Country, except that it was surrounded by the dark navy uniforms and black ski masks of the Ertzaintza. There was white police tape stretched around several police cars, blocking off the entrance to the apartment building. A crowd had gathered, pushing against the tape.

The second photograph of the series was dated two years earlier, the blackened shell of a sedan smoldering in a parking garage.

The car was so completely destroyed that it was impossible to even tell the make, while the windows of the two cars next to it had melted in the explosion. There was a white sheet placed on the driver's seat of the sedan, though it was difficult to imagine that there was anything to cover up; even the car seats seemed vaporized entirely. And again the dark figures of the Ertzaintza milling through the background of the photograph. The scene looked vaguely familiar, as if I might have seen it on the news when the explosion had taken place two years earlier. The caption read: *Spanish Intelligence Officer Killed in ETA Car Bomb, June 12, 1995.*

As I examined the final photograph I experienced a physical reaction, a tremor of nausea and a tingling along the pink seam holding in my borrowed kidney. The picture, the largest of the series, was a police photograph. It showed a young man in his midtwenties. He had dark hair cut short. His ears were a little on the large size and his nose drifted slightly to his right. He was wearing a T-shirt, and he smiled just enough to show his crooked bottom teeth.

The caption below read: *Iñaki Libano, ETA Terrorist Responsible for 1995 Assassination, Killed by Ertzaintza Tuesday in Mondragón.*

12. JONI

THE MORNING AFTER MY LUNCH WITH THE DUARTES I returned to work at San Jorge. The sun was just coming up over the foothills of the Pyrenees as I headed toward the main entrance of the school. I had made it a point to arrive before Robert Duarte, but when I found his new Renault already in the lot, I began to walk the perimeter of the schoolyard, finishing a cigarette.

Along the walls of the fortress, I saw evidence of the older boys: piles of broken sunflower seed shells, the crooked necks of a thousand cigarette butts, names and insults etched crudely into the stone walls with ballpoint pens. Farther up the wall, above what would have been the moat's waterline, large divots were chipped out of the stone, scars from Franco's Falangist tanks as they entered Muriga in 1937. By the time I completed my lap around the school, stopping once to light another Chesterfield, several other teachers' cars had appeared in the parking lot.

I arrived early that morning in order to look over the day's lesson plan so that the new American Robert Duarte would be impressed by the old man's sagacity. I was already aware of my desire to impress a man who was half my age, a man who I knew had come to Muriga to take my place, even though Goikoetxea hadn't gathered up the nerve to tell me as much. But the American had defeated me even in this small contest. I considered passing by his door, rather than stopping in to say good morning. Reminding myself that I was to be his mentor for the remainder of the term, I paused outside his small office. Robert answered the door almost as I was still knocking. The windowless room was bare except for a single chair and desk, upon which rested only a spiral notebook and a ballpoint pen. Taped to the wall above the desk was the room's only decoration, a small charcoal drawing of a young woman that I recognized to be Morgan Duarte.

"I was hoping it'd be you. Goikoetxea has been checking on me every five minutes for the past half hour."

"I think he's just eager to impress our new American," I said. "We get a few Americans in Muriga—college students, the sons and daughters of cousins that have moved away to the States—but none that intended to stay, Robert. You and Morgan are the first in a long time."

Duarte nodded solemnly, as if understanding his role in a new light, even though I hadn't meant the comment to mean much. "But Goikoetxea," I continued, "he's an old neurotic. He can't help himself. He'd tuck you into bed at night if you let him."

The American laughed, then sat back casually on the corner of the desk. "So what's the lesson plan for today?"

"Well, I can't remember offhand," I admitted. "My notes are all in my office and haven't been updated in thirty years, I'm afraid. But if memory serves me, the tenth-year students will be continuing with the imperative."

"How is the class?"

"Intolerable," I answered. "They're all preoccupied with their college entrance exams this spring. Studying vocabulary is the last thing they're concerned with. There's a particularly tough lot of boys this year. You'll see."

"I did my student teaching at a low-income high school, mostly Latino kids," Robert said.

"It's different," I started. "The kids with money can be even harder to deal with, in a way. We always think the poor kids don't have anything to lose, which is scary. But these kids, sometimes it's like they're *trying* to lose it all. They think they have the most to prove. That's *really* frightening."

Again, the American nodded as if I'd said something very wise. I offered a smile; it's always a pleasant surprise when people assume you to be a wise old man, instead of just an old fool.

"Don't take me seriously," I said. "They are, after all, just children. They're nothing to be afraid of."

"I'm not afraid," he said. "I just want to know what to expect."

Now, I think back to the empty seats in my twelfth-year English class, where Iker Abarzuza and Asier Díaz were missing that morning, and I wonder how things would have played out if this had been the case—if we'd any idea what to expect.

13. MARIANA

THE SUNDAY AFTER THEY FOUND THE BODY I'D CORNERED
Joni Garrett at a rally against political violence organized in José
Antonio's honor. It was the end of a week in which I'd slept no
more than an hour or two a night, in which I alternated between
hours of crying followed by long stretches when I noiselessly
mouthed the Lord's Prayer into the dark.

I had seen Garrett through the crowd at the rally, had backed
him against the wall on the far side of the Plaza de Armas. An offi-
cial from the Party tried to calm me, but I pushed him away and
kept moving toward Joni Garrett. I shoved a finger in the American's pale old face, held my hand above his head as if I were beating a dog. I said things I shouldn't have, even if they were true. I
told him that he was a selfish, perverted old man who had no business here in the Basque Country. That he'd betrayed me in a way
that was unforgivable. That I wouldn't speak to him, that I would
never even look at him. That he would never as much as speak to
my daughter again. That if I saw him on the streets of Muriga he
should turn the other way.

But time is the best antiseptic, as my grandmother used to say,
and when I saw him at Beatriz Martínez's wedding in April, six years

after José Antonio's murder, I had to actually remind myself why it had been so long since we'd talked. Recently, it seems that time has become less and less dependable.

I went over to the old man after the reception was over, when most guests had already left. The tablecloths were stained purple with wine, and the waiters had begun to clear coffee cups and dessert plates. A handful of people still had no place to go (or at least were in no hurry to return), and they sat at the tables just at the edge of the lights in drunken groups of two or three. I refilled my glass with the last of a bottle of cava and made my way through the clutter to Joni.

"I saw you at the ceremony earlier, when you arrived," he said awkwardly, standing to greet me as I approached him. "It's good to see you. How is Elena?"

I shrugged my shoulders.

"Fine. With my mother until tomorrow," I said. "My mother, who insists that I stay out. That I *socialize*. That's what it's come to, thirty-five and already a recluse."

But Joni didn't smile at my little joke. There were several empty glasses on the table in front of him, and I wondered if he'd had as much to drink as I had. If he was drunk, it was a different kind of drunk than mine. He seemed somber, contemplative.

"And Rimbaud?" I asked.

"Dead," he said flatly. "I put him down last October."

I couldn't help putting a hand on his shoulder. He'd had the dog since before I could remember; might have been the old man's only true friend here in Muriga, even after all those years.

He brought his glass halfway up to his mouth, then put it back on the table, as if changing his mind. He reached into his jacket pocket and took out a pack of Chesterfields. He tapped two out and placed them between his lips before lighting them both. I've never been much of a smoker, but when he held one out I took it. It reminded me of the last cigarette I'd smoked, a Lucky Strike

I shared with Robert Duarte's wife, Morgan, the year José Antonio died.

"Can I ask you something?" he said as I dragged on the cigarette. "It's something I've been wanting to ask since José Antonio was killed. Since before that, maybe."

"You don't waste any time with small talk, do you?" I said. I paused for a moment, wondering what he might ask, and then I shrugged. It was too late for defenses. "Sure. Why not?"

He ran a hand over his mouth the way drinkers do when you ask them if they'd like another, but he didn't say anything. The song "Pictures of You" was playing, and a few young couples rocked slowly to the music. It was a song that always reminded me of my first boyfriend in secondary school, Paulino Murillo.

"Did you love him?" Joni asked suddenly.

"Who?" I asked, thinking for a second that he meant Paulino.

"The American," he said. He didn't look me in the eye when he said it. "Duarte."

IN THE six years since José Antonio's death, I've decided there are two ways to be unfaithful. I tried to explain this theory to Cristina, an old friend of mine from *secundaria*, in the months after the funeral. But it wasn't something that she wanted to hear. Her eyes wandered between Elena, who was digging through the damp soil in the park planter, and a thread on the sleeve of her sweater that she was picking nervously.

A few years later I tried again to explain my theory, this time with the therapist I'd agreed to see twice a month—to appease my mother after José Antonio's death—but the therapist dismissed it as symptomatic of lingering, malignant guilt.

"You still feel as if your affair with the American—Duarte—brought about your husband's death," he said, and when I tried to clarify what I meant, he put it down as further proof that I was in denial.

"You're not listening," I said. "It's more complicated than—"

"No, *you're* not listening, Mariana," he interrupted. "I'm beginning to think you don't *want* to move past your husband's death."

OF ALL people, it was Joni Garrett who finally listened.

I breathed in two full lungs of Chesterfield. And instead of saying yes or no—neither would have been entirely true—I explained.

The first kind of infidelity, I told him, is the most common and always involves another person. It's a way of testing out another version of what life might have looked like, if chance or fate or God or whatever you'd like to call it had turned the world slightly in one direction instead of the other. These are variations that we've come to know from movies like *Casablanca* or from stories our friends tell after swearing us to secrecy: a drunken fling after a conference with the coworker, the neighbor whose boyfriend works evenings, and so on. Or you are introduced to a handsome young American right when your husband begins to spend weekends in Bilbao, as just another example. These are the stories that we're used to, and even if we don't necessarily approve, at least they're familiar. Maybe that's why it's so easy to participate in this kind of infidelity.

Joni only nodded. He seemed far away, and when I followed his eyes there were only two kids, maybe sixteen or seventeen years old, dancing to Jarabe de Palo. The girl was Ander Martínez's daughter, but the boy I didn't know.

"But there's a second kind of infidelity?" Joni asked.

"Yes," I said. "And I have some experience with this too, I'm afraid."

14. IKER

WE BEGAN TO GO TO THE NEIGHBORING TOWNS AT NIGHT, on weekends.

When we were fourteen or fifteen, it was only to see a band play in some basement bar or to try for one of the girls we'd met the weekend before. Asier began to play the guitar—a fact that he liked to advertise when girls were around—and I inherited my brother's old drum kit when he moved to Gijón for work. Even though Asier was tone-deaf and I had the rhythm of a broken washing machine, we could technically say that we had a band, that any day now we'd be playing in a basement or storage shed near you.

Soon, however, we began to plan our trips around other events. We went to a real political meeting in Gasteiz, not just a few kids drinking and smoking in an abandoned bunker. University students and professors spoke about the independence movement and the unfair treatment of ETA prisoners, describing them either as prisoners of war or political prisoners or as martyrs for the revolution. A concert was planned to raise money to fight the Spanish government's outlawing of Herri Batasuna, the political wing of the ETA. We met people whose friends were in prison for political crimes. "He got five years for passing a pamphlet out in front of city hall in Donostia," they would say, or "They put him in a prison in the Canary Islands for writing an article for *Egunkaria* in support of the right to self-governance." And even though we couldn't quite imagine someone being sent to prison for passing a pamphlet, and we didn't understand exactly what the "right to self-governance" meant, we shook our heads and said "fucking fascists." Then we rolled another joint or mixed another two-liter of wine and coke.

After a while we could tell that Ramón was full of crap, just another big fish in a small pond, his posturing about José Antonio just something to get our attention. Sometimes, we would go with Ramón in his broken-down Fiat to the nearby towns. But more often, I'd ride on the back of Asier's moto, and we would lean in against the cool nights and winding mountain roads. We told Ramón that it was just easier for us to leave on our own, when we were able, but the truth was that once we began to meet kids from the other towns, we didn't really need Ramón around. And in fact we were a little embarrassed to show up with him at all. Nere had ended things with him at the beginning of the summer, though she was still around.

It was always the same kids that traveled from town to town, and after a few months we knew them all: the Zabala brothers from Bermeo, Mikel and Alain from Mundaka, Tito from Nabarniz. (A couple of these names may sound familiar. In the years after José Antonio Torres, Tito Zabala was arrested and convicted of extorting business owners in Getxo, while Marutxa and David Oresti are the primary suspects in the bombing of a police station in Cataluña in 2000 and are thought to have fled to South America.) Most of us cut our hair short, leaving two or three long chunks that we would braid or dread, which was the style among young nationalists. We would talk politics or hand out pamphlets or spray-paint street signs with pro-ETA slogans, and then we would drink and fool around in the alleys behind bars or in the dark corners of parks. They were our comarades-in-arms and our coconspirators, but more importantly, they were our friends and our lovers.

Nere was Ramón's age, five years older than Asier and me—this fact alone made her more beautiful and mysterious than the gray-uniformed girls of San Jorge—and she even had a real job. While Asier and I were drinking cans of beer in the bunker (it seems now that my life will always revolve around either of two concrete bunkers: the crumbling walls above the cliffs in Muriga and the chipped yellow cage of the Salto del Negro), and Ramón Luna was in a university classroom in Bilbao, she drew vials of blood from old women's arms and delivered bowls of runny gelatin and lukewarm soup at the hospital on Calle Nafarroa.

If I could guess, I'd say Asier and I had fallen in love with her the first time we met her at the bunker, when we were fifteen. And not just because she was older, or because of her looks, though she's always been a classic Basque beauty. She turned thirty just before her last visit to the prison in March. I suppose she looks her age now, which isn't a bad thing. She stopped dyeing and chopping her hair a long time ago, and now there are light freckles on her nose where she's stayed out in the sun too long. But it's been four months since her last visit and still Andreas, from his top bunk, likes to talk about her perfect ass after the lights go out in the block.

Certainly her looks helped, but there was much more to her. She was as sharp as anyone in our cuadrilla, passionate about her Basque heritage and about her political activism. While changing her patients' catheters or taking their blood pressure, she would carry on about the injustices against the Basque people. She'd remind more conservative patients of the government's death squads, the ones that had executed more than two dozen Basque activists in the 1980s, or of the most recent student protesters to be detained in Pamplona for exercising their right to free speech.

But by the final year of *secundaria*, the three of us seemed to catch up to her. We had grown into something approaching adult-hood. When Ramón traded in his punky T-shirts and piercings for collared shirts and wool sweaters, Asier and I took over as infor-mal leaders. By then, we thought we were big-time; we had made out with practically every girl in San Jorge and many more from Bakio and Getxo and the other nearby towns. Through all this Nere seemed frozen in time, preserved in the formaldehyde of small-town Basque life. Her constantly changing hair and her quick tongue became more familiar, more approachable each time we saw her. When she kissed me the night after our first show (in an aban-doned house just north of town along the river), I was surprised but not so surprised that I didn't kiss back.

"I hope you don't worry about Ramón," she'd said.

"Why would I?" I said back, in the cocky way young men do after they've killed their kings. I was already replaying her mouth against mine, already realizing that I could love her. "Fuck Ramón."

OUR FIGHT for Basque independence was, in a way, also a fight for our own autonomy. Slowly, we began to gain some of this independence—from our parents, from our older brothers and sisters, from the teachers at San Jorge. We'd head out of town on Asier's black scooter, backpacks full of supplies for the trip: egg and potato sandwiches that my mother prepared for the two of us wrapped in tinfoil, two or three boxes of Don Simon table wine, whatever cigarettes we could take from our parents' half-empty packs.

We spoke only in Euskera, refusing to talk to people that started a conversation in Spanish (which was rarely a problem in Muriga, or even much of a statement, since for most people Euskera was their primary language). To avoid a moral compromise that last year of school, we simply skipped our English classes at San Jorge. It didn't seem like the old man even noticed we were gone, and the new American they'd brought in to replace the old man when he fell over dead—he wasn't going to say anything. It was clear the new American sympathized with our ideas. I'd recognized several titles from a stack of books he'd left on his desk one afternoon, the same books that we'd been reading in the bunker. The way Asier and I ran the school our final year, leaving class whenever we wanted, smoking openly on the front steps of the school, no one questioned our bravado. I wasn't sure if the new American was afraid of us or if he wished he were tagging along.

And, finally, by my last year at San Jorge the contents of our backpacks had begun to evolve. We added spray paint and fireworks, xeroxed pamphlets announcing rallies and strikes, clipboards with petitions. But even these items continued to change, until finally our packs were also filled with dark hooded sweatshirts, black bandannas to cover our faces.

It was something the newspapers like to call *kale borroka*. Twenty or thirty of us would get together late on a Friday or Saturday night, when the streets were sure to be filled with people drinking, tourists, families finishing dinner. We loaded our pockets with rocks and fireworks and cans of black spray paint. Then we tied bandannas behind our heads, put on sunglasses, and pulled up our hoods. This was our armor. Each time I pulled the drawstrings on my sweatshirt, I would turn and look at my reflection in Asier's sunglasses, and he would do the same, and I would like how frightening I looked: entirely faceless, anonymous, and dangerous. I wasn't a militant. Under the hood, under the sunglasses, I knew that. But the costume was convincing.

Here's how it would go: we'd gather out of sight of the crowded streets until one of the older university students gave a whistle. Then we would be off, running down the main streets, throwing rocks through windows or at streetlights, spray-painting long black lines along the old stone walls, yelling our slogans, throwing handfuls of pamphlets into the doors of the bars. This had been going on for years; before us, it was Ramón's older brother and his group of friends, and before that it was another group, or a band of college students from Bilbao or San Sebastián who had driven in. The only things that changed were the spray-painted names of the political parties as one party after the other was outlawed by the national government.

I'd seen these early versions of *kale borroka* when I was a kid myself, maybe seven or eight. I was with my parents, Iñigo Cortéz's parents, and a couple of other families at Natalie Lizaso's restaurant on Calle Miramar, when a heavy, empty boom exploded a half block down, followed by the whoops and yells that I'd later get so used to. The adults had been talking over cups of coffee and snacking on small plates of cheese when the firework exploded. They barely looked up from their conversation, as if nothing at all had happened. Natalie's father lowered the storm doors and windows, and it was suddenly quiet inside the bar. He went back behind the wooden bar and began pouring brandy into short, fat-bottomed glasses as the yelling and chanting made its way through the cracks in the storm doors and into the restaurant. Still, my parents and their friends continued their conversations. It was only the clank of a rock against the door that got any reaction at all, a quick "*Hostias*," from Natalie's father behind the bar.

I remember a siren and then a loud popping, as if someone had set off several fireworks at once, and the sound of yells, of feet running on the wet stone streets (maybe I'm inventing some of this, now that I've been on the other side so many times), before my mother looked to my father and said, "Ertzaintza. Finally."

The Ertzaintza were the Basque police force, and on nights like these (which they were used to just as much as the restaurant patrons and owners and as much as the kids in the bandannas and sunglasses), they would be sent out to scatter the rioters, fire off a few rubber bullets. Really, they just wanted to make sure a handful of troublemakers didn't turn into something worth worrying about.

To come home with a rubber bullet—or even better, a black-and-purple bruise from where the bullet had struck—was a badge of honor. We would act infuriated, thinking of ourselves now in the company of Gandhi and Guevara and Castro and not the bored kids that we were. I don't think we ever knew exactly what was worth fighting for—or at least I didn't. ("Against the abuses of the Franco regime, for an autonomous state!" I would have said, had you asked me then.) We were just kids playing a game, the same game that the Ertzaintza was hired to play, the same game that the shopkeepers played each time they shut their storm doors or scrubbed away graffiti. This would go on and on until, inevitably, one team or another broke the rules.

IMAGINE IT like a football game. On the red team, young nationalists. On the blue team, the Ertzaintza. They agree to unspoken rules. Broken windows are OK. Broken bones are fair game. Graffiti is acceptable, as are rubber bullets and tear gas. An unjust or overly lengthy prison sentence was against the rules. Killing, by either side, was always against the rules.

The newspapers served as the referees. Whenever these rules were broken, we would read about it in the four-page paper printed in Muriga each morning. The headlines would read, "Ertzaintza detains two youths from Aulesti for unprovoked attack on local market," and we would know to shake our heads over our coffee at the acts of these senseless thugs. Yellow card to *kale borroka*.

A month later the paper would announce, "Two college students from Bermeo beaten and arrested during peaceful demonstration," and this time around the Ertzaintza were to blame. The old men in the shops would spit on the ground and talk about how the Ertzaintza had too much power, about how they were just the same as the Guardia Civil. How they should leave our good boys alone—this was supposed to be a democracy now. Yellow card to the Ertzaintza. Another warning.

Retaliation for breaking the rules comes quickly: Ertzaina who break the rules are found dead against the tires of a Volkswagen in the parking garage of their apartment building, their heads burst open by two close-range pistol shots. And the unlucky kids who get caught breaking the rules, who are unfortunate enough to be labeled *etarra*, well, their penalties aren't any less severe. (As I later found out, even if you never actually had contact with a real member of the ETA, once you've broken the rules you are also, by virtue of association, an *etarra* for life.) These are the kids in their twenties who are shot down by the Guardia Civil in a raid or extradited from France and disappear for decades into a far-off prison like the Salto.

15. JONI

"WHAT DO YOU RECOMMEND, JONI? WE'RE IN YOUR HANDS."

The new American couple had been in Muriga a month, and Morgan Duarte had just begun to pronounce my name the way everyone else in Muriga did, with the *j* pronounced as a *y*, as if my name were an adjective describing one who yawns. (When I used to make comparisons such as these, the woman I had fallen in love with would accuse me of being overly poetic, batting her eyes sarcastically and saying, *Aye, que guapo eres, no?* Oh, you're so pretty, aren't you?) I wondered what had brought about Morgan's sudden change in pronunciation, but it was easy to speculate. Robert smiled at her when she said it, the way someone might smile when they've taught their dog a new trick. "Is there anything that you'd prefer not to eat?" I asked. We were pushed up against the wooden bar of the Boliña and in front of us was plate after plate of *pintxos*, colorful and oily. Thick pieces of bread stacked with Serrano ham the deep red of cabernet or bright-green *pimientos de Guernica* topped with sardines and lanced through with wooden toothpicks. "You don't care for seafood, if I remember."

"We've made a pact, Joni," Robert said, smiling at his wife.

"That's right," Morgan said, pushing closer to be heard over the din around us, the conversation and whine of the Formula 1 engines from the television in the corner of the bar. It was past ten, and the old men who had started making their rounds of the local bars at noon were by now yelling their jokes and insults. "We've decided, Joni, that we're going to try anything that's offered to us while we're here."

There was an excitement to her voice, as if she were sharing some sort of secret. "While we're here," she had said. In these three words the agreement that Robert Duarte had struck with his wife was clear: make the best of the situation, of Muriga, and in return I promise that we'll leave. And Morgan was telling herself: soon this will be over and it can be the wild two years of our early marriage when we lived in the backwoods of the Basque Country, where Robert played the role of the Euskaldun come back to the homeland, to Euskal Herria as he will say when we return to our air-conditioned home and outsized cars and our friends we've known since high school. We will tell them about the fiestas that last until five in the morning, and I'll wear the Basque rope-soled shoes when I pick peppers and green beans from the garden, and in return all I have to do is try to enjoy it. This was the deal, of course.

"You seem to be much more comfortable over here than when you first arrived," I said. She wore the ecstatic look of a prisoner whose sentence had just been overturned. She smiled her delicate American smile.

"I am, Joni," she said, giving Robert's arm a squeeze. He winced, as if those thin hands could cause him physical pain. "I'm much more comfortable here. I've been painting more—did Robert mention that I paint?" she said. When I nodded my head, she invited me to their apartment to see some of the sketches she'd done of Muriga since she'd arrived. Then, pointing to the trays set out on the bar, she asked, "So what should we eat?"

"*Chipirones*?" I asked Robert. "Squid in its own ink, if you're feeling adventurous?"

"You have to at least try one," Robert said to his wife. "My mother used to keep frozen packets of squid ink in the freezer when I was growing up."

I ordered a half dozen *pintxos* for us to share, including some less exotic plates, which Morgan mostly favored. People went in and out of the door of the bar, just another stop as they hopscotched down the street from one place to the next, saying hello to a friend behind the bar before emptying their glass and heading to the next restaurant. At any given time there were three or four generations of *Murigakoak* at the bar, old men with their traditional black berets and starched white shirts, young parents having a glass of wine or a bite to eat while their children slept precariously in strollers surrounded by tipsy teenagers in torn jeans. As they left the bar, Santi Etxeberria and Alonso Irujo stumbled over to invite me to the pelota match the next afternoon.

"Bring the *Euskaldun*," Santi said, clasping Robert on the shoulder. He'd already become a minor celebrity in the town, the Basque American with the blond wife. Perhaps derisively, somebody had begun to call him Euskaldun—which simply meant "someone who speaks Basque"—and the name had stuck.

When Robert responded to Santi in Basque, the only words I recognized (after forty years in Muriga) in the jumble of unlikely consonants were *Oso ondo* (Very good) and *Bihar arte* (See you tomorrow).

"How could I forget that the Euskaldun speaks Euskera?" Santi asked in his high-pitched wheeze, before waving his hand over his head.

"I hope you don't mind," the American said when they had left. "I told them I'd love to come along to the pelota match tomorrow."

"Of course not," I said, though I *did* mind, for reasons I wasn't able to articulate yet. "You both can come to my house around eleven, if that's all right with you."

"I was thinking that just the men would go," Robert said, as if

Morgan wasn't still clinging to his arm. "I don't know if you would like it much anyway," he said, turning to his wife. "A lot of sitting around drinking."

Her face dropped, and then, as if remembering their recent agreement, she said, "Don't be ridiculous. It sounds like a boys' day. And I was planning on going to the store anyway, if you'd like to stop by for dinner, Joni."

Before I could answer, the deep boom of a firework exploded down the street, followed by yells, shoes slapping against wet stone, the rattling of metal.

"Fuck me," I heard the bartender say, more annoyed than anything. There are no real swear words in Basque, so he had resorted to Spanish. People were streaming into the bar, cursing, carrying their children. The bartender walked around the counter and stood by the door. When the noise from outside grew louder, and the small bar was so crowded that there was no standing space left, he reached up to pull a grated metal security door down, then closed a wooden door behind it. Inside there was a restless jostling of bodies, some people swearing while others laughed and shouted, trying to order beers from the bar. Outside the noise increased as well, a wave rising from the end of the street, making its way toward the bar.

"What's happening?" Morgan said anxiously. "Is there some sort of attack?"

Robert was sipping at the last of his beer, trying to remain composed, as he always seemed to. But I could see apprehension stirring in the young American, as if the ground had begun to move beneath his feet. He touched the small scar at the corner of his lip with his index finger, like he was scratching an itch, and waited expectantly for an answer.

"Not really," I told Morgan. By now we could hear sirens from the other end of the street and the hollow pops of rubber bullets. From the wave outside, we heard a crest of cries as the bullets arrived, then security doors rippling as people outside jammed themselves into the closed doorways, out of the line of fire. "Just a few kids. It's been happening for years, though it's been particularly bad this year."

In the few times that we had seen each other socially since their arrival in Muriga, this was the first time we'd talked about politics. The political situation wasn't discussed in public among Muriga-koak, particularly with visitors, and I'd adopted this code a long time before.

"Is it the ETA?" Morgan asked. "Are we being attacked? Is that what's happening?"

"Of course not. Don't be ridiculous," Robert said, though he was still looking anxiously out the window we were pressed up against. I could see him fighting to regain his sense of control.

"Come here," I said, guiding Morgan closer to the window. "Do you see that one there? Hiding behind the garbage can? That is Isabela Cabrera. She has been a student of mine since she was eight. Her mother works as a manager in the Todo Todo on Calle San Francisco. And that one over there against the wall, holding the spray paint? Asier Díaz, another San Jorge student. He was wearing that same sweater after class this morning."

They both looked at me, confused.

"Why don't you report them to the police?" Morgan finally asked.

"The police know just as well as I do who they are," I said as if this were common sense, though I knew how ridiculous it must seem. I'd learned early on that this was one of the requirements of living in Muriga—to act as if the inexplicable were simply unnoteworthy. I had come to Muriga in the Franco days, in the days when the *etarras* were seen as heroes in the Basque Country, responsible for bringing about the end of the dictatorship. I knew that even if people in Muriga were annoyed or bored by these little riots, they continued to show their support by simply accepting their existence. "This is a small town. If the Ertzaintza arrested all of these kids and threw them in prison, then there would be real trouble. It's easier to shoot a couple of rubber bullets and wash off a little paint."

A few minutes later, before the people at the bar finished their drinks, it grew silent in the street. A few yells, the isolated pop of a rubber bullet leaving an Ertzaina's rifle. People continued to shuffle where they stood in the bar, growing impatient, while Robert kept his place at the window, squinting into the dimly lit street. Finally someone yelled for the bartender to open the door, and we stepped outside the way people do after taking shelter from a sudden thunderstorm.

16. MARIANA

"YOU'RE FEELING SORRY FOR YOURSELF," JOSÉ ANTONIO said the week before I lost consciousness in the bookstore on Miracruz. Over the previous weeks, he had complained when I stayed in bed while he dressed for work or when I fell asleep immediately after putting Elena down. He'd been promoted to deputy in charge of rural campaign recruitment not long before, and slick self-satisfaction still clung to everything he said, especially to me. "You'd feel better if you left the house every once in a while. Take the girl out for a walk. Something."

THERE'S NOTHING like acute organ failure to remind you how small your world is, how limited your future has become. We'd been back in Muriga nearly a year. *A temporary thing*, we had said in Sevilla. I had been pregnant for five months, and José Antonio still hadn't been able to find full-time work. *A temporary thing*, I told myself when we had moved into my old room in my mother's apartment, and again when José Antonio accepted the position with the Partido Popular. But it was becoming less and less temporary, no matter what we told ourselves. I could feel the mortar setting, the bricks of my life locking into place in Muriga as they had for my own mother and for her mother before her.

I regained consciousness in the back of an ambulance after passing out at the bookstore on Miracruz. I recognized Maite Urrutia's younger brother leaning over me in one of the dark-blue jumpsuits the paramedics wear, fitting a series of adhesive wires against my bare chest. There was something hard and angular under my arm, and when I lifted it, I saw it was *Lady Chatterley's Lover*, the book I had been waiting to buy at the book-store.

"Lawrence," Maite Urrutia's brother said, noticing I had come to. "One of my favorites."

I wanted to reply but felt a cold hiss over my mouth and real-ized that I was wearing an oxygen mask. He shook his head, indi-cating I shouldn't answer, then took my left arm in his hand and placed two cool fingers against my wrist to take my pulse.

"You passed out at the store," he said, looking down at his watch. "It's probably nothing. Low blood sugar maybe. We'll take you to the hospital as a precaution."

I nodded under the clear plastic mask.

"I'm going back to the Uni after my year of civil service," he said, as if we'd just run into each other at the corner store. "For litera-ture, I think."

HOW OFTEN do I imagine what things might have been like if it had just been a precaution. If it *had* just been low blood sugar or the heat of the bookstore. Would I still be in Muriga? Would José Antonio still be alive? And always, the ultimate question: which real-ity would I prefer?

But, of course, it wasn't a precaution.

Instead, it was the beginning of four months of tests. Of con-versations that began with the endocrinologist taking my hands in hers and sighing. Of ruling out donors: first my mother, then my cousins in Zumaia and in Gijón, each one secretly relieved when the doctor told them they were not "viable." Of donor lists and new diets and lists of Things I Should No Longer Do. Driving a motor vehicle. Strenuous activities that might unduly stress the body, such as running. Heavy lifting. Sex.

"It's a different story after we find a donor," the doctor said. "After that, your life will more or less return to normal."

"And when will that be?" I asked.

She shrugged.

"Who knows? Sometimes a week. Sometimes a year. Sometimes more."

"And if a donor doesn't come in time?" José Antonio asked.

The doctor scowled, but I didn't know which she didn't like: the question or the answer.

"It'll come in time," she said, squeezing my hand in hers.

＊ ＊ ＊

"IT'S JUST a recommendation," I said, pushing against José Antonio under the sheets, reaching between his legs through the dark. It was six weeks after the episode in the bookstore, the night before he was supposed to leave for Bilbao for a four-day set of meetings with the Party. "She said that I should *try* not to exert myself. We'll be careful. . . ."

"Jesus, Mariana," he said, grabbing my hand at the wrist. He rolled away, toward the bedroom wall. "You heard what the doctor said. Are you really being this reckless? We can wait for a few months, for God's sake."

I lay on my back in the dark, felt that great weight that had been pressing against me more and more frequently since we'd moved back to Muriga. Even then, I knew that this sense of dread had nothing to do with the diagnosis and everything to do with the man sleeping next to me. The encroaching walls of the apartment. The breathing sound the sea made as it crept up the sand.

I held my breath and waited, listening to the sound of José Antonio's chest rising and falling, rising and falling. I thought of the girl in the room next to us, and then of the stories my grandmother would tell, of burned witches and schoolchildren lost in shadowy forests. My hand snuck out from under the sheets, briefly touched my forehead, then the middle of my chest, then quickly to either side. It was the first time I'd made the sign of the cross in twenty-two years.

I lay, waiting, and after a while it seemed that the weight began to lift, if just a little. That the walls of the apartment had leaned away from me. That the sea had pulled back from the shore, stopped its encroachment. It was silent in the room, perfectly silent. My hand crept out, up through the dark to touch my forehead again.

IT WAS six months after the surgery that Joni introduced me to the new American. Or actually, it'd be more true if I said, "It was six weeks after the operation that Joni introduced me to the new American *couple*." In the time since José Antonio's death, I've often wondered why Joni had wanted to introduce me to Robert Duarte and his blond wife. Was he simply worried about me? Did he want to offer me the company of people my own age? Or maybe he thought that I'd be a good guide, someone to introduce them to the town. Or something else. Did he know that this simple introduction would lead to everything that followed?

If it was worry that prompted that first meeting, it was Joni's worry over my growing obsession with the donor of my newly attached organ. In fact, he suggested the meeting (was this an American idea, like the "blind dates" in late-night American movies that keep me company when I can't sleep?) during one of our coffees at the Boliña, just after I described how I had determined, through intense scientific investigation, that the kidney had almost certainly belonged to a twenty-eight-year-old ETA member.

"I don't see why you insist on playing this game, Mariana," he said.

"Here, hold her for a moment," I told him, lifting Elena from her seat on my lap (how long ago, it seems, are these days when she would sit quietly with me). The old man lifted Elena onto his lap, bouncing his knee just slightly; as soon as she was situated, she asked if he would buy her an ice cream.

"She already knows how to get what she wants from men, doesn't she?" he said.

"She learns from the best," I said.

With Elena in his lap he seemed confident, like he was imagining himself as something more, an uncle or a grandfather. He nodded happily at Ursula Hemen as she passed the front of the Boliña, sipping at his coffee with his free hand as he bounced Elena.

"I don't *really* believe it," I said. "But certainly, it is an interesting game to play, isn't it?"

"No, I don't see the fun in it at all," he said, stopping the jogging of his knee.

"*Gehiago*, Joni," Elena said, looking up at the old man.

"In Spanish," I told her.

"More?" she said. The knee began bouncing again.

"It's difficult to explain," I said. "But I feel like there is something it's trying to communicate to me. A message, or a memory. Something . . ."

"The memories that you've told me about—the *membrillo*, lighting the cigarette for the girl—they don't *have* to belong to this person, this terrorist. They are just little ghosts stirred up from some old memory of yours. A couple that you saw at the beach one day. *Membrillo* set out for the holidays at the grocery store," he continued. "Has it occurred to you that you're forcing all this onto some very normal sensations?"

"Sure, but what fun is there in that?" I asked, trying to change the tone of the conversation. "Just imagine how upset José Antonio, Mister Conservative, Mister Partido Popular, would be to discover his wife is secretly a militant Basque nationalist. That he's been sleeping beside a terrorist for the last six weeks."

But Joni didn't laugh. He stopped bouncing Elena on his lap, kissed the top of her head, and set her on the chair between us. Elena began immediately to pick at the chipped white paint on the armrest.

"Have you met the Americans yet?" he asked abruptly.

"The one who came to replace you?" I asked.

I'd seen the couple around Muriga, of course. They were impossible to miss, the woman with her blond hair and small mouth, the husband's short pants and hairy legs as he ran each afternoon along the beach and up into the hills west of town. "Joni, you know I would never betray you by talking to your enemy."

The old man laughed his nervous little laugh.

"I've spent a little time with them. The husband, I can't quite figure him out. But the wife—her name is Morgan—the wife, I find myself feeling sorry for. I think she feels very alone here in Muriga."

"Well, that's something I can understand," I said, though I instantly wished I hadn't. Joni gave me a little shake of the head.

"So I thought that you might want to meet them," he said. "You could maybe show them around, introduce them to a few people. As a favor to me."

With José Antonio gone for half the week, I couldn't say that I didn't have the time. And besides, the idea of meeting someone from outside Muriga didn't sound bad.

"The husband," I said. "I've been told that he speaks Basque."

"It's true," Joni said. "I don't know how much. Certainly, he speaks enough to defend himself. But the wife, she doesn't even speak Spanish. She's trying to learn—a couple phrases only. You could teach her a little Basque, if you wanted to."

"What do you think?" I asked Elena in Euskera. "Should we become teachers?"

THE TRUTH is that I didn't feel guilty about the affair with Robert Duarte until after my husband's death, and even then it was guilt for José Antonio's murder, rather than for the affair itself.

After my first meeting with Joni and the Americans (an unnoteworthy lunch, other than Robert's strange, antiquated Euskera and his wife's almost total silence), Robert arrived alone for our coffee date the following week, explaining that his wife had felt ill and would not be able to join us. We stayed at the Boliña long after the first two cups were empty. Robert described his parents' immigration to Idaho in the 1960s from Nabarniz. I asked him to translate the words of old American songs I had never understood (Toto's "Africa"; Bruce Springsteen's "Hungry Heart"). He occasionally reached across the table to touch the back of my hand with his wide fingertips, and there were moments of silence in which I found myself leaning in closer, and in which he had done the same. By the time I finally excused myself to pick up Elena from my mother's apartment, we had migrated from opposite sides of the small table to sitting with our knees nearly touching. When we made plans to meet again the following Thursday afternoon (after José Antonio had left for Bilbao for the weekend), it was understood by both of us that we would meet alone.

❋ ❋ ❋

IN THE week leading up to that next meeting with Robert Duarte, the impulses from what I was now referring to as my "terrorist kidney" were more intense, more explicit. I'd order a hot chocolate for Elena, then find myself asking the waitress to throw a shot of brandy into my cup of coffee. I'd intentionally leave José Antonio's breakfast to burn on the stovetop, let Elena cry herself out while I soaked in the tub, a bit of José Antonio's scotch in a coffee cup. I'd wake José Antonio up in the middle of the night, rubbing a hand up and down the front of his boxer shorts, and when he leaned in to kiss me I'd roll away and pretend to go back to sleep.

"I left my wallet back at my apartment," I told the American when we met the next Thursday.

"It's fine," he said. "I have money."

"No," I said. I could feel the voice from under the scar speaking through me, pushing me on. "I have to go shopping after. Come back to the apartment with me. It'll just take a minute."

I wasn't sure what I expected to happen when we arrived at the apartment; it was odd to have a stranger, a man, walking along the same hallway that José Antonio had rushed down that morning, hurrying to make the first train for Bilbao.

"Your husband is a politician, is that right?" Robert said. He wandered around the apartment comfortably, looking at photos, as if taking inventory.

"He thinks he is," I said. I took José Antonio's scotch down from the cabinet above the stove, poured two water glasses a quarter full. It was early in the afternoon, but when I handed a glass to the American he didn't seem surprised. We both sipped at our glasses, and I felt the warmth of the scotch run over my tongue, down the back of my throat. The voice whispered inside me, urging me on.

"He's fallen in with the Partido Popular," I said. I set my glass on the tile counter, reached out to grab the American at the top of his dark-blue slacks. He took a step forward, pushing against me so that I could feel the hard corner of the counter against the small of my back. I felt the roughness of his neatly trimmed beard against the side of my face, the smell of stale coffee on his breath. He put a hand on my hip, pushing me harder against the counter. I took the hand in mine, pushed it under my skirt, between my legs.

"*Bai*," I heard Robert Duarte say, and it matched the whisper rising up from under the scar at my side. *Bai.*

17. IKER

IT'S WORTH SAYING THAT OUR GROUP—DANIEL, ASIER, and I—never had a formal connection with the actual ETA, no matter what the papers later wrote. The men and women we saw on television who held press conferences wearing black hoods— these weren't the people we were organizing our raids with. We'd moved our meetings to a couple of bars in town that sympathized with the cause; by now we had gained notoriety in Muriga and even in some of the neighboring towns. And though we had never met with the actual "terrorists," we didn't do anything to dispel our schoolmates' perception that we took orders from them. We never said so, but we all hoped to gain the attention of these higher-ups— the real *etarras* who we'd seen so many times on the news.

"I'd tell them that they've become too cautious," Asier said one afternoon while we swam in the bay. He said this during a calm in the heavy, breaking waves, before sliding headfirst into the water. He swam so far down that the white bottoms of his feet disappeared. When he came back up he spit a mouthful of seawater in my direction, something he knew pissed me off.

"I'd tell Ibon Gogeaskoetxea that this can be a protest that lasts another fifty years without change, or it can be a war that gets real results," he continued. "And quickly."

"I'd ask Jiménez if he knows where Francisco Irastara and Marcos Sagarzazu escaped to," I said.

We fantasized about these meetings the way other seventeen-year-olds might imagine a conversation with their favorite footballers. Their cause was our cause, and the cause of our parents and our grandparents. Even if Muriga hadn't decided on the future of the Basque Country, we all knew we had suffered and been persecuted for the past two generations. As Ramón Luna used to say, Muriga had been built on the bones of the Basque cause since the Civil War.

But we didn't talk about the future, at least not in any real sense. It was becoming clear that Asier was expected to follow his father into finance, and by then I had started to think seriously about studying literature at the university, but we never discussed these long-term plans out loud. We daydreamed, instead, about advancing in the ranks of the movement. For me, it was always pure fantasy, though for Asier I suspect it was something more. The closest we came to meeting an actual ETA member was when Gorka Auzmendi arrived in Muriga in the summer of 1996.

BY THAT time, Asier and I had taken Ramón's place as the head of our group because we had thrown the most rocks, been hit with the most rubber bullets, and messed around with more girls than any of the other ten or so kids who we met up with regularly. We abandoned Ramón's rambling history lessons, and now Asier made a short political speech at the beginning of each of our meetings. These little speeches seemed to add some legitimacy, to allow me to say "meeting" rather than "fucking around." But I'd find Asier outside the bar before our meetings, smoking a cigarette and looking over a page of notes that he'd brought along. When Gorka Auzmendi arrived, unannounced and alone, to one of these meetings at the Bar Txapela,

Asier and I instantly handed over whatever small leadership roles we had gained.

If Ramón Luna had been Muriga's discount version of Ché Guevara, Gorka Auzmendi *was* Ché. He was tall and athletic, and if he hadn't been an intermediary for ETA-militar, the military branch of the ETA that was responsible for the bombings and assassinations that made the headlines, then he might have played center halfback for Athletic Bilbao. I had seen him speak at a couple of university rallies in Getxo and Hernani; he was a confident and articulate speaker who seemed more moderate in his arguments than many of the others that had taken the stage. His brother Xabi had been arrested and convicted for an attempted car bombing in Madrid five years earlier, and when Gorka arrived at the Txapela he was wearing a T-shirt with Xabi's image printed across the chest.

"Gorka." I found myself calling him by his first name. "It's an honor to have you here with us in Muriga." I was suddenly speaking so formally, as if I were introducing him to receive a prize. "I'm Iker and this is Asier—"

"Sure," he said. He was smiling, seemingly amused by the entire scene. "The group in Bermeo tells me that Asier rolls the best *porros* around. Is that true?"

Asier pulled a joint from behind an ear and offered it up. Gorka lit it with a blue lighter he'd already taken from his pocket. The room had gone silent, and we watched Gorka take a couple drags, then offer it to me. Finally it was Daniel who spoke up.

"So why are you here?" he said. I think he meant to sound strong and assertive, but it came out more like an accusation. Even Daniel looked surprised. Auzmendi didn't take any offense, though; instead he held his hand out to Daniel, asking for the *porro* back like they were old friends.

"I was visiting my aunt in Bermeo, so I was in the area," he said. "But in fact, I keep reading in the newspapers about the shit happening in the streets around here. I talked to some comrades—a word Asier and I put into our rotation after Auzmendi's visit—in Bermeo, and they said I'd find you at this bar."

This was enough of an explanation for us, and most of our friends' attention returned to their drinks, to the sandwiches on the table, to gossip about who was going to try to sleep with who when we traveled to Deba the next weekend.

Asier and Daniel pulled their seats closer to Gorka to hear him over the racket of the bar; I lingered between the groups for a moment before Asier caught my eye and nodded me over. The purpose of his visit, Gorka said, was to get to know people behind the movement in the smaller towns. He told us that although he himself was not directly involved with the ETA-militar, he certainly knew people who were looking to recruit comrades for the Jarrai, the nationalist youth groups in cities like Mondragón or Gasteiz. He told us he'd be speaking at a protest the following afternoon in Bilbao, at the campus of the University of the Basque Country, and invited us to join him and his friends after the demonstration.

Asier was already nodding his head, telling him that we'd be there, that there was no way we'd miss it. With that, Gorka lifted his beer and drained what was left in his glass, then stood to leave.

"This is something," Asier said while we watched Auzmendi's broad shoulders go out the door of the Txapela. "They're starting to hear about us. I'm telling you, Iker, this is really something."

"We can't go tomorrow," I said. "We have a test in calculus. And in composition."

"A test?" Asier said, almost laughing. He waved his hand, brown smoke trailing from his fingertips. "Do what you want, Iker. I'm going to Bilbao."

18. JONI

AS SOON AS DUARTE AND I ARRIVED AT THE PELOTA MATCH
the following afternoon, Irujo ordered us a round of whiskeys on
ice before dragging Robert away, leaving me to pay. The fronton,
which predates Franco's invasion of Muriga in 1937 by a hundred
years, is tucked into an alley behind the Plaza de los Fueros, and
on the days between matches the small door looks as if it might
belong to a closed bakery or a moldy storage cellar. But on the days
of the pelota matches, one passes through the door and enters a vast
room, empty except for the small rows of concrete stands lining
the right-hand wall. The pelota court itself is what gives the room
its vastness, a smooth concrete floor fifty meters by ten meters, with
two looming walls that reach up ten meters.

As I entered the room with Robert Duarte I found myself remembering my first time there, with the butcher Aitor Arostegui's sister. We had been living together openly for two months, one of
Muriga's great scandals in that wonderful year of 1949.

Wonderful for me, anyway. By all other accounts, it had been a
difficult year in Muriga; people barely had money for food and
clothes, and several of the town's men who were in their teens and
twenties struck out for the United States and South America to try

their luck as sheepherders or cattlemen. A prominent *bertsolari* had been arrested for performing one of his improvisational poems in Euskera at his father's funeral, and the Guardia Civil had set up roadblocks on either side of the town, where people coming to and from Muriga would be searched for arms or propaganda. Both her brothers had threatened me, and her mother refused to make eye contact when we passed on the street, but we were untouched by the outside world, lost in the cocoon of new love.

When we crossed through the large stone doorway into the fronton, I had realized she was the only woman present; several of the men in the stands had begun to shake their heads or to make a clicking sound with their tongues. I learned later that three of these men were Nerea's uncles. Can I begin to call her Nerea now? If I've avoided her name this far, it's only for my own safety. But it's beyond the point of ridiculousness. *Nerea, Nerea, Nerea.*

WHEN I left the fronton three hours later with Robert Duarte—the *Euskaldun*, as Etxeberria and Irujo had called him all afternoon— I was drunk and it was raining.

"You're joining us for dinner, aren't you?" Robert asked. "Morgan is expecting both of us."

"I'm not sure," I said, though the idea of Morgan Duarte serving a warm meal was much more appealing than returning to my empty flat to walk Rimbaud and reheat the soup I'd made three days earlier. It's times like these when I realize I've adopted too many of Muriga's mannerisms, to turn down an offer at least once before accepting.

"She's trying to roast a chicken—I'm not guaranteeing it'll be the best meal you've ever had, but she'll be disappointed if you don't come."

"Sure," I said. I was drunk and happy now in the rain, and company sounded good. "As long as we can stop in Martín's shop so that I can pick up a bottle of wine or two."

Morgan Duarte had been expecting us to arrive drunk, it seemed.

When she opened the door, it was obvious that she had been drinking as well. She greeted us with a water glass half-full of white wine, and by the time we had shaken off our umbrellas and removed our wet shoes, the glass was empty. We joined her in the kitchen, the counters covered with carrot greens and grains of dry white rice and a compact disc player that played an American song I'd never heard before, as well as the empty wine bottle standing next to a corkscrew and two spent corks.

Behind her, in the living room looking out toward the harbor, the walls were broken up by large sheets of drawing paper filled with charcoal landscapes and portraits. I recognized a face or two—Gotzone Urueta, Pantxo Ortiz de Urbina—sketched out in a minimalist style, dark lines making economic use of the negative space. A coffee table was barely visible under several open notepads, stacks of books on the legacy of Spain in the twentieth century and the Basque independence movement. I wondered vaguely why he would be so interested in the Nationalists, before reminding myself of the obvious appeal this history would have to a young American like Duarte. The romantic appeal of armed struggle for someone who'd never seen it up close before.

"It smells wonderful in here, *txakur txiki*," Robert said, a hint of surprise in his voice. Morgan swung her arms up to grasp him behind the neck, to pull his bearded face down so that she could press her lips to the scar just below his nose.

"I love it when he calls me that," Morgan said, turning to me. "It's Basque for 'my little dog.'"

AS ROBERT had warned, the chicken had been left in the oven for too long and the rice was undercooked, so when there was a pause in the conversation it was most often to allow the parties a chance to chew. Robert and I continued to pour tall glasses of *tempranillo* throughout dinner, and by the time Robert put on a pot of coffee, Morgan's chin was in her hand and her eyelids were beginning to waver.

"Tell me something, Joni," Morgan said as her husband came back into the dining room. "You used to be married, right? That's why—"

"Morgan," Robert interrupted her. He now seemed entirely sober, as if he'd never been drunk at all.

"Did Juantxo warn you not to bring it up?" I said. "It's all right. It was a long time ago. The truth is that I don't talk about it much. People here are afraid to mention her to me, I think."

It was silent for a moment, and I felt my head sway in the apartment's heavy warmth, weighted down by the heat of the oven and the dark smell of the coffee brewing.

"Who was she?" Robert asked.

"Her name was Nerea. Do you know the butchers in Goiko Plaza, across from the Elizondo? The fat one with the red nose and the handsome one? Those are her brothers."

Robert nodded. I could feel him watching me closely. His wife reached over the table and divided the last of the *tempranillo* evenly into our two glasses.

"Is that why you came to Muriga?" she asked, almost hopefully.

"It's not *why* I came," I said. "I came here to teach at San Jorge, because I was young and wanted to get away from my parents, and because I read too much Hemingway as a teenager. But I stayed because of her."

Another silence.

"Juantxo told you what happened, I'm sure," I said.

"Just that she died when she was very young," Robert said.

He said it in a manner that was free of affect or emotion, so there was no way to tell exactly how much they had been told. I reached for the glass of wine on the table but instead of drinking from it just held it in my lap.

"It was a car accident," I said. "It was 1955. God, we were practically children, when I think about it now."

While Robert stood to retrieve the coffee, I placed my wineglass on the table. Morgan was poking absently at the silverware that was still on the table. Her jaw was sliding slightly back and forth, a nervous habit I hadn't noticed before, and then I realized that she was about to cry.

"Does Robert ever teach you any Basque?" I asked her, trying to change the subject.

She shook her head.

"He should," I said. "Have you heard the saying around here? That the best way to learn Basque is to look at a Basque ceiling?"

Her jaw stopped its strange movement, and she looked at me questioningly.

"It means that the best way to learn Basque is to sleep with a Basque," I explained. "Lucky for you, you're already married to one."

She smiled, and I kept talking. I found that I enjoyed making Robert Duarte's wife smile. And because I had been drinking, I spoke about the woman.

"She taught me a few words of Euskera, you know. Nerea did," I said.

"Yeah?" Morgan said, brightening.

"Sure," I said. "*Eskerrik asko.* That means 'Thank you.'"

"Even I know that one," she said. "And what else did she teach you?"

"Well," I said, looking around the room. "Let's see. 'Table' is *mahaia.*" I patted my hand on the table. "*Mahaia.* Try it."

"*Mahaia,*" she said. Her small voice filled with delight at this new game. "*Mahaia.*"

"How about this?" she asked, holding up her empty wineglass.

"I'm not sure about that one," I said. "We never got to that lesson. Euskaldun!" I called into the kitchen. Robert looked up from where he was carefully pouring hot milk into the three cups of espresso. "How do you say 'wineglass' in Euskera?"

"*Edalontzia,*" he said. He was smiling now, thankful that the conversation had veered away from Nerea.

"This is a fun game," Morgan said, laughing. "How about this?" she said, holding up a wooden-handled knife. She pointed it toward my chest in a mock threat.

"*Aiztoa*," I said, my heart dropping as I said the word.

"*Aiztoa*," Morgan Duarte said. "*Aiztoa*."

Suddenly I didn't care for this game at all. "*Bai. Aiztoa*," I said again, standing to leave.

19. MARIANA

"SO WHAT IS THE SECOND FORM OF INFIDELITY?" JONI GAR-
rett asked me.

I had spent the years after José Antonio's death imagining what
I would say if I ever spoke to the old man again, things that I hadn't
remembered to say when I cornered him at the rally. A laundry list
of things carefully crafted to inflict the most damage, to cause the
most pain. But now it felt good to simply chat again as we used to.
The last of the crowd at the Beatriz Martínez wedding was still milling around half-empty bottles, still picking at their desserts; the
dance floor was nearly empty. I took a breath, readying to tell him
something I'd never revealed to anyone.

The second form of infidelity, I told him, is more disturbing. And
not because of the physical activity itself (which might not even be
as bad as the more "normal" infidelities) but because it isn't a version of love at all. It's something completely selfish.

"You've had one of these infidelities?" Joni asked. He was watching me carefully now. "The second kind?"

"Yes," I told him. He handed me another Chesterfield and an
orange lighter. "Yes, I think I have."

*** * ***

IT WAS a Thursday—I remember this for several reasons. I remember that when the alarm went off, our apartment smelled of the pork soup that our neighbor Doña Maite still starts each Thursday morning. And José Antonio was packing his suitcase to leave for Bilbao, which always happened on a Thursday. In addition to knowing it was a Thursday, I can tell you it was also the second week of March 1998. Ten days later José Antonio's body would be found washed up on the rocks below the old bunkers on Monte Zorroztu. Those are weeks you remember, whether you want to or not.

I had gone about my morning routine: first, coffee on the stovetop. Then I fed my new kidney a handful of antirejection medication. (By now, I had discovered that not only did my kidney tie his shoes differently, but he also loved *membrillo* and the smell of spilled wine mixed with garbage in the streets the day after a fiesta.) Next, I would change Elena and warm a bottle, and if the girl wasn't fussing I would leave her with José Antonio and retreat to the bathroom to shower.

Once the bathroom door was closed I would strip naked. After I had locked the door, I would angle the mirrors so that I could examine myself from all sides before showering. The affair with Robert Duarte had been going on for nearly three months, and I liked to remember the places where the American's hands had been—from the knees up, there wasn't a part of me that he had missed. On that particular Thursday morning José Antonio ironed his four dress shirts—always checked and with starched collars—folded them on the bed, and squared them into the black suitcase that we bought when we moved from Sevilla, hurrying to make the 9:08 train to Bilbao.

(This scene always replays itself in slow motion, as if submerged in warm honey. I know that José Antonio will leave the apartment to board a train that will arrive, shortly, not at the San Mamés station in Bilbao but at the rocks below the bunkers on Zorroztu. It can be so easily averted—I only need to offer up a warning, an instruction to leave the train in Getxo, before it arrives back in Muriga. And yet each time I play it the routine remains the same. I don't warn him. I don't call the office in Bilbao, distracted as I am from thinking about the American's hands.)

While José Antonio finished packing the suitcase, pulling tight his dark-green tie, I lay back on the bed still wrapped in a damp bath towel, Elena now asleep (as was our habit after breakfast, before our morning walk) with her head tucked under my arm.

"Do you have to lie there like that?" he suddenly asked, looking at me through the mirror. He said it in such a way that for a second I thought he was talking to himself.

"Like what?" I finally said. I felt Elena move under my arm.

"After the shower, on the bed with my daughter."

"What does it matter?" I asked.

"First of all, your hair is getting the pillow wet," he said. I was still trying to understand this tone. I couldn't place it.

"And secondly?" I asked. For all his talk of politics, of his plans to run for city council in Muriga, José Antonio had always been afraid of confrontation. In a way I liked this new José Antonio reflected at me in our mirror, as if a stranger had been living under our bed, in our closets for the last three years. I found myself trying to provoke him, trying to prod him out into the light of day. Instead, he only pulled again at his tie, then turned to zip closed the black suitcase.

"Do you realize that you spend more days a week in Bilbao than you do with your daughter—with me—here in Muriga?" I hadn't planned to say it; it wasn't even a point I really wanted to make. In truth, I enjoyed the days when José Antonio was away considerably more than those when he was around, when we were forced to act like a family, when he felt obligated to take off his underpants (just the underpants, always leaving the shirt on) and to lie on top of me every Monday night after Elena had been put to bed.

It occurred to me, of course, that he had found out about the American, that this was what had brought about his sudden aggression. But I didn't care if he knew or not. I'd been less careful over the last month, leaving the American's wineglass unwashed in the sink, a pair of my underwear pushed carelessly under the corner of the bedspread. He must suspect something, I thought, and I wanted to goad him into showing his hand. I *wanted* a reaction, a fight. Over the previous few days, as Elena and I waded through the small cold waves of the harbor, or while I tied braids through her thin brown curls, I had gone so far as to imagine *telling* José Antonio about Robert Duarte. Not just that something had occurred between us or that I had feelings for him, but in a way purposefully designed to cause the most harm, the most anger. Not a confession but an attack. That we had made love on the small bed in his daughter's room that morning, and again the day before in the shower where José Antonio kept his razor. That the American said things to me—filthy things—in Basque, a language José Antonio couldn't even understand.

But when he stood up, it was the old José Antonio again. The José Antonio who had waited in the hallway as the sculptor grabbed at my breasts and pulled at my hair inside my apartment in Sevilla. He had the infuriatingly serene face of a martyr with his body riddled with arrows, still looking apologetically out at the world.

"My time in Bilbao—is that what this is about?" he said, and I remember "this" meaning many things at once.

"You should go," I told him. "You'll miss your train."

"I DON'T understand," Joni said. "So that's your second infidelity?"

I shook my head.

"It's just the prologue, I guess," I said.

"We'll need reinforcements, then," the old man said, reaching for one of the half bottles of wine left on the next table.

AFTER JOSÉ Antonio had boarded his train for Bilbao that morning I left Elena with my mother, telling her I had errands to run. Robert had said that he would come to the apartment after his morning class if he was able to, but when he hadn't arrived by noon I was anxious to leave the house. It had been raining for eight days straight, but on this particular Thursday a three-day stretch of sun began in Muriga (and again ten days later, the Sunday that José Antonio's body washed ashore), so I put on a swimsuit and tucked a towel and tanning lotion into an old straw beach bag and walked the three blocks to the beach.

Because it was a Thursday, and because it was an hour and a half before siesta began, the beach was relatively empty: only a few middle-aged women already roasting their bare and hanging breasts, a couple of younger mothers with their children and an armful of colorful plastic shovels and buckets, a few groups of teenage boys who had taken the good weather as a cue to skip school and smoke cigarettes. I waved to Doña Estefana, a friend of my mother's, and rolled out my towel in an empty area at the end of the beach, just before the sand turns to heavy gray boulders.

The scar curling across my abdomen wasn't something I had thought about since the surgery, even when Robert Duarte undressed me for the first time. But now, on the beach in the full light of day, I felt self-conscious. When I pulled my shirt up I noticed just how big it was, how the scar was still healing and you could see the holes where the surgeon's needle had dove and surfaced. I left the shirt on over my swimsuit top and rolled onto my stomach, opening a magazine in front of me. Flipping through the glossed-out photographs, I thought only of my next meeting with the American, Robert Duarte, and how I seemed to have more in common with him than with my own husband. Didn't Robert speak to me in the same language as my mother? Didn't he believe in the same politics, share more of my blood? I reached down to the place in my stomach that held my new kidney, my Basque kidney, and thought nonsensically that the kidney would approve of Robert Duarte. He even fucks like a Basque, I said to myself.

I woke up a half hour later, my face stuck with sweat to the first page of the magazine. I sat up, drank from a bottle of water in the beach bag, watched the old women wading just at the water's edge. When I reached behind me for the tanning oil, I noticed a young man—a boy, really—sitting on the wall at the edge of the beach, watching me. There was enough distance between us—thirty meters at least—that we could each look at the other without threat, and so I stared back, watching the young man like you might watch a bird picking at a discarded sandwich.

His hair was dark and straight, and I could see that it was once cut neatly but that it had grown messy through neglect. The arguments he must have had nightly with his mother about that hair. He wore the dark-gray slacks and light-blue oxford from Colegio San Jorge, and his uniform jacket was folded carelessly on his lap. When I turned to get a better look at him, he glanced quickly down the beach, as if to make sure that we were alone, and then continued staring back at me. *A challenge*, I thought.

I pulled the light linen shirt over my head, folded it, and placed it in the beach bag. My stomach was surprisingly pale in the sunlight, but still the curl of the scar stood out, beginning only ten centimeters or so below my swimsuit top and continuing down below the striped green fabric of the bottom. I thought that my Basque kidney might appreciate some sun on such an unusually warm day. He, of anyone, would appreciate the rarity of it, would know that it could be another five months before he might enjoy sun like this. Still watching the boy (who was still watching me), I reached behind my back to unfasten the top of my swimsuit.

It's not uncommon, of course, to go topless at the beach, but it's not something I ordinarily do. Ever since the affair with the American became public knowledge, people in Muriga think I can't wait for the lights to turn off so I can lift my skirt. Nobody's said as much, of course, but it's true. I'd think the same thing if it wasn't about me. The truth, though, is that I've always been shy by nature. But that morning I felt different, bolder. I wasn't just tanning at the beach. I was undressing in front of this boy.

It was a response to his challenge, to intimidate him. My breasts and my scar were out in the sun, telling him to fuck off. It was as if the kidney hadn't just restored me to my complete self but had somehow added to me, made me something greater and more powerful than I was before. I imagined a voice radiating from my abdomen, soothing me, encouraging me on. I glanced quickly around. The old women were still floundering at the water's edge. A couple of overly sunned old men rallied with *paletas* and a tennis ball at the far end of the beach. I locked eyes with the boy, who was still watching me from the low wall at the edge of the sand, and then I leaned back slightly, one hand out behind me on the towel bracing me, and pushed the other hand down inside my swimsuit bottoms.

We sat like that, the boy frozen on the stone wall watching, as my hand moved slowly under the damp cloth of the swimsuit. I closed my eyes, felt the heat of the sun through my eyelids, heard the small voice of my kidney coming from within. *Yes. Go ahead. Bai. Yes. Bai.*

When I opened my eyes the boy was gone.

"SO THAT'S an example?" Joni asked. The last of the guests— Ander Martínez's daughter and the young man I hadn't recognized— had disappeared ten minutes before, and now the staff was folding up tables, disconnecting cords from the public-address system.

"Yes," I said. "That's one example."

"I'm not sure I see the distinction," he said.

20. IKER

AS I SAID, *KALE BORROKA* IS A GAME WITH CERTAIN RULES; even if they're not written down, they're understood. And when one team breaks a rule, well, that's when you get penalized.

In the end, I stayed in Muriga to take the two midterms while Asier went to see Gorka Auzmendi speak at the University of the Basque Country in Bilbao. When I saw him before school the next morning it was clear that he had barely slept, and yet he was so excited that he could hardly stop talking.

"Fucking mind-blowing," he said, before even saying hello. "I've never seen anything like it. Three thousand college students. Three thousand comrades. At exactly ten in the morning, the students rushed into each of the university buildings, forced everyone to leave. Once the buildings were empty, they chained the doors closed. Fucking incredible."

He was nearly out of breath, as if it had just happened five minutes before.

"And Auzmendi?" I asked.

"A genius," Asier said. "After the buildings closed all of the students gathered outside the School of Architecture. They built a stage, with a microphone and everything, and people came to speak to the audience. Gorka was the last to speak—he talked for forty minutes and no one in the audience interrupted even once. I wish I could remember five percent of what he said."

I found myself strangely jealous of Gorka, of the way that Asier fell over him, seemed to want to *be* him.

"And what about after the protest?" I asked. "Did you meet with him?"

"Of course," he said. "And none of this bullshit about sitting in a bar drinking *kalimotxo*, either. He took a few of us to a friend's apartment—a professor of sociology—and we stayed until five in the morning, drinking red wine and discussing the Situation."

There was something that annoyed me about the way he said "the Situation." I had gone to the same meetings as he had, read the same pamphlets, and listened to Ramón's history lessons for almost three years. And now, after a night drinking cheap wine in some old man's apartment, Asier seemed to say that he understood things in a way I didn't.

"He gave me some books," Asier said. "The professor did. You can borrow them when I'm done."

"Are we still going to Bermeo this weekend?" I asked, trying to change the subject.

"Yes, of course. But there's a change of plans. We'll meet after school to discuss it."

"I can't," I said. "I have plans already." Which was true, actually. I'd made plans to meet Nere at her house at five, since her parents didn't come home from work until late on Thursday nights.

"Well, change them," he said. "Daniel is already planning on it, and he's telling other people to be there as well."

"Listen," I said, getting frustrated. "I can't make it. Just tell me now what this 'change of plans' is."

And then Asier was smiling, as if he had just now realized that our friendship had been transformed, but if we acted quickly enough we could switch it back. "Sure," he said. "Of course. So here's the thing: it's a lot like what you and I were discussing the other day, actually. When we were swimming. I was talking with Gorka and Jorge—Jorge is the sociology professor—and we decided that the problem with the independence movement in general, and with the activities in the street in particular, is that things have become stagnant. The activities are always the same, and so people become complacent."

I could tell that these words, "stagnant," "complacent," weren't his words but Auzmendi's or the professor's. But still I nodded my head.

"What needs to happen is *change*. Something to catch the people's attention again."

We both knew what he was saying: we needed to break the rules.

"So this is what I was thinking," he said, and then he told me the plan that Auzmendi had diagrammed for him.

※ ※ ※

THAT FRIDAY afternoon, as usual, I excused myself from Irala's class to go to the restroom, then left out the front doors, along the empty moat where some of the younger children were running laps for their physical education class, and out to the parking lot where I'd parked the motor scooter my father had given me for my birthday that year.

Once I'd driven out onto the road that leads down to Muriga, I cut the engine, as I would often do, and let the moto coast around the shoulders of the mountain. I had spent the entire morning at San Jorge grinding my teeth thinking about what would happen that night. And although I knew the tenets of the cause, I wasn't wondering if what we were about to do would alter the future of Basque autonomy. I was worrying about how it might change *our* lives. But now, listening to the ticking of the two wheels spinning underneath me, breathing in smoke from the farmers' summer burn piles, I let myself relax. I didn't think about the past or the future—about Muriga's past, the rotted soldiers buried under San Jorge, or my own future away from Muriga, in classrooms discussing the great Basque and Spanish novelists, or in the beds of women I hadn't yet met. For the couple of minutes it took for the moto to roll down the mountain I was in a radiant free fall.

The three of us, Asier and Daniel and I, met at the gas station on the ground floor of Asier's apartment building. Asier had gone to Bilbao again the night before and hadn't been at school that morning.

"OK," he said. "We all understand the plan, right?"

Daniel and I both nodded. I pushed my moto next to Asier's so that they were beside the gas pump but also blocking it from the view of the cashier inside.

"I'm going to go pay," Asier said. "Get ready."

After he said it, he just stood there for a moment, looking out across the boulevard toward the harbor, where the fishing boats were floating at their buoys. Daniel had taken off his backpack and was pulling out the empty two-liter bottles.

"Asier," I said, and he snapped back to attention.

"Right," he said. Then he turned and went into the gas station.

I sometimes wonder what little debate he was having with himself in that moment. Whether he realized that he might be pushing the pebble that would start a landslide, or whether he was just going over Auzmendi's plan one more time in his head, taking into consideration all the details he might have overlooked.

When he came back out of the gas station, Daniel took the hose from the pump as if he were going to fill the tanks on the two motos.

"It's fine," I whispered. "There's no one around."

Daniel filled the two empty bottles with fuel, spilling a small puddle on the concrete underneath. Asier was sitting on his bike, looking nervously around. The smell of raw gasoline seeped out from the open bottles.

"Who was it?" I asked. "Behind the counter."

"Benito," he said. "The guy was so stoned he barely recognized me."

A dark-green Renault turned off the boulevard and stopped at the pump next to us. Its driver reached into the glove box for something, over the lap of the thin blonde in the passenger seat. I recognized the driver as Duarte, the young English teacher from school.

"OK," I told Daniel. Asier put on his black helmet and slid down the wind guard. "Time to go."

Daniel had already put the bottles into his backpack and was zipping it closed when he looked up at the Renault.

"*Hostias*. Did I ever tell you that I love blondes?" Daniel said.

"I thought brunettes. Or was it redheads?" Asier said.

"Those too," Daniel said, swinging behind me onto the backseat of the moto.

✳ ✳ ✳

WHEN ASIER told us about Auzmendi's plan, he'd made it clear that the most important thing was to keep the operation simple. "The Operation," he kept saying, another one of Gorka's terms, I guess. But it did make what we were planning more legitimate. So in an alley behind the basketball courts in Bermeo, when Asier gave the whistle to the forty or so of us (our friends from Bermeo had brought along ten or fifteen kids from their school), only the three of us from Muriga were aware of the real plan.

There had been a rowing competition in the bay in Bermeo earlier in the day, and the streets in the old part were filled with people from neighboring towns who had come to cheer their teams on and of course to eat and drink after the regatta. But even with the crowded street, everyone knew the rules. When our first fireworks went off—before we even made it a single block—people pushed into the doors of bars and restaurants and the metal sound of storm doors slamming closed came to me from all sides. Soon enough the streets were nearly empty, except for a few drunks. Just before we reached the main boulevard we ran past two old men who had been locked out of their bar by the storm doors and were huddled in the stone entryway holding small glasses of beer. I felt a pang of guilt about the whole thing, about breaking up the evening for these innocent people. But then Asier was grabbing me by the shoulder, and there wasn't time. Asier, Daniel, and I broke off from the stampede, changing course toward the series of benches along the boulevard where two buses waited at the curb.

The first bus was filled with passengers, old women and mothers with their children, teenagers too young or too drunk to drive back to their towns, and so we went directly to the next bus, as was our plan. The driver was a middle-aged man with a huge gut, and when he saw us, three men with dark glasses and bandannas covering their faces, he stood from his seat and pushed forward the box that held the fares he had collected that night. Asier took the small aluminum box and threw it out the bus door, pointing for the bus driver to follow it out onto the street.

If I'm honest—and I have no reason to lie now—I felt a change taking place in Asier. The voice that came from under the bandanna, ordering the few remaining passengers out the back door of the bus—first in Euskera, then in Spanish—seemed entirely foreign. It wasn't the voice of the boy who cried at his tenth birthday when his cousin punched him in the stomach, or even the one that had yelled to me over the waves at the beach the week before. Daniel was kneeling down in the aisle, pulling the two-liter bottles out of his backpack, and I simply stood in the empty doorway watching the scene clicking forward.

Daniel took one of the bottles and ran to the back of the bus, while Asier removed the remaining bottle and put it under the steering wheel. You could see the small wet treads where the driver's feet had been just moments before.

"Ready?" Asier yelled to Daniel in the back of the bus. It was surprisingly quiet in there, just the three of us, and then Daniel nodded back. Asier took a lighter from his pocket, and Daniel did the same. It was a strange dance, the way they moved in time with each other. The rags that hung from the tops of the bottles lit simultaneously, and still the bus was quiet.

"OK, let's go," Daniel said from the back of the bus. "Fuck. It's done."

And then we were back on the streets, running past the bus driver and the couple of passengers who were still standing outside, and then we were back into the night, taking a side road to catch up with the rest of the group. I waited for the two explosions, but instead all I heard were the sirens of the Ertzaintza as they arrived in the old quarter of the city.

21. JONI (1948)

NEREA WAS ONLY TEN WHEN SHE WITNESSED HER FATHER'S execution. She told me this in bed after the first time we made love.

It was pouring outside my apartment that afternoon; the ticks of rain on an aluminum shed outside sounded like letters being typed on the old Hermes I kept in the corner of my bedroom. But even with the rain, blown in by a storm settling in on Muriga from the Bay of Biscay, she insisted we keep the window open to allow out the smoke from my Dunhill. It had become an obsession of hers, this idea of letting the smoke out, as if the apartment itself were capable of respiration. As if the building might die if it were not allowed to breathe.

"Do you remember it? When your father was killed?" I asked her. We were still in that wonderful first phase, when you are more honest with each other than you ought to be and when you convince yourself that it will always be this way. I didn't yet feel uncomfortable asking. I knew she would answer.

"Of course," she said. She laid her head across my forearm and inhaled deeply, as if she was trying to store the smell of my arm, or of the sheets, or of my bedroom, in that same vault that held the memories of her father. "He was short. Probably not any taller than

I am," she said. "That's what always stands out about that day. How short my father was compared to the others."

I flicked the flint of a lighter to start another cigarette. It was the same lighter I had bought in the airport in San Francisco the day that I left the United States, one that I still have today, in the back of some desk drawer. I ashed the cigarette into a water glass on the nightstand.

"Was he a prisoner already?" I asked, touching her thick black braid with the hand that did not hold the cigarette. "Did they already have him at San Jorge?"

"No. They came for him the same morning that he was shot," she said. "Things like this are supposed to happen at night, aren't they? The bad men are supposed to come when it's dark, and they are supposed to do their killing out of sight, where no one can see."

Gooseflesh rose up from her shoulder blades, down over the notches of the ribs on her back. I pulled the sheet up over her shoulders, but she shrugged it off, so it settled in a pool at the small of her back.

"No," she said. "I'm not cold."

Neither of us said anything for a moment, and it was as if the ticking of the rain outside were the sound of a film being projected in her mind. I pinched the lobe of her ear, which was our little game, and still she said nothing.

"I don't know where my mother was when he was shot," she said. "It's something I've never asked her. When they came for him I was in the bedroom, and my brothers and I all sat in our beds and listened to the voices from the next room. We heard my mother say something and the sound of a bucket being tipped over or of silverware falling onto the kitchen floor. Then a shout that I always imagined was my father's, but I can't be sure of this. I don't even remember what his voice sounded like, Joni."

"It's normal," I said, suddenly uncomfortable. "You don't have to tell me this."

"Of course I do," she told me, putting her lips to the underside of my wrist. "I love you, and so I have to tell you this," and it was then that I knew that I loved her too. I wonder how often it happens this way, to realize that you are in love only after hearing it said.

"*Barkatu*," I said. "I'm sorry."

Nerea smiled at my awkward pronunciation. It always made her happy to see our Euskera lessons being put to use in conversation. She held out her hand toward mine, as if she were pinching the air. When I offered the half-burned Dunhill, her thin fingers pinched the filter just above mine.

"You smoke now?" I asked.

"Today, I smoke," she said. She took a small drag off the cigarette, just enough to fill her tiny mouth, and quickly exhaled the smoke toward the open window. She passed the cigarette back to me, then suddenly turned onto her back. "I'll never understand this habit of yours," she said absently.

"So you love me," I said, not because it was a question I needed answered but just to draw her away from the discussion of her father.

"Of course," she said. "Do you realize," she continued, "that you are the first person I have told this story to?"

I watched the ceiling with her and said nothing. When she continued, she told me that after the voices in the kitchen left, her oldest brother, Aitor, had opened the bedroom door. The kitchen was empty, as if her mother had only walked down the street to buy a loaf of bread and her father had already left to teach his morning class, except that a cup of coffee had spilled across the white tablecloth of the kitchen table, and the front door was left open into the hallway. Across the hall their neighbor, Doña Mercedes, stood in her open doorway. When she saw the three children she ordered them back into the house, telling them that their mother would be back in the afternoon. But as soon as he heard her door click closed, Aitor led his brothers and sister out into the hall and down the two flights of stairs to the entrance of the apartment building.

"There were people in the streets, like on a festival day," she said. As Nerea described how they had followed the crowd up the hill to the fortress at San Jorge, I imagined a procession of peasants with pitchforks and torches, something from *Frankenstein*, moving with slow conviction up the same road that I drove each morning in our Peugeot.

"You already know that Muriga isn't a big city," she said. "But in 1937 it was much smaller even. Just a few thousand. It seemed like everyone in the city was walking to the barracks at San Jorge that morning. It was the week after Easter Sunday, and there wasn't one cloud to block the sun."

When they arrived at San Jorge a crowd had gathered along the north wall of the barracks, facing the bay below. The men were milling about uncomfortably, as men often do before a funeral begins, and several women in the crowd were crying. Nerea remembered someone pointing out that there wasn't a single fishing boat in the water that morning. She and her two brothers had pushed themselves through the wavering, quiet audience, past the legs of uncles and cousins and friends of their mother and father, until they were standing just behind the front row, where they had a clear view of the stage but were still hidden. By the way people looked at them, the children knew they shouldn't have been there.

Nerea described how the single iron door on the north side of the barracks opened—the door that now leads to the gymnasium—and how her father and three other men were led out the door, followed by a dozen Falangists carrying rifles with bayonets, their folded hats worn tilted across their foreheads.

"You are probably imagining it was like the movies, where there is a firing squad and the captain says, 'One, two, three.' But it wasn't like that. Not at all." She was still staring up at the ceiling, past it, twenty years behind the ceiling. "Most of the men with the rifles were facing the crowd, while a few of the others pushed our father and the three other men against the wall. This is where I have the image of my father as a short man. He didn't even come to the shoulder of the man standing next to him. When the Falangist captain pulled his pistol from his belt, my father was the first man he shot."

22. IKER

WE NEVER HEARD AN EXPLOSION, BUT IN THE NEWSPAPER the next morning the front page contained a photograph of the bus in Bermeo radiating flames five meters high. In the picture, the fat bus driver stood with his hand on his bald head as he watched the bus burn, his little aluminum box still tucked under an arm. As I read the article my mother clucked her tongue in that disapproving way. "*Qué gilipollas*," she said. She placed a plate of toasted bread in front of me, on top of the newspaper. When I moved the plate and continued to read, she seemed to watch me more carefully.

"Where did you say you were last night?" she asked, pouring coffee into the cup she had set out for me. At the place next to mine was my father's plate, dusted in crumbs, and his empty cup.

"I told you," I said. "With Asier and Daniel. We were writing new songs—we're playing in Guernica in two weeks."

Well, the first part was true. I *had* been with Asier and Daniel. I stared at the picture of the driver in front of the flaming bus and began to worry about just how far things had progressed.

That morning I drove my moto to the turnoff just before the road begins to climb to San Jorge, to the small clearing in the woods where Asier and I would meet each day before school. Asier was already there, sitting on the black vinyl seat of his Honda and smoking, flicking his ashes onto last year's rotting leaves. He was in a pair of jeans and a ripped Misfits shirt, his favorite. He held the joint out to me and I took it.

"Not going to school?" I said.

"Are you kidding me?" he said. "After last night? Did you *see* the newspapers? It couldn't have gone more perfectly. Gorka called my house this morning to congratulate me."

"You?" I asked.

"Us," he said. "You know what I mean. Don't be a pussy about this, Iker. Last night was huge. It could mean huge things for us."

I wondered what "huge things" could include. Lately I had been talking more seriously with Nere about applying to university in San Sebastián. It was farther away, too far to make the drive every day, as most kids from Muriga did when they attended university in Bilbao. But living away from home was something I found myself thinking about more and more. Nere had a cousin there, and we planned to visit after I finished final exams, maybe look at some apartments. None of these, of course, were ideas I mentioned to Asier. They didn't have any relevance to his "huge things."

"I have to go," I said. I straightened the collar on my uniform and pulled the red tie close to my neck. "The fucking American professor called my mother last week. Said I wouldn't graduate unless I did extra work to make up for absences. He didn't call your parents?"

"He did," Asier said. "I don't give a shit about his class, or about San Jorge. And neither should you, Iker. We're working on much more important things now. The bus in Bermeo—that will be on the news tonight. Just watch. Things are really going to change for us."

He still looked like the kid I had grown up with, the floppy brown hair and the crooked tooth that only came out when he smiled. But

I didn't know this person standing in front of me at all, and I wondered if he was thinking the same thing about me.

"Sure," I said. "Sure. All the same, I'm going to see the *guiri* professor. Should I tell him you're sick?"

"Tell him whatever you want. Tell him to read the newspaper."

✳ ✳ ✳

IN THE last two months I might have gone to Garrett's class twice. I'd always liked the old man, though; in *primero* he would dress like Saint Nicholas for class pictures, handing out plastic bags of candy to each of the students. It's strange what you remember about someone. Even now, when I think of Professor Garrett, I remember the white plastic hairs his fake beard would leave on your sweater at Christmastime.

I arrived at San Jorge a half hour before the opening bell. There was a strange quiet that I wasn't used to. Only a couple of boys stood behind the chain-link fence surrounding the play area for the little kids in *primero*. The ones who'd been dropped off early by their parents, before the buses arrived. They reminded me of goats at the zoo, the way they walked aimlessly, kicking at the dirt or climbing for a second up the slick metal of a slide, only to slip just before the top and land in the dirt. The good-looking young teacher that had been hired a year or two before, the one with the tight curls in her hair and the baggy sweaters that made her look older than she was, watched the children absently as she smoked a cigarette from the edge of the playground.

He had been my English professor since I was eight, and I can only ever remember him as being old. Fifty? Sixty? Ninety? It was all the same. But the man that opened his office door that morning seemed to have aged twenty years in the last few weeks. His eyes were rimmed with red, and he'd missed a button on his shirt, so I could see clear through to his bony chest.

"Good morning, Iker," he said in English. He looked behind me into the hall. "Our friend Asier isn't going to join us today, I suppose."

"He is sick," I said, the English words rolling awkwardly in my mouth. Garrett sat on the edge of his desk and motioned for me to sit down on a chair.

"Do you know why I asked you to come here?"

The answer seemed obvious enough, but he wanted me to say it out loud. He wanted to shame me this way.

"Because"—I struggled for the words in English, words that I'd known before, for one exam or another—"I am missing the classes."

He leaned forward, as if to tell me a secret. When he spoke, it was in his Spanish—grammatically perfect but with its heavy American accent.

"Yes," he said. "You are missing classes. But the better question is, 'What are you missing these classes for?'"

It was then that I noticed the newspaper on his desk, the yellows and blacks of the burning gasoline almost standing up off the page. I waited for him to play his hand.

"I understand how this town works, Iker. Nobody thinks that I understand its little rules, but I do understand them. I've been here for forty years, more than twice as long as you've been alive."

I'd never heard anyone talk like this, let alone an adult. A professor. An old man. An American. He hadn't asked me anything yet, so I kept my mouth shut, waiting to see where he was taking this conversation.

"It's the way this town works, isn't it? To stand by and do nothing while people throw their lives away? To act like we each have our private lives, when in reality we all know everyone's business."

"I don't know," I said. The last of the hash was still tangling my thoughts. What should I have said to the old man? I couldn't understand what he was asking me. I began to wish that I hadn't come, that I had gone with Asier.

"Of course it is. But I can't anymore." He sat down in the chair at his desk and drew it closer to me so that our knees nearly touched. I could smell the stale coffee on his breath, could see the slight purple tint to his teeth. He reached behind him toward his desk, then swung the *Muriga Daily* onto his lap.

"Everyone knows, of course." He tapped his hand on the flames of the bus. "Not about *this*. I don't even know if you and Asier are responsible for this. But I do know that you are caught up in it. I've seen you—everyone has—running around like criminals with your masks and glasses. It's the great game, isn't it? To be the revolutionary?"

I hoped that if I kept silent it would be over sooner.

"What exactly is it that you two are fighting for, anyway?" he asked.

I remembered the way that Gorka had described our cause: a people's right to autonomy, the right to self-determination, the need to fight against a government that put people in prison just for expressing their political ideas. But all of these seemed too far removed from the empty school at the top of the hill, from my gray slacks and my navy jacket. The old man carried on: "Your father is a banker, isn't that right? He bought your scooter, pays for your school. And Asier—everyone knows who his father is. I understand that people in the Basque Country have suffered, and continue to suffer. Believe me, I understand that better than you think. But your lives are *easy*," he said. "So what exactly *are* you trying to accomplish? What's your goal?"

"I don't know," I said. And in fact this was true. I didn't know exactly what I had wanted to accomplish or what Gorka or any of them had wanted from all of this. From running in the streets, from torching the bus. On the cover of the newspaper, next to Garrett's hand, I could see the bus driver watching his bus burn, the fare box tucked under his arm.

Garrett sat back in his chair looking satisfied, and I felt like I could breathe again.

"Let me ask again," he said. This time he took the newspaper and tossed it into a small metal garbage bin next to his desk. He waited until I looked up from my lap, and when finally I did, I could see that he was smiling. It wasn't a condescending smile, or the smile of someone who had beaten you in a game of *pala*. It reminded me of the look my father would give me before each of my football games when I was in *primero*. "So, Mr. Abarzuza, what is your goal?"

I held my breath for a moment, and when I finally let out the air in my lungs, words began to come out with it. I told him that more and more, I just wanted to leave Muriga. That I had been reading lately, writers like Bukowski and García-Márquez and Lorca. Books that I would steal from the bookshelves in Professor Irala's classroom while the old man was in the bathroom, that I would read alone in the old bunkers above the cliffs between San Jorge and Muriga.

They were words, ideas, that I hadn't shared with anyone, some that I hadn't even admitted to myself. I told the old man about Nere and about the cousin in San Sebastián and the possibility of leaving Muriga to go to school there. About maybe studying literature or trying to write myself. And all through this, the old man maintained his smile, as if he had expected this all along. If I had to put a word to it, I'd say he looked satisfied.

"You're not going to pass the English exam at this rate," he said. "You know that, right?"

I nodded, looking back down at my hands on my lap. I remembered the things they had held in the last few days: motorcycle helmets, brown turds of hash, Molotov cocktails, a translated book of poems by Allen Ginsberg, Nere's short, dark hair. All of the plans I'd just said out loud—the move to San Sebastián, studying literature—seemed stupid now, nearly impossible.

"But you have another three months before exams," he said. "I'm willing to work with you. I can't guarantee that we have enough time, but I'm certainly willing to try if you are."

I looked up from my hands, which seemed so full and so empty at the same time.

"Please," I said. "Please."

✳ ✳ ✳

WE SPENT the next ten minutes creating a schedule: since I had attended so few classes, the best course of action would be to start from the beginning, compressing the entire course into a six-week class. I would be assigned three chapters a week from the textbook, and we would meet twice a week after school and once on Saturdays to review and work on conversation. By the time we'd finished planning, I had two pages of notes listing what I would be responsible for. Garrett leaned back in his chair, seemingly satisfied, and took a pack of Chesterfields from the top drawer of his desk. He drew one out and put it between his lips, then offered the pack to me.

"It's not like no one knows you smoke," he said when I hesitated. "We see you and the rest sitting around the other side of the school, in the old arches."

I took one of the cigarettes and lit it with a lighter from my pocket, and for a moment the two of us just sat there, not looking at each other, smoking, thinking.

"You know, I had a Nere too, once," he finally said. Outside his window, the playground was now filled with the small children from *primero*, playing their games with the serious faces that children always wear. He took a drag off his Chesterfield, then scratched at a small stain on the lap of his shirt. "She's what made me want to stay in Muriga, why I'm here now, I suppose."

It was something I'd never asked—why Garrett was here in Muriga. He'd been there all my life. Whenever Garrett did come up in conversation, my parents would refer to him only as "the American" or "the English teacher." "I saw the English teacher at the butcher buying two cuts of pork," my mother would say. "One for him and the other for that dog of his." And now he was giving me a clue. More than that, maybe. He was confessing something.

"What happened to her?" I asked. The bell rang for first classes to begin, but Garrett made no motion to get up.

"She died," he said. "She died in a car accident in 1955. She was driving the road between here and Bermeo. You know the curbs that drop all the way down to the ocean?"

The old man was staring out the filmy window, through the haze kicked up by small fires in the fields to where the green ocean water came up to the edge of Muriga, as if he were looking for a specific boat in the harbor. I tried to imagine him as a young man at the funeral of his wife, but it was impossible to pull a younger Garrett out of the dry-skinned, white-haired man in front of me.

"The car went off the road right there." He moved his open hand in front of him, as if it were traveling around a bend in the road. "Our daughter was in the car with her."

FOR A long time after that morning, I tried to figure out why the old man told me about his wife and daughter. Maybe it was to gain my trust. To make me think that we were becoming friends. But now, six years later—after the death of the Councilman and after the trial, after the transfer to the Canaries—I understand the old man's confession differently: it was simple honesty. I see it in some of the men here at the Salto, men serving life sentences or men who would rather stay in the prison than ever be free again. It's the honesty that hangs like a stench around broken men, men who no longer have anything to take.

23. JONI (1951)

WE HAD BEEN LIVING TOGETHER FOR TWO YEARS WHEN Nerea became pregnant. By then we had moved out of the cold-water apartment above the grocery store and into the guesthouse of Kattalin Gorroño's farm on the northern edge of town. Here, in the small house with its garden backing up onto the Ubera River, we would stay awake until the early hours of the morning sipping coffee at the kitchen table and reading aloud to each other the works of Miguel de Unamuno or Alfonso Sastre, artists and play-wrights who had been censored by the dictatorship. In the sum-mers I would return from a day at San Jorge to find Nerea in the kitchen beating a half dozen eggs—a fork in one hand, a new trans-lation of an Orwell novel in the other—wearing one of my old work shirts unbuttoned and open against the afternoon heat. These are the days against which I have measured the remainder of my life.

But even the blinders of forty years don't block out the darker days from this time. I often suspected that the old women's whis-pers as we walked through the plaza weren't prompted only by the impropriety of a young Basque woman living, unmarried, with a foreigner but by the presence of Nerea herself. "Be careful with that one," Santi Etxeberria told me once after the fiestas of the Virgin's Ascent. "She's never been right in the head since her father was killed."

And in fact, when I look back on those brief years, I force myself to remember not only the good days but also the days when Nerea would close herself into the spare bedroom, refusing to eat or even bathe. On these days, which seemed to occur more often during the chilly, overcast winter months, I would pry the lock and open the door to a cold, damp draft, Nerea wrapped in the duvet and huddled against the wall underneath an open window.

"Should I get your mother?" I asked on an evening when I was feeling particularly helpless, particularly over my head. I'd only met the old woman once, during the wedding of one of Nerea's childhood friends, and she seemed as uncomfortable with the introduction as her daughter had been. But now I only wanted someone else in the house with us, this house that now felt cold and removed and as if it had never held the warmth of a summer afternoon. I wanted someone to put on hot water for coffee, to rattle around a couple of pots and cough once or twice while I lifted Nerea's thin body and carried it to the bathroom, where I had filled the tub for her. But Nerea laughed at my suggestion, as if I had asked to invite Franco himself over for dinner.

"Is that it?" she said. There was a harsh edge to her voice. "You've been talking with her? Is that it?"

"No," I answered. I tried to bring her closer even as she pulled away. "I don't even know her. But she's your mother. I just thought that—"

"Are you planning?" she said, beginning now to cry. "You're planning with her, aren't you? To send me away."

"No," I said, feeling her body go limp, her diaphragm shuddering as she surrendered herself over to the sobbing. "I could never let you go."

BUT THESE dramatic swings seemed to trail off with news of the pregnancy. In the spring of 1952, the guesthouse along the Ubera River was again a place of warmth and excitement. The doors of the house were thrown open to clear the gloomy air that had accumulated over the winter. Nerea wore her hair pulled back, spent whole days planting beans and peppers in the garden, absently touching her stomach's small roundness. She invited friends over for dinner, dragged me by the hand to the market early on Saturday mornings. There was a constant stream of potato omelets in those months, so that even now when I am ambushed by the smell of onion and fresh garlic beginning to brown in a frying pan, I am brought back to that kitchen we shared.

"Do you ever want to get married?" I asked her one evening in bed. The coolness of the night air was slipping over us from the open window, and when Nerea turned to me, it was with a look that suggested both amusement and sympathy.

"*Eta zuk?*" she said, poking me playfully in the chest. *And you?*

"It doesn't matter to me," I said. And it was true; I hadn't been raised in the Church, and though I knew I had never loved someone as I did Nerea, I felt no need to marry. My only desire was to keep the life we had been living that summer. But I was also aware of the town gossip. About how Nerea's brother Aitor had cornered her outside the Bar Nestor and called her a *sinvergüenza*, about how small towns talk. And so I asked her again.

"But do *you*, is the question. I would if it was important to you."

"You should know me better than that by now, Joni," she said. "I don't care what those people say." She waved her hand dismissively in the direction of the town center.

"And your family? And the Church?"

"I haven't been to confession since the day my father was killed. And besides," she said. "The only God I believe in is the one that wants us to be happy in this little house."

✳ ✳ ✳

THE CHILD arrived in late November, just as the first winter storm blew in from the North Atlantic. In the office of Don Octavio, Muriga's nearsighted doctor, Nerea labored from Monday morning until Tuesday afternoon, at which point Octavio sterilized a silver forceps and pulled the boy's motionless body onto the bloody sheets.

When Nerea had finally fallen asleep after a second shot of morphine, I left the child with the doctor and midwife and made the short walk along the Avenida de San Lorenzo. From inside the shuttered restaurant came the sounds of tipsy patrons cheering Zarra and Iriondo on in the Athletic game, and the glow around the window frame seemed warm and inviting as I shuffled past. The wind swept down the narrow corridors of the cross streets and left my umbrella useless. When I arrived at the door of the Arosteguis' apartment, I was soaked through to my underclothes.

I had never been to the apartment before; during my first few weeks in Muriga, in which Nerea and I compulsively strolled the streets, talking and pointing, she had once stopped in front of the building and pointed up to the second-floor apartment.

"This is my mother's house. It is the house I grew up in," she had said. The windows were obscured by white curtains, and the iron railing along the balcony was lined with small pots of red and purple geraniums. This was before she had told me of her father, of how later on her mother had sent her to live with the sisters at the hermitage near Bermeo when she was thirteen, and so I asked if she wanted to stop in.

"No," she had said. "No, I don't think I'll ever set foot in that goddamned apartment again."

And now I found myself on the landing of this same apartment, a steady shiver settling in. The yellow hallway lights buzzed, and from one of the apartments above I heard a woman tell her husband to turn off the radio. I realized, absently, that this was the same hallway through which her father had been dragged by the Falangists on that morning in 1937—I could almost see the scuffs left by the small man's shoes as he struggled to return to the apartment, to his children, to the life that he'd already lost. And then, as if of their own volition, my knuckles struck the wooden door.

The sharp rap was followed by silence. Then shuffling behind the door and some muffled Basque, a language I knew I'd never understand. Footsteps, and then a slight crack of the door, before it quickly closed shut.

I knocked a second time. This time there was no muffled discussion from within the apartment, only heavy footsteps moving purposefully down the corridor toward the door. Before I had time to guess what was happening inside, the door flung open and I could see Aitor, his broad shoulders darkening the doorway.

"Why are you here?" he asked.

I took an involuntary step back into the hallway. It was a terrible way to meet her family—unannounced, shivering, a small puddle forming under my feet. It occurred to me, for the first time, that I was facing a real possibility of physical violence. Aitor wasn't known to shy away from a fight; he'd bloodied Primo Trujillo's nose over a spilled cup of Rioja just a few weeks earlier. But I had been two days without sleep, and any fear was outweighed by sheer exhaustion.

"I am Nerea's friend," I said.

"I know who you are," he said. "Again. Why are you here?"

"She was pregnant," I said.

"Of course she was pregnant. I saw her pass my butcher store every morning. Shamelessly unmarried, pregnant with the bastard child of a *guiri*. So I'll ask you one more time why you are here."

I began to speak but felt my knees give. I leaned back and let myself slide down against the wall until I was seated on the floor of the landing and held my head in my hands.

"The child is dead," I said. "I thought that you'd want to know."

24. IKER

AFTER WE BURNED THE BUS IN BERMEO I BEGAN TO KEEP my distance from Asier and Daniel. I made good on my promise to the American, met him directly after school to review the extra homework he had assigned me. I was grateful for the extra work, in a way; it allowed me to separate myself, just a little, from these things that seemed to threaten a different life that was slowly emerging: Gorka and his political manifestos, the cans of black spray paint, the bus driver holding his small box with the afternoon fares.

The bus had been a tipping point—everything before the spark of Asier's lighter was anchoring me to Muriga, while everything since was in preparation to leave it behind. In my mind, I was now only waiting to be away at the university, to leave behind the rotting smell of the harbor and shake the last of the sand from the beach out of my shoes. The only bit of Muriga I wanted to take along with me was Nere.

This is a revisionist history, you might say. After all, the Councilman is dead, and I have spent the last five years here in the Salto del Negro, as far away from any universities or books or women as a person can be without leaving the surface of the planet. But isn't history always revisionist? Doesn't the truth lie somewhere between?

"WHOSE IDEA was it?" Garrett said once, in the middle of a practice examination. "The bus, I mean. I've always wanted to know how those things come about."

I put my pencil down. The old man was sipping at a paper cup of coffee from the teachers' lounge, a finger tapping on the empty envelope of sugar on his desk.

"You don't have to tell me, of course."

But there in his office, the radiator filling the room with a sleepy warmth, over our cups of coffee, I found myself more comfortable, safer, than I had in a long time—the old American and I were friends, I realized.

I told him about the visits from Gorka Auzmendi, the way that the bus bombing had really been his idea, but presented in such a slow, suggestive way that it soon began to feel like our own. I recounted every bit for the old man, the way we'd filled the bottles with gasoline, the way the fat bus driver had retrieved his box of fares after Asier had thrown it out the bus door. And as I spoke I began to see them in a different way.

"It sounds stupid, doesn't it?" I asked the old man. Rather than answer immediately, he sat back in his chair, as he often did when I asked his opinion on something.

"No," he said. "I don't think it does. It's what I miss most about being young. The ability to believe in something despite all evidence to the contrary."

It wasn't until my second year here in the Salto del Negro that I began to understand what he meant.

25. MARIANA

WITHIN THE FIRST WEEK OF THE AFFAIR WE HAD A ROU-
tine; we had rules. Always at my apartment, always on the days that
José Antonio was in Bilbao. We were careful that the neighbors
never saw him enter the apartment, that we were never seen leaving the building at the same time. We planned our next meetings
in person, never over the phone. When Elena and I passed Robert
and his wife, Morgan Duarte, in the street one afternoon I waved
hello but made no effort to speak to them.

If José Antonio's lovemaking was characterized by his tenderness, the American's was best characterized by its mix of
affection and brutality. It had been less than eight months since I
inherited the new kidney, and my strength hadn't fully come
back; yet I found myself being pushed into pillows, slid off the
bed or the sofa and onto the hardwood flooring, my hair seized
in his hands and his in mine. He would say things to me in Basque
while we made love—sometimes sweet things, sometimes filthy
things I'm embarrassed to repeat. He would call me his whore, or
his love, or his little dog. And always, afterward, he would touch
me in a way that was almost clinical, inspecting the pale webbing
between my fingers, smelling the damp hair at the back of my

neck, running his fingers over the raised pink line across my abdomen.

"How do you say this in Basque?" he would ask, pressing his lips to the scar, in that way of his that seemed affectionate but might have just been simple curiosity.

"*Orbaina*," I said.

"Of course," he said. He had been asking me for the Basque translations of peculiar words like these since the first day we met. He spoke Euskera well, but his vocabulary had holes in it, lacking, for example, a whole range of words that dealt with pain or toil, as if his family home where he had learned his Basque was free entirely of grief, or tenderness, or aching.

His inquiries, however, seemed to be unrelated to any real interest in my life, but rather only to advance his own version of what it was to be Basque. He often asked silly questions such as "What do the Basques think of the election of Aznar?" or "The death of François Mitterrand doesn't seem to have much importance here in Muriga, does it?"

"I have no idea," I'd say. Or I'd make up an answer, just to humor him or to confirm his sweeping generalizations. "Yes," I'd tell him. "It's true. Basques don't like spicy foods."

After that first day in the apartment he never once asked about José Antonio, or about Elena, for that matter. When Robert occupied my home for those brief afternoon hours in which our affair existed, I never again caught him examining the photographs on our walls of our honeymoon in the Canary Islands or of our only trip to Córdoba, when we had introduced Elena to José Antonio's parents. Instead, he would sit uncomfortably on our couch, flipping through José Antonio's old football magazines and fidgeting impatiently, smoothing down his dark hair with his fingers. When once I mentioned that he had to leave, that my mother would soon be bringing Elena home, he seemed almost grateful to be allowed to escape the apartment.

After we had been sleeping together for a few weeks, however, I found myself struggling not to interrogate him about his wife. It wasn't jealousy—I knew that she was more beautiful than me, that she was doubtlessly more compatible with Robert than I was. But I wanted to know the most commonplace details of their lives. (Where do you store the olive oil, on the countertop or under the sink? How often do you change the sheets on the bed? Does your wife change them, or do you, or is it something done together? Did you bring peanut butter from the United States to eat while you are in Muriga? Do you brush your teeth at the same time?) Maybe this is what we both gained from the affair, this voyeurism.

The one time that I brought myself to actually say his wife's name, it was to ask where the two had met—the most commonplace of questions, something you might ask an old friend from primary school if you saw him in the street. We had just collapsed onto the sheets of my bed when another of the memories came to me (as they often did during my afternoons with the American), a brief flash of a young woman with dark, short-cropped hair leaning back against a stone wall, the salty, rotted ocean air pulled into my lungs, and suddenly I was talking. Against all my expectations, Robert answered immediately, as if it was the question he most wanted to be asked.

It was at a barbecue the day after his graduation from the university in Idaho, he said, on the beach of what was called Lucky Peak Reservoir. He had seen her earlier in the afternoon, sipping at a can of beer and refusing to swim in the cold water, but it wasn't until the sun had set and the party began to wind down that he gathered the courage to approach.

"She looked just like she does now," he said, to himself as much as to me. "Her older sister was a friend of my cousin. Even after we had been dating for several months, she said that she wouldn't sleep. When she told me that, I knew that I had to have her."

26. JONI

THE ELECTIONS WEREN'T FOR ANOTHER SEVERAL MONTHS, but after José Antonio's death in March 1998 the few placards and campaign posters that he had plastered along the granite walls of the old part of town were left behind, an unspoken homage. José Antonio's dark suit seemed a little too large for his thin build and he was framed in bright lettering proclaiming, "Torres, a New Vision for the Basque Country." Mariana had told me it was a campaign slogan that had been devised by the party in Bilbao. It was the same slogan being used by a wave of young conservative party candidates in small towns throughout the region, she said, one that had tested well in market research from Madrid.

But even after his death, and after the nationwide protests and the calls for justice, after the trials and the sentences, the peeling posters betrayed Muriga's conflicted psychology, spray-painted over with the usual nationalist slogans. In sloppy handwriting across a José Antonio poster at the corner of Calle Nafarroa and Calle San Francisco, it read, "Fascists Stay Out of the Basque Country," and on a poster outside the town music store, José Antonio's forehead was tattooed with a red swastika. The last traces of the posters finally peeled away during the winter rains of 1999.

"QUÉ SINVERGÜENZA," Robert said one Saturday afternoon that January, walking past one of José Antonio's newly hung posters on the way to the handball court. In a small town where reputation is everything, to call someone "shameless" is perhaps the worst insult one can level.

"That's a strong word," I said to the American.

"I'm sorry, Joni," he said, kicking at a crumpled Coke can with the petulance of a pouting young boy. "It's not our place, I know. You and me, we're outsiders. But I can't help but take sides here."

I nodded. He was right, of course. If anything, he was more easily accepted because of his Basque heritage.

"My grandfather was a political prisoner during the Civil War," he said suddenly. "I never told you that before."

"No," I said.

The American reached his hand out, skimming the wet limestone with his fingertips as we approached the fronton.

"He was a barber in the Republican navy. His ship was captured in thirty-seven, two years before the end of the war. They kept him and his brother until the war finished, and when they were released they borrowed money to come to Idaho as sheepherders. They were indentured servants, more or less; it took my grandfather five years to save enough money to bring my mother over to the States."

"You know about the massacre at San Jorge?" I asked. I realized I had made my home in Muriga during the height of the dictatorship that had taken power after the war, while Duarte's family had been forced into exile by it.

"Of course. I did my master's thesis on the role of the Church in the Civil War. It's one of the reasons that I chose to apply at San Jorge."

I struggled to make sense of this new information; it was, I felt, the first moment of true candor I'd heard from Robert Duarte, and

I didn't know what had provoked it, what its implications were. Had Duarte come to Muriga as something more than a curious young man exploring his heritage?

"And José Antonio?" I asked.

His bearded lip curled up involuntarily, emphasizing his scar.

"Torres and his party are just the next version of Franco and the Falangists. I've been talking with Mariana," he said, then stopped himself, as if realizing he'd overstepped a boundary.

"She's mentioned as much," I said. He watched me closely.

"You wouldn't believe the things he's said to her. 'Spanish unity.' 'The Nationalists are a bunch of terrorists.' The same thing my parents tried to escape from. We act like things have changed, but they haven't."

By this time, we had arrived at the fronton. Etxeberria and Irujo were waiting for us at the front gate, as had become our habit over the last several weeks. Already Etxeberria was slurring his words, tottering over to slap Robert Duarte on the back and speak to him in Euskera. Irujo grinned dumbly at me, then offered a flask from his jacket pocket.

IT WAS a disappointing match, with Mendoza and Ortza, the grandson of the legendary player Txikito de Iraeta, losing quickly to two young *pelotaris* from Ustaritz. When the crowd dispersed it was still early afternoon, and the match had put our foursome in a collective foul mood. As we emerged squinting into the afternoon light Etxeberria spat on the street, flicked his hand at us in an attempt at a wave, and headed up the hill toward his apartment behind the cathedral. The three of us—Robert, Irujo, and I—wandered aimlessly through the stone streets of the old part of Muriga. Finally, after we had passed the elaborate stonework of the city hall, Robert broke the afternoon's silence.

"What do you know about Iker Abarzuza?" he said in English.

I glanced over to Irujo, who was still wearing the same drunken, beatific smile he had arrived at the pelota match with, oblivious that someone had spoken at all.

"What do I know?" I asked.

"I've spoken to him a few times after class. He seems like a bright kid. Pretty idealistic. He thinks the world of you; he's told me about your private lessons."

I was unnerved by the tone in which the American spoke; gone was the soft intimacy of our discussion on the way to the match, when he had spoken about his family. Instead, his clinical coldness had returned.

"Yes," I said cautiously. "He's very bright. I've been helping him prepare for his English exam at the end of the year."

Irujo touched me softly on the shoulder, then turned into the Boliña, leaving me again alone with Robert. The streets were empty for a Saturday afternoon. Most people were at home watching the Bilbao match against San Sebastián. Only a few old women were out, pulling their small carts full of the weekend's groceries.

"I've also spoken a few times with his friend Asier," he continued. "Funny kid, won't speak a word to me unless it's in Euskera."

"I suppose that's why he hasn't been in my English class for a month now," I sighed.

"He's an interesting kid. Imagines himself to be quite the expert on Basque politics."

"We have a few of those kids every year," I said. "Luckily, they grow out of it."

"What's lucky about it?" Robert said, defensive.

"Well, I just worry about them sometimes, is all. Idealism is great, especially when you're young. But it's an intellectual vacuum in small towns like Muriga, and I've seen kids get lost."

Robert didn't say anything for a long while. When we reached the bridge out of the old town, I stopped.

"I think I'll head back and meet Irujo for a *patxaran* after all,"

I said. Robert nodded. We shook hands, but as soon as I turned to leave he called to me.

"Joni!" he said, jogging back over. "I know it's not my place, to get involved in people's lives here. But there's a point in which you can't really help it, isn't there?"

"Yes," I said, and the image that came to me as I said this was not of Iker and Asier with their Molotov cocktails nor of José Antonio's new posters wallpapering the streets, but rather of Mariana, at home with Elena, allowing the young girl to run her tiny fingers over the bright pink scar across her mother's abdomen. "Yes, I suppose you're right."

27. IKER

"I HAD A DREAM LAST NIGHT," ANDREAS SAYS THIS MORN-
ing from his upper bunk. Each day, the Salto del Negro is woken
by the clanging of the cafeteria and the squawks of shorebirds circling the garbage bins just outside the prison walls, and after eighteen months together Andreas and I have settled into a habit, where
the first to wake says loudly, "The worst part of this shit-covered
prison is the fucking shorebirds!" (Or, on mornings where one or
the other is less inspired, simply, "Fucking shorebirds.") But this
morning it's too early for the shorebirds, and there's only the dark
of the Salto del Negro, the sound of a thousand men breathing and
snoring, and now Andreas's high, childlike voice.

"Are you there, Iker?" he whispers. "Are you awake?"

"Yes."

"Do you want to hear about the dream?"

"No," I say. "But you're going to tell me anyway, so go ahead."

There is a pause, as if he's considering whether to be pissed off
by this answer. But he wants to describe his dream more than he
wants to act offended, so he continues.

"At the beginning, we were fishing, my grandfather and me,
along the Río Atuel back home in Argentina. Except that the man

who was my grandfather was my own age—no older than thirty. I knew that he was my grandfather because he wore the same blue handkerchief around his neck and because he called me Pepo. The river was black and flooded and filled with debris. Fences. Plastic soap containers. Old books so fat with water that they were open like the wings of a bird. A woman's shoe. I remember all of these things. Dead animals. A young girl's addition tables."

"So how was the fishing?" I ask.

"The fishing," he says, still dead serious. "This is what I was about to tell—this is the worst part."

I hear a clicking noise from Andreas's top bunk, as if he is tapping a ballpoint pen against the concrete wall.

"We were standing at the edge of the river, just where the roots of the Fitzroya trees were exposed by the water. The water was up over our feet, and my grandfather was pointing across the river, showing me where to cast. His hand was on my shoulder, and he would point across the debris in the river to a target as if he were a military general telling me where to shoot. I whipped the pole out over the river, and when I felt the hook set my grandfather would clamp his hand on my shoulder and yell at me to reel in."

Suddenly I want Andreas to stop. I don't want to know what monstrosities are waiting on the end of his grandfather's line. But it's too late. The story is in motion, and now it will arrive.

"He pointed to a small gray shape just under the surface of the water, and I cast my line. When the line went tight I reeled and reeled. The pole bent so much that its tip was touching the river. I pulled for what seemed like hours, my grandfather yelling and cursing in my ear the entire time, and when I finally managed to bring my catch into the shallows I saw that it was the altar from the San Juan Cathedral, where my grandfather had been buried.

"My grandfather swore at me and waded into the river to release the hook from where it had been set around the leg of the altar. The river was still rising, so by now I was waist-deep. I had to lean upstream against the current. Before I could even gather my strength my grandfather was at my side again, pointing at a smooth brown hump against the far bank of the river. Without thinking, I cast. The first cast missed, and my grandfather whispered more and more quickly in my ear, but the second cast landed cleanly on the brown hump, and I felt the line come alive as the hook set. It was quiet for a moment, as if the river itself had stopped flowing, and then the line jerked toward the bottom, knocking me off-balance. I felt the current carrying my feet from the river bottom, and then my grandfather's hand landed square between my shoulder blades, pushing me into the river with the thing at the end of the line.

"Are you there, Iker?" Andreas asks. "Are you awake?"

"Yes."

A pause, and then:

"The debris in the water battered me without mercy. Have you ever been in a car accident, Iker? It was like a car accident. I held on to the bamboo pole as if by instinct—I knew it would be the only thing to save me. Finally, the river emptied into a great muddy lake in the valley where my town, Santa Rosa, had been. The streets were filled to the streetlights with the brown water, and I swam onto the roof of my aunt's bakery.

"I was still holding the bamboo pole, and when finally I had wedged myself between two stovepipes sticking out from the roof, I felt a small tug on the line, as if to remind me. This time, when I turned the reel, the thing on the other end of the line twisted slowly. The water was dark brown, nearly the same color as his skin, and it wasn't until he was within reaching distance that I realized it was Imanol. It was my son."

The clicking sound from Andreas's bunk continues, and then it is joined by the first shrieks of the shorebirds.

"Do you think it means anything, Iker?"

"No," I say. "Except that maybe you should have been a fisherman instead of an amphetamine dealer."

When he laughs, Andreas's lightheartedness comes back. There is a racket from the outside courtyard.

"Fucking shorebirds," he says.

28. JONI (1951)

THE NIGHT THE CHILD ARRIVED STILLBORN, NEREA'S mother had come with me back to the doctor's house, walking the quarter mile in the blowing rain without a word. In the dark rain-slicked streets, the woman seemed older than I'd ever be, though in fact she was no older than her midfifties. When we arrived at the doctor's house she told me to wait at the doorway, and a moment later the old doctor joined me.

Her mother stayed at the guesthouse on the Ubera River for ten days. For the first four days the old woman refused to allow me to see Nerea at all. Instead, I slept on the sofa with the sloping cushions and watched Nerea's mother shuffling in and out of the bedroom, opening the door just enough to allow her thin, bent frame to pass through. She cooked for hours at a time, Aitor stopping by every few days to leave groceries and to sit around the kitchen table for coffee. There was a constant smell of garlic frying in olive oil, a steady train of food carried into the bedroom and, often as not, brought out untouched.

I wish I could say that in these ten days I was eventually accepted by the Arosteguis, but the best that can be said is that we reached a functional civility. The first two days I barely moved from the couch, coming in and out of sleep, dreaming of the boy's waxy body, the look the doctor gave me as he tried to draw the child out with the forceps, the sob that arose from Nerea when the midwife took her hand and whispered in her ear. The morning of the third day, I woke to fingers of sunlight reaching around the corners of the blinds. I heard a quiet murmuring from behind the bedroom door, and I went to the kitchen to fill the Cuban press on the stovetop. When the old woman came out twenty minutes later, I poured her a cup of the thick, dark coffee. She accepted it without a word.

"Do you take milk?" I finally asked.

At this, she seemed to soften just a little. She shook her head, but as if in response to another question.

"You can't go in today," she said. I nodded, holding my coffee stupidly in my two hands. "She's not ready yet. Maybe tomorrow, but not today."

"What can I do?" I asked, feeling helpless. "Can I get anything? What does she need?"

"What she needs . . ." the old woman said, anger suddenly sparking up in her before she calmed herself. She continued on, her Spanish heavy with the rolled *r*'s and drawn-out *s*'s of her Basque accent. "What she needs is rest. She's a fragile girl. You know this, I hope?"

I nodded, remembering the paranoia of the previous winter.

"She's always been that way. That's why I sent her to live with the sisters," she said, looking keenly at me. "I don't know how much she's told you."

"Practically nothing," I lied.

"Anyway, today you cannot see her. Go to work—you work at the private school, no? Go to work. Today you cannot see her, but perhaps tomorrow."

WHEN I'D called San Jorge two days earlier, the old secretary told me that they had already heard the news. (The doctor was, after all, the headmaster's brother-in-law.) I told her that I would be taking off the rest of the week, and when there was no answer on the other end of the line I realized that she was crying.

"It's OK," I'd said, somehow. "These things happen. It's something that we'll get through."

But now I heeded the directions of Nerea's mother, if only because following directions allowed me to not think about the body of the boy, and about what would be left of the woman I loved when our bedroom door finally opened.

On the way to San Jorge, I drove to the doctor's house. I pulled the car over onto the curb and let myself through the front gate into the garden. When Octavio answered the door, he looked surprised to see me, perhaps even frightened. He took a step back into the house before speaking.

"Joni," he said. I tried not to look into the open house behind him, but my eyes wandered past him, through the living room, into the back bedroom where Nerea had labored for nearly two days.

"I'm not sure why I stopped in," I said.

"Come in, please. Come in," he said.

"No," I said. "I can't stay. Like I said, I'm not sure why I stopped."

"Of course," the old doctor said, pinching the bridge of his nose tiredly. We stood there awkwardly for a minute, just the cold clean air blowing through the few leaves that hadn't yet fallen in his garden.

"I should go," I said.

"Of course," he said again, more quietly. When I turned to leave, he said, "Joni, how is she?"

I turned to look at him there in the doorway of the house. He was wearing a heavy knit sweater that was a little too big for him, the sleeves rolled up so as not to cover his hands. He seemed undersized and vulnerable standing there like that.

"I stopped by the next afternoon, but her mother turned me away. Did she tell you?"

"No," I said.

"And yesterday I sent the midwife, but she was turned back as well."

I nodded. We stood there for what felt like a long time, the two of us in the small garden with only the wind blowing between us.

AFTER I left the doctor's house, I drove on the road leading to San Jorge—the same road, I reminded myself, that Nerea and her brothers had climbed the morning that their father was executed. When I entered the office, the secretary walked across the room and put her arms around me, and I thought that she might start crying again. I collected a few pieces of mail, then left a note for the headmaster to tell him that I would be back teaching the next afternoon. I started down the hallways toward the exit, but before opening the doors that led onto the parking lot I turned down the hallway of *primaria*.

I was hired to teach *secundaria*, so I rarely had an opportunity to see the youngest students at San Jorge. And now, as I walked down the halls decorated with cutout cartoons and alphabet letters, I stopped at the door of one of the classrooms to peek inside. The children wore the same gray slacks and oxfords as their older counterparts, and behind the small glass windows in the doors the children's mouths moved soundlessly. I wondered what tiny conversations they were having, what they found so important to talk about even as their teacher tried to quiet them.

THE NEXT morning I woke early. The house was still dark and silent. I padded in my socks around the kitchen to start the coffee and then went out onto the front step and lit a cigarette just as the first light was arriving. When the bedroom door finally scraped open an hour later, I had already showered and dressed.

That morning, Nerea's mother seemed more hunched over than I had remembered her the day before, and she appeared, for the first time, a woman who had lived through tragedy several times over. The whites of her eyes were shot through with red, and there was a pale crust at the edge of her mouth. I poured her coffee again and this time added hot milk. She nodded, then sat heavily at the kitchen table.

"Not today," she said, offering a tired smile, again shaking her head. "I'm sorry. Not today."

29. MARIANA

IN THE MONTHS BEFORE JOSÉ ANTONIO'S DEATH, IT ALL seemed to boil up to the edge, as if Muriga were the cauldron in the kitchen of the Boliña, and Elena's emerging teeth were the scallions, and the American Robert Duarte's sweat against my chest was the stock, and the peeling edges of José Antonio's campaign posters were pale bits of cabbage, and it was all a great stew that was suddenly heated too quickly. Or maybe this is just how I see it now that the pot has already spilled over. It's possible—likely, even—that at the time, there was no stew and no heat (perhaps not even the cauldron of Muriga as I remember it now) but only the broth of real life, its parts blurred into each other a long time ago.

What I can say for certain is that ten weeks before his body was found (still wearing his only suit), José Antonio called from the Party offices in Bilbao to inform me that a committee had formally approved his bid to run for Muriga's city council the following November. That same night, alone in the bedroom with the window cracked open so I could smell the sea foam whipped by a two-day storm, I woke no fewer than four times. The series of dreams that visited me that night seemed to belong to someone else (who else, of course, but my new pet? Even now, I can't help but touch the light line at my belly button as I recall that night). When I went to the kitchen just before five to put a pot of coffee on the stove, I could only remember the skeletons of the dreams, tiny images connected only in their violence: a young woman with no eyes at all, attacked by two men with red ribbons instead of arms; a calf struck down by a white postal van; and finally, only the black sensation of drowning.

"Iñaki," I said quietly that morning, waiting in the dark for the coffee to brew. It was the first time I had addressed the organ directly. By now I was certain that the young terrorist was in fact growing, becoming stronger, fighting for space inside me.

And did my new kidney answer? Did the dead speak through my own mouth, with my own tongue?

Of course not.

But I continued on anyway. At first I spoke so quietly that it was barely anything more than the moving of my mouth. I asked about the dreams, and I asked about his life before he was killed by the Ertzaintza. I thanked him for his gift to me. I asked him about the image of the young girl that had come to me several times, the girl with the short, dark hair who was handing me a cigarette. About whether she had been his girlfriend, or perhaps a cousin or a coworker. Had he been in love with her? Had she broken his heart, or did he break hers? I asked if the smell of *membrillo* that came to me when I woke from the surgery was the same smell of the *membrillo* that his grandmother would set out after Easter dinner. I asked him if it was true that he had killed the intelligence officer in Madrid, and if so, then why? I asked if he ever regretted it. I asked what he missed most, now that the only part of him left on this earth was in the dark pit of me.

By now a gray light was beginning to come in through the open shutters of the living room, and I could see that the sill was wet with the fine mist that we call *txirimiri*. As I tapped out the spent grounds from the coffeepot and refilled the small reservoir with water, I told him about the affair with Robert Duarte and about how I had never once felt guilty. I asked if this made me a bad person, and when he didn't answer, I continued on. I told him that I knew what my old friends, the ones I had grown up with, were saying behind my back, about Mariana, who had brought the pestilence of Madrid to Muriga in this husband and his posters about his "New Vision for the Basque Country." I talked about my old life in Sevilla, and I admitted that I sometimes fantasized about something bad happening to Elena so that I could be free entirely of José Antonio.

I wondered out loud what Iñaki would have thought of my husband and his Partido Popular, if he would have spit on the posters of José Antonio. If Iñaki might have lain in wait outside of *our* apartment, had he not been killed in a shoot-out with the Ertzaintza. If he might have slid between the tires of our car at three in the morning to secure a packet of explosives that would ignite when José Antonio turned the ignition (perhaps with me and Elena in it). Or if perhaps he might not wire the bomb correctly, if maybe in the dark of the night and in the excitement of the task he might connect a red to a green, or a green to a blue, and in the morning as we started the car to drive the twenty kilometers to my aunt's house in Guernica, the explosives would not detonate. Would the small gray package of explosives ride with us along the steep road to Guernica and then back to Muriga; would it fall harmlessly as the car passed over a bump in the road?

Elena slept late. I drank cup after cup of coffee and reached out the window to feel the cool mist against my palm and wrist and talked and talked until, just after eight, there was a knock. When I opened the door, I found my neighbor, Maite, in her dusty pink housecoat.

"Is everything all right?" she asked.

"Yes," I said. "Everything's fine."

"I've heard voices over here since five. The only time people talk at that time of the morning is when someone has died."

30. IKER

SOME DAYS THE COUNCILMAN WOULD COME OUT OF THE train station looking like shit, his dark suit wrinkled and his eyeglasses sliding to the end of his nose, his black briefcase pulling one shoulder down so that he leaned to one side. On others—if it was one of the odd warm days we get in Muriga in late September—he would bounce down the steps onto the curb, the navy jacket folded under an arm and the white of his dress shirt rolled up, showing his hairy arms. Or he would step out into an afternoon rainstorm, holding the morning's copy of *El Correo* over his head in a way that reminded me of my father. But always, he would come off the 6:24 train from Bilbao.

We continued our lookouts throughout the summer before our final year at San Jorge, even after Ramón Luna had left Muriga for university in Bilbao. What started as a game had taken on a different tenor without Ramón. Asier and I would meet Daniel at the bridge that crosses the Ubera on Monday afternoons, where we knew the Councilman would pass on his way home from the station. As we waited for his familiar form to walk out of the string of people coming off the train, we would lean over the low stone wall, out over the river. When the tide is low during the summer months, the silver flashes of river trout jump out from the brown river bottom. Waiting for the Councilman, we'd flick the shells of our sunflower seeds from the bridge and watch the fish rise to the surface, mistaking the husks for an insect wing before spitting them out into the river to be carried into the bay.

Starting down the Avenida de Getxo, the Councilman might stop in at a newsstand or a café before walking the seven blocks across the plaza, in front of the city hall, and along the Paseo de los Robles to his apartment building at the corner of Atxiaga and Zabaleta. From the mailboxes in the apartment entryway, we had learned that they lived on the fifth floor on the left side of the building facing toward the bay, which was blocked by another row of apartments. The three of us would sit in the entryway of Santi Etxeberria's musty hardware shop, watching the window and talking about Lizarazu's off-season trade from Athletic until old Etxeberria would run us off. Sometimes, a few minutes after the Councilman had disappeared into the entryway of the apartment building, we would see his white sleeves reach out and swing closed an open window five stories up.

I OFTEN think back to a Sunday afternoon the spring of the Councilman's death. Nere and I were finishing our coffees in Estefana Torretxe's bar when we saw the Councilman pass by with the little girl on his shoulders, his wife following a few steps behind them. For all the times I'd seen him in the past months, it was the closest we'd ever been to each other. He added a small bounce to his walk so that the girl sprang up with each step, which made her laugh inaudibly outside the window of the bar. Behind her, the Councilman's wife seemed unaware of her family, and if I hadn't known better I wouldn't have thought the three were related. As she passed the door of the bar, she reached a hand into the doorway to wave to Estefana.

Her voice was soft and worried as she said, *"Agur, Estefana, agur,"* into the almost empty bar. The old woman waved back from behind the counter, but the family had already continued down the block toward the plaza.

"*Gaixoa*," I heard Estefana say to herself. *Poor girl.* I was wondering whom she was referring to, the wife or the daughter, when Nere squeezed my leg under the table.

"Let's follow them," she whispered.

"Yeah?" I asked, trailing them down the street with my eyes.

"It'll be fun," she said. "We can observe our subjects in their natural habitat."

"How much do I owe?" I said to the old woman behind the bar. She wiped her hands on her apron, then waved them in front of her.

"Tell your mother I say hello," the old woman said.

I left two one-hundred-peseta coins on the counter anyway and followed Nere out the doorway into the bright afternoon street. She hooked her thumb onto the front pocket of my jeans, as she always liked to do. (*I want to keep you close*, she used to say. She did this, her little anchor on my pocket, for her first visits in the Canaries, when we were allowed to walk around the visiting courtyard together. *I want to keep you close.* She kept it up until the start of the third year, when we both realized that the Salto del Negro was how it would always be. She still visits, but she no longer hooks a thumb in my pocket.) Ahead of us, the Councilman and his family mixed in with the Sunday afternoon crowd. The girl's bobbing brown hair made it easy to follow them, and as we walked, Nere began to talk about the coming year.

"If you're accepted to San Sebastián, we can stay with Carolina. Her roommate is leaving in August," she was saying.

"Sure," I said, imagining afternoons reading in cafés by the beach, nights out in the city's old part with its hundreds of bars and streets running over with young people.

"She has a friend that works at the hospital there," she said. "She might be able to help me get a job."

The Councilman and his wife stopped in at the Arosteguis' butcher shop, the Councilman pointing to the halved pigs hanging by their feet in the back of the store and pinching his daughter's stomach playfully while the wife ordered cuts from the handsome butcher behind the counter.

"Do you ever worry about what your parents will say?" I asked.

"When we move to San Sebastián?"

She didn't answer immediately. Instead, we kept walking past the plaza to avoid drawing the attention of the Councilman. When we had reached the large stone archway leading out onto Calle Nafarroa, she stopped, using her hooked thumb to pull me toward her. She leaned up to kiss me, stepping on my shoe to raise herself up (another thing that stopped during the third year at the Salto del Negro), and then she leaned back against the wall of the archway.

"Of course I worry," she said. "Don't you?"

"Yes."

"My father will be furious."

I nodded. I'd met her father once or twice at her house. He was a short man who seemed incapable of anger. The first time we'd met, when I stopped in to pick up Nere on the way to a concert in Lekeitio, he had insisted that his wife make me a ham sandwich before we left. My father, on the other hand, was much easier to imagine angry. He had made clear early on that he expected me to apply to the economics program at the University of Deusto, and Nere, with her dyed hair and piercings, didn't have any place in that future. I hadn't yet dared to tell him about my plans to live with the twenty-three-year-old girlfriend he didn't know existed or that I had decided to study literature instead of engineering.

"But anyway, let's not think about it just yet," she said.

"Sure," I said. I squinted against the afternoon sun. The dull pressure was starting just behind my eyes. I felt the taste of metal on my gums.

"Are you all right?" Nere asked, taking me by the arms. "Another of the headaches?"

I nodded, leaning back against the wall. The pain was radiating, brittle behind my eyes, and the pops of light had already begun. I slid down against the wall and held my head in my hands. Nere knelt next to me and rubbed the back of my neck. Around me, I heard the shuffle of feet, disembodied conversations. Soon the flashes faded, and the pain began to lessen. When I finally looked up, it was just as the Councilman and his wife walked past us in the archway, so close I could have touched him.

31. JONI (1951)

A WEEK AFTER SHE MOVED INTO KATTALIN GORROÑO'S guesthouse with us, Nerea's mother emerged from the bedroom waving away the coffee I had prepared for her.

"You smoke, no?" she said.

I nodded. She held out her small hand, and I handed her the blue box of Dunhills from my chest pocket. She pinched one of the cigarettes out of the box, then bent down to light it on the gas range. In the previous seven days, I'd never seen any indication that she smoked. She opened the kitchen door and blew a plume of smoke out into the gray morning. She took another pensive drag, then turned toward me as if noticing my presence for the first time.

"Maybe today, young man," she said. She nodded as if answering a question she had asked herself. "Maybe today."

※ ※ ※

WHEN I returned from San Jorge that afternoon I found Nerea standing at the stove in one of my old dress shirts worn over a cotton blouse, the sleeves rolled up on her thin arms, stirring potatoes in a cast-iron pan. Her slender legs were hidden under a dark, heavy skirt. Her mother was seated at the kitchen table, stemming a pile of green beans and puffing on another of the Dunhills. Hearing the front door, the two women turned nearly in unison as I entered the kitchen.

"*Arratsalde on,*" she said, smiling weakly. *Good afternoon.* "You've made a smoker of my mother, I think."

She hardly looked like the woman I knew: not only had the bulge at her stomach all but disappeared, but she seemed thinner, more gaunt, than even before her pregnancy. Her cheeks were hollow, her usually dark skin sallow, the color of spoiled milk. Her black hair, which had become even thicker—impossibly thick—during her pregnancy, seemed sparse and uneven, as if entire handfuls had been ripped from her skull. (Later, I found that this was exactly what had happened.)

"*Arratsalde on,*" I said. I stood in the doorway, trying to keep myself from rushing across the room that smelled of garlic and onion and was finally, after what seemed like years, warm. We stood like that, she at the stove in the oversized shirt, me hovering awkwardly in the frame of the door, the old woman smoking, her hands working quickly over the green beans.

"The stove," the old woman said, looking up from the bowl of beans. "The potatoes are burning."

And then the spell was broken, and Nerea was coming across the room to me, and it was as if the thing that had happened in Don Octavio's office eight days before were only a story we had been told about another couple, about two unfortunate other people. I held her thin frame in my arms and we rocked like that, neither of us crying, just rocking and rocking until the old woman said again, "Nerea, *mecachis*, the potatoes!"

WHEN AITOR came to drive his mother's bags back to the apartment on San Lorenzo, nothing suggested his opinion of me had changed any in the past ten days. He nodded curtly when I answered the door to the guesthouse, then pushed past without waiting for an invitation to enter. In the living room, Nerea and her mother sat stiffly on the couch that I was still sleeping on, sheets and blankets folded neatly between the two of them. Nerea smiled at her brother, who offered her the same gruff nod that he had given me at the front door.

"Well," the old woman said. "Joni, perhaps you can help carry my bags to the car. Aitor, you stay here with your sister."

Her two children looked at her inquiringly, while I had no choice but to follow her into the back bedroom. As soon as we entered, she wheeled around and closed the door behind us.

"She's not well," she said in a low voice. "You think that she is, but she's not."

The room was the cleanest I'd ever seen it; the hardwood floorboards shining brightly, the comforter pulled tight to the bed and folded neatly at its head, the top of the dresser cleaned of empty cigarette packs and discarded tissues.

"She's tried to kill herself before. Of course she didn't tell you this." She was whispering now, her small hand gripping my forearm. "It was why I sent her to the sisters in Bermeo."

I nodded, glancing quickly toward the closed bedroom door.

"You think that she's well, but she's not," she repeated.

"What can I do?" I asked.

The old woman shrugged her shoulders, as if to say, *She's your problem now.*

"Watch her, I suppose. I've been trying to help her for the last twenty-five years, and look at me now," she said, holding her hands empty in front of her.

THAT HAD been on a Tuesday. That same afternoon, from Kattalin Gorroño's house, I called the school to tell them I wouldn't be in for the rest of the week.

"Of course, Joni," the headmaster had said. "Take all the time you need."

When I walked across the field from Kattalin's to the guesthouse, I found Nerea sitting on a downed log at the edge of the river. Long shadows stretched out across the newly mowed hay, the final cutting of the season, and she was wrapped in a heavy wool shawl that her mother had left.

"You'll catch cold out here," I said as I approached along the small trail leading to the water's edge. She smiled sleepily at me and patted the space next to her.

"Why is it you never fish the river anymore?" she asked me.

"Do you want me to fish again?" I said, thinking back to the summer afternoons when I'd string up an old pole borrowed from Kattalin Gorroño and toss a line out into the current, occasionally pulling up a shivering river trout.

"Not necessarily," she said. "But I wonder why you don't anymore."

"I don't know," I said. I thought about it for a moment. "It's out of season, for one. But I think I just forgot about it, with this summer."

Immediately I regretted saying it. *This summer.* It implied so much more than a season. Another life. The excitement of Nerea growing out of the small cotton skirts she had always worn. The warmth of the summer air at night when, lying naked on top of the sheets, I would hold my ear to her stomach. It was the life of the other people. She leaned her head down onto my shoulder, one of her hands reaching up to grab a handful of her dark curls.

We sat like that for a long time, her head resting against me, and when I eventually said her name she didn't answer. I felt her small frame shaking under the wool shawl. Just when the last of the afternoon light vanished, she stood and walked the skinny trail back to the house. I stayed sitting on the downed ash tree, watching the dark shape of her silhouette move silently through the low grass. Nerea entered the kitchen door, and from the river, I saw her through the window as she closed and locked the door to the bedroom and then turned off the light.

32. MARIANA

THE REPRESENTATIVES FROM THE PARTY INSISTED THAT I have José Antonio buried in Muriga. For my part, I hadn't cared one way or another what they did with the body, whose dirt they covered it with. Where the body should be left was a concern that seemed to ignore the real question: why was there a body in the first place?

But the representatives didn't stop there. They brought meals, put their cold hands on my arm, directed the photographers and newspapermen away. They asked their questions in quiet, slow voices, saying my name often, as if I were a very young child.

"DO YOU know, Mariana, if he would want to have been buried in the Church?"

"No."

"SHOULD THE casket be open, or do you prefer closed?"

"It doesn't matter."

"DO YOU have any clothes you would like him to be wearing?"

"I'll have to look."

"There is a rally at the city hall at four, Mariana, to protest political violence. Will you be able to attend?"

"I'm not sure."

"WOULD YOU say just a few words about your husband during the rally?"

"No. No, I don't think so."

"JUST LEAVE her in peace," I heard them finally whisper. So they approached José Antonio's parents about where the body should be buried. His parents had arrived at the airport in Bilbao on Wednesday night and seemed to have aged ten years since I'd seen them last, David, small and withered under his navy-blue sweater that we had sent him for Christmas the year before, his teeth somehow appearing too large for his head, Susana's chlorine-blue eyes in their deep, darkened recesses.

His parents wanted to take the body back to Andalucía to be buried. They would hate Muriga forever for killing their son. Not just the men who had fired the two pieces of metal through their son. Even now, six years later, David and Susana haven't returned to Muriga, not even to visit their granddaughter.

The very serious men explained to them even more slowly, and more quietly, how important it would be to the Party if the body remained in Muriga. That it would be a showing of strength. That José Antonio would have wanted it that way, they were sure of it, until finally David nodded his head weakly. I imagined them beginning to dig the hole at the exact moment David nodded his head, more of these serious men in their serious clothes stomping shovels into the black soil of the cemetery, turning up old bones in order to make room for the new.

33. IKER

DURING THE TRIAL THEY MADE A BIG PRODUCTION OUT OF the rifle. The *fiscal* had it brought into the courtroom by an assistant on the second day. It was wrapped in brown butcher paper and clear packing tape, as if it had been sent to the court through the mail. The *fiscal* was a small man, and when he tore off the paper and held it by the nicked wooden stock in his undersized hands, it looked bigger than it actually was. He had Asier's father tell the courtroom that it was his old hunting rifle, given to him by an uncle who lived in the country. Asier's father looked weak and helpless as he answered the prosecutor's questions, as if he were trying to come up with a response that was true and yet did not implicate his son. He told the *fiscal* that the gun had been stored in his bedroom closet, leaned against the back corner with a half-empty box of cartridges.

Asier had handed me the rifle the morning after we had taken the Councilman. Gorka and Daniel were supposed to have returned to the bunker hours earlier, and when the sun began to rise, we decided that I would stay with the Councilman until Asier could determine what had happened. The night had been clear and cold, and the Councilman was shivering in his dark suit jacket, seated against one of the concrete walls with his hands tied behind his back. The small room was lit only by the shaky beam of the flashlight Asier carried. I blew into my hands to warm them before Asier passed the rifle to me. It was heavier than I expected, but I tried to handle the gun casually, to give the impression that I was familiar with it. I pulled the bolt action back, then pushed it into place, as I had seen Asier do several times earlier. Asier gathered his camera, the remainder of the laundry line we had used to tie the Councilman's wrists, and his rolling tobacco from the floor.

"He hasn't come back because they've caught him," the Councilman said suddenly. Asier's hand stopped on the bag of tobacco.

"What did you say?" Asier asked. He took a step closer. The Councilman's lips trembled with the cold.

"It's not too late," the Councilman said. "They've probably caught your friend. But nothing has happened yet. You can still let me go. It's not too late."

Asier squatted down so that he was eye level with the Councilman. He set the flashlight on the ground, then rubbed his palms on his knees. He picked the flashlight back up. The Councilman squinted against the glare.

"That's what you'd like, I guess?" Asier said. "To go home to your wife. Mariana, right?"

The Councilman's head straightened at his wife's name. His shivering stopped.

"Asier—" I said.

"And your daughter, Elena?" Asier said. "We know a little bit about you, José Antonio Torres. We might even know more about your life than you do."

"Get that goddamn light out of my face," the Councilman said.

Asier flicked the switch off, and the bunker was lit with only the dim morning light. Outside I could hear the scraping sound of the surf against the cliffs and the high shrieks of the first gulls circling below.

"For example," Asier continued, "you might not know that your wife, Mariana, has been having an affair for the past two months."

As Asier said this, the gun suddenly felt small and stupid in my hands. I wanted him to stop, to do what the Councilman had said: to go home, to set him free, to set things back a day or a week or a year. But it already had a momentum that could not be stopped by me, or by Asier, or by the Councilman and his pleas. We all understood this, I think. We understood it but we didn't want to accept it.

"Three days a week, while you are working in Bilbao," Asier said. The Councilman sat motionless. The cuffs of his dark slacks were splattered with mud from the night before. "In your own apartment, even."

Asier inched closer to the Councilman.

"Do you think you know who it is?" he continued. "It's the new American, of all people. Duarte. He's been fucking your wife for two months now. We've seen him in your window. With Mariana."

"You should go," I said. "It's already five thirty."

Asier rocked back on his heels, then stood up.

"Keep that gun on this son of a bitch," he said, switching back to Basque. "If he tries anything, put one between his eyes."

I nodded, adjusted the rifle in my hands. Asier took his bag from the floor and put it on his shoulder. Standing there in the bunker's crumbling doorway, he seemed like an intruder in this place where we'd spent so many afternoons.

"I'll be back in forty-five minutes. No later than an hour. You're all right here?"

"Sure," I said, looking at the Councilman leaning against the wall. "Sure."

ASIER HAD been gone for nearly an hour when the Councilman finally spoke.

"What's your name?" he asked. "The other one is Asier, I heard you say. But I didn't hear your name."

I didn't say anything back. I leaned the gun against the gray concrete wall, then shook a cigarette from the pack Gorka had left in the bunker.

"Not going to tell me, eh?" he said. "It doesn't matter. You know, I recognize you now. Asier, I don't think I've seen him before. But you—yes, now I remember. Your mother is friends with Estefana. From the Boliña."

I checked my watch again, then looked down the empty trail that wound through the damp morning grass toward Muriga. The sun had come up over the mountains behind the cliffs, softening the night chill.

"Do you think I could have one of those?" he asked.

"No," I said.

He shook his head, then stared with me out the door toward Muriga. I dragged on the cigarette, waiting for the whole horrible morning to be over.

"It shouldn't surprise me," he said as I snubbed out the cigarette on the floor of the bunker. "The affair, I mean. If what your friend said is true. It shouldn't surprise me but it does."

"I'm not really sure," I said, although I had seen it myself in the window of their fifth-floor apartment.

He shook his head again.

"No," he said, "I can see it now and I'm sure that it's true."

"I'm sorry," I heard myself say.

"The funny thing, of course, is that I was doing the same."

He was still staring off through the doorway, strands of his dark hair falling into his face.

"Her name is Isabel," he said. "She works at the Party headquarters in Bilbao."

I picked up the rifle from the wall, slid the action forward and back again.

"Why are you telling me this?" I asked. "Stop talking."

The Councilman regarded me gloomily.

"I don't know," he said. "I guess I'm just feeling the need to confess."

"Stop your talking," I said, nearly yelling.

And then I felt the dull pressure behind my eyes, one of the headaches building. I shouldered the rifle and looked down the sights, one eye closed like I had seen in the movies. On the other end of the barrel the Councilman stared back with what seemed like boredom, as if all things had already been done. I dropped the rifle back down into the sling of my arm. The morning sunlight coming through the empty windows dimmed as the pain gathered strength. I stepped toward the door so that the Councilman couldn't see me, the taste of copper arriving under the edge of my tongue.

I turned and pointed the rifle again at the man crouched against the wall, who was staring hungrily at the cigarette butt I had put out on the cracked concrete floor below him.

"Not another fucking word," I said.

34. JONI (1951)

MY FIRST YEAR IN MURIGA WE HAD TAKEN A BOAT FROM
the marina—a small rowboat that Nerea claimed she'd been given
permission to use by one of her uncles. I had rowed us across the
bay, around the western harbor to a hidden gravel beach she knew.
We ate lunch and made love on a blanket we had brought for this
purpose, and later fell asleep in the midday sun.

When I woke I was shivering. Thunderheads bruised the afternoon sky, and the sea had turned gray, jagged. The boat scraped
against the rocks of the beach. I shook Nerea's shoulder, but even
as the first rains of the storm arrived, she shrugged me away, pulling the blanket happily over her.

"We have to leave now if we're going to beat the storm," I said
through the rain. Already there was a heavy break along the shore-
line, bucking the boat. I waded out to my knees and held the gun-
wale tightly, trying to wrest the boat against the onslaught of waves;
when I turned back toward the beach I saw Nerea tucked in her
blanket, laughing.

"It's already here!" she yelled gleefully through the rain. The
delight in that laugh, as if she were incapable of worry. I began to
laugh with her, even as the boat lifted out of my reach.

"Let it go," she said, still laughing, gathering our things for the long walk back to town. "There's no outrowing a storm that's already here."

THE LINE became a favorite that we used to say to each other in the year before the boy. In our first week at the guesthouse we would point to the drips falling from the ceiling joists, *There's no outrowing a storm*, and it would all be just an inconvenience, just a game. Drop a plate? You can't outrow a storm.

But the weeks after her mother left us, it truly was as if we were trapped on this same boat, adrift in that summer squall. Everything was unsteadiness, the world itself seeming to pitch unnaturally. There were moments when our boat would crest a wave, when Nerea would emerge from her room and allow me to sit with her on the sofa or perhaps to make her a ham and cheese sandwich, and I could see the clearing skies on the horizon and know that we would survive. I would remind myself that we had survived storms before. That soon the winds would pass and the waves would settle, as they always did.

And then there were times when our little boat would slip grotesquely down the face of a swell, and we saw neither the sea around us nor the black sky above, only our stern pointing toward the sea bottom. These were the days when I would find Nerea curled on the floor of the bathroom, holding her stomach and insisting that it was the doctor's fault, that he had conspired with her mother to kill the child. On these days I was chained to the house, afraid of what Nerea might do if I left. I turned away the friends that came to visit, only opening the door enough to speak to them. I used every excuse possible with the headmaster at San Jorge, a kind man who was not without limits to his sympathy.

"Joni," he told me over the phone after the third week. He spoke to me with empathy, as if he were speaking to a son. "I don't pretend to know what is happening with you. I don't. But the students have been three weeks without an English class."

"I understand," I said. I walked the phone to the end of its cord so that I could look out of Kattalin's kitchen window toward our house across the field. "I will be there on Monday."

THAT WEEKEND Nerea seemed back to her old self, or at least some version of it. We slept in the same bed for the first time. She walked with me into Muriga on Saturday, and we spent an afternoon at a restaurant, snacking on fried calamari and *patatas bravas* and sipping at a few beers with Marina Inestrellas and her cousin, who was visiting from Portugalete. On the way back to the house, I told her that I would have to go back to work on Monday.

"Of course you do," she said. "Someone needs to make some money around here!" She was playful, almost happy. As we passed under a low oak limb on the Paseo de los Robles, she reached up to shake the branch's water on my head. I ducked my head and cringed, and as the cold rainwater raced down the crook of my neck I heard the high shriek of Nerea's laugh, and then she took off at a delighted run.

Her mother's words still sat with me, had grown in the time since she'd left. *She's tried to kill herself before.* I was certain that her mother was telling the truth.

And so, the Sunday before I was to return to work, I woke in the dark of early morning and felt my way from the bedroom. While Nerea slept, I wandered our small house and tried to think of every way she might do it. The living room ceiling was exposed beam, and so I gathered the laundry line, the extension cords, the garden hoses, and carried them to the outbuilding at the edge of the pasture. I looted the bathroom cabinet of two bottles of aspirin, then poured out the few bottles of liquor that we kept above the refrigerator. When I was gathering the bleach and ammonia from under the sink I realized that there was no end. We were surrounded by deadly tools. A milk bottle could be broken, creating a thousand handy knives. A radio cord could be ripped from its casing and strung up on the dining room light. The gasoline cans along the side of the house. A wine key.

When I returned from the outbuilding after several trips, the sun was already up, cutting at the edges of a morning fog. The light in the bedroom was on, as was the light in the kitchen. I found Nerea at the stove, stirring milk into the top of the Cuban press.

"*Egun on*," she said, smiling. Her hair was tied back with an old piece of string as it always was in the mornings, her eyes still heavy with sleep.

"Good morning," I said back.

"You were up early," she said. She tipped the coffeepot into the two cups she'd set out on the tile counter.

"I had to use the bathroom, and then I wasn't tired," I said. "I went outside to watch the sun come up."

"You should have come to get me," she said, handing me one of the cups. She held the coffeepot in a towel to protect her hands, then carefully unscrewed the base from the top and shook the spent grounds into the sink. She began to run the water, then opened the cabinet under the sink for the dish soap. She paused, kneeling there with the cabinet open, and I knew that she'd realized the bleach was missing. I sipped at my coffee, then took a half baguette from the countertop and broke off the end.

"What should we do today?" I asked. "It's my last day of freedom before I have to go back to San Jorge."

She stood at the sink and began to run a yellow dishrag over the coffee press. She shrugged her shoulders, and I could tell she was turning over the evidence in her mind: the missing container of bleach, the knives removed from the silverware drawer. "Whatever you want," she said. She turned toward me, the hot water steaming in the sink. I bit down on the hard crust of the baguette and felt the bread cracking under my teeth.

"Did you have a chance to practice your Basque with my mother while she was here?" she asked.

"A little," I said, guardedly.

"Do you still remember the word for this?" she said, holding up her brown coffee mug.

"Yes," I said. "*Katilua*."

"And how do you say 'hair'?" she asked, pinching one of the wine-dark strands that had fallen over her eyes.

"*Ilea*."

"And 'knife'?" she said, watching me closely. "Did I ever teach you the word for 'knife'?"

"No," I said. I looked down guiltily at my hands.

"*Aiztoa*," she said quietly. "*Aiztoa*. Now you try it."

"*Aiztoa*." As I repeated the word, I realized the terrible stupidity of thinking I'd be able to hide all the objects in the world that could take her from me.

She set the dishcloth on the counter and reached over to me.

"*Aiztoa*," I said again.

Her hand was wet and warm in mine, and she pulled herself in close to me. I could smell the coffee on her breath and the warm scent of sleep, and she said, simply, "There's no outrowing this storm, Joni."

35. IKER

THE IDEA WAS TO HOLD THE COUNCILMAN FOR FORTY-eight hours, as a show of strength against the Partido Popular in the coming election. The genius of the plan was its simplicity, its foolproofness: an anonymous abduction, an announcement, and then we would release him. There was no discussion of a ransom, of a swap for prisoners. These were complications known only to Gorka, though I've often wondered how much Asier knew and never told me.

Asier called my house several times the week before, leaving messages with my mother. But all of my time after school was occupied by the sessions with Garrett, and when I wasn't taking sample grammar tests or filling out verb tense charts I was with Nere, and so the messages went unanswered.

After a week of unreturned phone calls, I met Asier face-to-face. I was parking my motor scooter outside Nere's parents' house when he sat up off the curb. Daniel was with him, and I saw Asier motion for him to stay sitting on the corner.

"I guess you got my calls," he said.

"Yes," I said. "I haven't had the time to call back. I've been studying for the English exam."

"Studying with the American," he said accusingly.

"Yes," I said. "Studying with the American."

He nodded, then kicked at a flattened Coca-Cola can that had been left in the road.

"I'm applying to university in San Sebastián," I said. "If I'm accepted, Nere will go with me."

He kicked again at the flattened can. His hair was longer, a single churro dangling awkwardly behind his ear. Daniel stayed on the curb smoking his cigarette.

"She has a cousin there who we can stay with," I said dumbly.

"That's good," he said. "That'll be good for you."

"Yes," I said. "We always talked about leaving Muriga, didn't we?"

"*Bai*," he said. "In fact, I have plans to leave as well."

I tried to imagine where he would go. I couldn't picture Asier leaving Muriga without me, but I could so easily imagine the opposite. I had imagined leaving Muriga, growing older, becoming another person, walking the streets of San Sebastián or Paris or New York; but in this fantasy Asier always remained in Muriga, wandering the same streets, wearing the same torn blue jeans and black T-shirts silk-screened with band names, preserved forever as I knew him then.

"The other side," he said, nodding his head up the street, toward the steep foothills of the Pyrenees. "Iparralde."

"France?" I asked, nearly laughing. "You're moving to France?"

Asier scowled, the same scowl that appeared when we played table soccer and he was concentrating deeply.

"Yes," he said. "With Gorka, I think. There are friends there. We'll be in exile."

He said the word proudly. He knew its connotations—it brought to mind all the history from Ramón Luna's speeches in the bunker above the cliffs, of Basques who had lived in Mexico or Cuba during the Franco years, of the photographs we displayed during our protests of the young men and women who couldn't enter back into Spain because of what awaited them. I shrugged my shoulders.

"Well, I hope that what they say about the girls there is true," I said.

"Listen," he said, putting a hand on my shoulder. I felt Daniel watching us. "We're going to do it. With the Councilman, as we had planned before. It will be simple—two days only. We take him for two days, to let the Party know that they aren't welcome here in Muriga, and then we let him go."

I felt his hand tighten on my shoulder.

"You need to help us," he said. "You're going to leave Muriga, and that's fine. You have the right to. But you also owe it to Muriga to help us."

✳ ✳ ✳

I'VE SPENT a lot of my time in the Salto asking myself why I agreed to Asier's plan. Maybe I did owe it to Muriga. But more importantly, I felt I owed it to Asier. We both sensed the end of our friendship approaching, a period in our lives coming to a close. If there is one thing we're taught in Muriga, it's that we owe something to our histories.

I remember telling myself that I was also thinking of Nere, though I know now this was never the case. I thought of our new life together in San Sebastián and about the new person that I was set to become, and I imagined this as a part of the new person waiting out in the future. The younger version of myself would have run the streets of this village, thrown Molotov cocktails and burned a bus, and was responsible for the kidnapping of Muriga's Partido Popular candidate in 1998. At parties and in restaurants in San Sebastián, people would speak about these things quietly, nodding their heads in the direction of the new man from Muriga. They would know. Maybe I'd tell the story of the kidnapping; maybe I'd keep it to myself. But they would know. Nere would know.

Of course, it had never been about her. If it had been, I would have told her all about it beforehand. She almost certainly would have tried to talk me out of it—we had a future almost in reach. When she finally found out what we were up to, it was too late: I was calling her from a roadside pay phone on the highway to France with Gorka, and the Councilman's body was already being dragged out by the tide.

The important thing, of course, is that I agreed. During the trial, the prosecutor didn't care about *why* I had agreed. He didn't ask about Nere, or Asier, or about the future I had planned. The only important thing to him was that I had agreed.

Daniel testified about the conversation between Asier and me that afternoon. He told the court that I had been eager to go along with Asier's plan, that he'd tried to dissuade us but that we pressured him into helping. Gorka's lawyer, a public attorney appointed by the judge, slid his chair away from us when Daniel pointed, as if he were concerned that the judge might mistakenly include him with the two murderers. I struggled to stay silent, to not call Daniel a liar, to point out that he wouldn't even make eye contact with me as he was making his accusations.

But now I wish that Dani had looked up at me. If he had, I would have tried to tell him that I understood that he didn't love us any less, even though he agreed to testify in exchange for a four-year sentence. I keep thinking back to those early days at the bunkers with Ramón Luna; when he and Luken would return to the public school in Muriga while Asier and I hiked back up the hill to San Jorge, there had always been a gulf between us. I would have told Dani that I understood self-preservation is sometimes at odds with what we love and that to choose to survive is not to forgo friendship.

THIS IS just another one of the true but untrue accounts that I give from within the painted concrete walls of the Salto del Negro. We're all familiar with these evolving memories here. Manolito, the old gypsy who has been in the Salto longer than anyone, once came to our cell with a plastic bag filled with clear rum that a guard had smuggled in for him. After he passed the bag between Andreas and me, he leaned drunkenly back against the legs of Andreas's bunk. We all pretended that we were friends at a bar, telling stories. When the conversation died down and the rum got us thinking of old times, Andreas asked the old man what he had done to arrive in the prison.

"The truth is, I don't remember," he said. He picked at the elastic band around the neck of his shirt. "They tell me I stabbed a woman in Cádiz, but I don't believe it."

Andreas laughed. Manolito reached for the plastic bag and tipped it up so the last of the liquor dripped into his caved-in mouth.

"When I think of my time before the Salto, I remember living the life of a saint. Don't you?"

36. MARIANA

"SHE WANTS TO MEET WITH YOU," SAID THE VOICE OF THE American, Robert Duarte. He was stepping out of the receding steam of the shower as he said it. He took a blue towel off the rack—the same one José Antonio had used that morning—and began to dry his black hair. He rubbed coarsely, almost violently, in a way that reminded me of the way he made love, sacrificing pleasure for efficiency. I was so hypnotized, watching him, that his words didn't register at first.

"Who does?" I asked.

"Morgan," he said. There wasn't even a pause in the violent movement of the towel over his head, roughly down onto his neck and across the dark hair on his chest. "My wife."

"I know who Morgan is," I said.

Finally he stopped his drying. He wrapped José Antonio's towel around his waist and regarded me across the bathroom. I sat naked on the closed toilet seat, my hair still dry, waiting for the American to leave before I showered alone in the empty apartment as I liked to do.

"Well, she wants to meet with you," he said again.

"What for?" I asked, annoyed that I had to ask such an obvious question.

He shrugged his shoulders.

"I think she's lonely," he said. "She said she'd like to draw your portrait. But really, I think she just wants to have someone close to her own age to talk to. She hasn't had the best luck meeting people here."

"We don't exactly have a reputation for being welcoming," I agreed. "But you don't really think that's a good idea, do you? For the two of us to meet alone?"

He gave the same irritating shrug, then pulled a white V-neck shirt up over his head.

"Why not?" he said. "It's not like she suspects anything. And besides, it might be good for you as well."

"What's that supposed to mean?"

He leaned in close to the mirror, wiping the fog away with a forearm. He held his left eye open with two fingers, then plucked a contact lens with the other hand.

"Eh?" he asked. He put the contact on the tip of his tongue and rolled it briefly in his mouth, then pinched it out and put it back in his left eye. "These contacts always dry out if I wear them in the shower."

"What do you mean, 'It might be good for you as well'?" I asked again. I was annoyed by the question, but in a backward way I was flattered. It was the first time he'd shown an interest in my life outside the bedroom.

"You just seem to spend a lot of time alone," he said.

"I have Elena," I answered quickly.

"Exactly," he said. "You divide your time between a seventy-year-old and a two-year-old. You need to interact with people that you have more in common with."

"And your wife?" I said. "I suppose we do have at least one thing in common."

"I think you'd like her," he said, ignoring my barb. "And she loves children. She wants to start trying as soon as we get back."

It was the first time he had mentioned leaving Muriga, but it didn't surprise me. His time in Muriga seemed more like a safari than an attempt to start a new life. For all the weekends he visited his cousins in Nabarniz, there was a distance that he maintained between his life and those he lived among. Even when he watched me undress at the foot of the bed, he seemed more curious than hungry. For the first time, I thought about the end of the affair. Of what I would be left with when Robert Duarte left Muriga.

He suggested that I take his wife out of Muriga for the day, to a mountaintop sanctuary that I had mentioned once.

"In four months she's hardly been away from Muriga," he'd said. "It'll be good for her to get out of town. She doesn't even come with me anymore when I visit the family in Nabarniz."

She called my house the next morning. When I picked up, there was a hesitation on the other line, and I knew who it was before she even began to introduce herself in stumbling Spanish.

"Robert," she said. "My husband. He tells me that I call you."

She spoke in the same simple way that Elena did, looking for the easiest words, avoiding the past tense. I watched Elena gazing at the English-language cartoons on the BBC channel, shaking her arms in that absentminded way she used to do. I realized then that we were both being used thoughtlessly, without consequence, by Robert Duarte.

※ ※ ※

THIS IS how I found myself waiting for my lover's wife at the train station cafeteria.

"You're doing what?" José Antonio had asked the night before.

"You know the American couple," I said. "They are friends of Joni Garrett's. You met them at the grocery store a month ago."

"Yes," he admitted. "I remember them. But why are you taking her to Aizkorri?"

"Because she's bored here," I said. "And because *I'm* bored. It'll be nice to spend a little time with someone different than the usual three people I see every day."

I was startled to hear myself repeating Robert's words and even more surprised to realize their truth.

"Sorry if we aren't entertaining enough for you," José Antonio said, though in fact I hadn't even included him in the three.

"You know what I mean," I said.

"Well, if it's all the same, I'll just stay the night in Bilbao, then," he said. "You won't be back before dinner if you're going all the way to the *refugio*, and there's a strategic meeting early on Friday that I have to be at anyway."

I nodded, then abruptly reached over to take José Antonio's hand. "You don't think I've been ... different ... do you?"

He raised his eyebrows in that way he did when he was confused.

"Since the operation," I said. "Sometimes I feel like a different person."

"No," he said, kissing my hand quickly before picking up an envelope from the kitchen table. "You're still the strange girl I met in Sevilla."

I had arranged for my mother to take Elena for the day, and for the first time since he had begun working in the Partido Popular offices, José Antonio and I walked the five blocks to the train station together, José Antonio off to Bilbao and me to meet Morgan Duarte. The train to Bilbao left at a quarter to eight, twenty minutes before I was scheduled to meet Robert's wife, so after José Antonio and I awkwardly kissed each other good-bye, and he rolled his small overnight bag past the ticket collector, I went back to the train station cafeteria and ordered a coffee. I was out of place in my nylon pants and hiking boots, the surprisingly busy station filled with people dressed nicely for a trip to San Sebastián or Pamplona.

Robert's wife arrived five minutes early. She was easy to spot, the only blond head in the crowd. She was wearing a pair of blue jeans with the knees worn, so they were lighter than the rest of the pants, and her hair was pulled back in a way that made her look younger than she was. She carried an orange backpack with a water bottle strapped to its side, and when she passed the glass window of the train station, she stopped quickly to look herself over in the reflection. As she tucked a stray strand of blond hair back behind her ear, I became angry again with Robert Duarte for betraying this woman.

I waved her over to the cafeteria bar, where I was finishing my coffee. We kissed each other on the cheek, then stood in front of each other awkwardly, not knowing exactly what to say. I wondered if she knew already or if she could tell just from looking at me, touching me.

"Well then," I said finally. "To the mountain?"

She nodded eagerly, happy to have some movement break our inertia. We walked to the ticket booth and I bought two tickets to Orio.

"Robert tells me the *refugio* was an . . . escape . . . for the Republicans during the Civil War?" she said, searching for the word. How typical, I thought, for Robert to think of everything in the context of Basque oppression.

"I haven't heard that," I said. "My grandfather used to take us up there for the views when I was a kid. With the clouds today, we might not see much. But on a clear day you can see up to the peak of Balerdi."

She nodded, but I wasn't sure how much she understood. When the train to Orio started up a few minutes later we were sitting next to each other in silence, but Morgan seemed content just to be moving, content to watch old farmers with wooden scythes mowing the steep hillsides of hay, tractors driving across the yard of a concrete factory.

* * *

WE HIKED for nearly an hour before stopping at the *refugio* at the base of Aizkorri. It had just started to rain, as I expected it would, and inside the building we huddled around the fireplace with four other hikers who had taken shelter. The *dueña* of the *refugio* busied herself in the small kitchen, boiling a large dented kettle for coffee and stirring a sooty pot that roiled with vegetables and beef bones. My stomach tightened with hunger, and I felt the sensation of steam on the undersides of my arms that I now associated with my new kidney.

It was four kilometers of winding trail to the refuge—farther by double than I had walked since the operation. But it was good to be away from Muriga, away from Elena and from José Antonio and from Robert. For the hour of the hike, as well as the thirty-minute train ride, Robert's wife and I had spoken only a handful of times, just to point out an interesting building or an especially pretty mountain peak. But as the other damp hikers slowly reanimated in the warmth of the refuge, chattering and laughing, Morgan also seemed to relax. We ordered two cups of Rioja while we were waiting for lunch, and the wine was now warm in our stomachs. She took off the blue rain jacket she had put on when it began to drizzle and hung it over the back of a wooden chair, then leaned up against the stone wall of the refuge, smiling warmly at me.

"Robert tells me about you," she said, watching the *dueña* working back in the kitchen, cutting bread for the soup. I had been waiting all day for an accusation, and now I tried carefully to read her.

"What does he know about me?" I asked.

"What Joni Garrett tells to him," she said slowly. "The operation?"

We shared a look—I still couldn't figure out how much she knew. If she was setting a trap or if she was just struggling for something to talk about. A moment of panic drained through me as

I wondered if Joni had told Robert about my theory of the terrorist kidney. *How insane it must sound*, I thought for the first time.

"You are strong," Morgan Duarte said, holding her thin arms in a body builder's pose.

"Yes," I said, laughing. "I feel good today. I'm glad to be here with you."

She glanced across the fire to the group of hikers, who were passing around a pack of cigarettes. They were talking about Uzkudun, a boxer from the nearby town of Errezil who had been famous in the 1920s and early 1930s. One of the hikers squatted down at the edge of the fireplace and held a cigarette out against a smoldering ember, then dragged on the filter until the tip glowed red. Morgan leaned in toward me, held two fingers up to her pale lips, and shrugged questioningly.

"Why not?" I said. I asked the man with the lit cigarette for another, and he held out a pack of Lucky Strikes. I lit the cigarette against his, then thanked him. When I gave the cigarette to Morgan, she took it in one hand and used her other hand to cover a smile.

"It's not normal for me," she said before taking a tiny drag. I watched Robert Duarte's wife smoking, trying to get my head around this day.

"Not for me either," I said. She took another tiny puff, then passed it over to me. When I inhaled, the smoke tickled the back of my throat, and I tried to hold back a cough. Morgan laughed and took another drink of the Rioja.

"Robert," she said. "He say . . . he *says* Joni Garrett loves you. Do you know this?"

"Yes," I said. As she said the words, I realized I had known this all along. "Yes, I think I do know this."

37. JONI (1952)

WE CRAWLED OUR WAY THROUGH THAT HORRIBLE WINTER
of 1951, through weeks at a time when Nerea refused to leave the
house, others when we allowed ourselves to believe that nothing
had ever been wrong at all. We fought and made love intermit-
tently, and by June of 1952 she was pregnant again, her hair thick-
ening as it had the previous year, her stomach swelling in the same
places it had before. And yet we spoke about the new child hardly
at all. She never said the words "pregnant" or "child" or "due," as if
their mere pronunciation would be enough to hex us again.

We both knew we were incapable of surviving again the events
of the night at Dr. Octavio's the fall before, and so I agreed to the
silence. My mother had always been a devout agnostic, and in
the years after my brother's death, my father refused to even consider the existence of a God. I had only entered the cathedral in
Muriga once, to attend the baptism of a friend's son. And yet in avoiding those words, in shuttering away the sounds of Nerea's morning
sickness through the bathroom door, this seemed as close a thing
to prayer as I had ever experienced.

We didn't allow ourselves to speculate about gender, to consider
names, or even to unpack the boxes of children's things that I had

hidden away the year before. When I reached through the sheets of our bed, around her thin hips, Nerea would stop my hand with the swiftness of an animal protecting its young before it reached the tightening bulge of her belly. And so this was how we carried on, ignoring the child's very existence, the two of us living with an unborn ghost.

38. MARIANA

JOSÉ ANTONIO WAS KIDNAPPED FROM THE TRAIN STATION on a Monday evening by four men with their faces covered in bandannas and dark glasses. Several witnesses had seen them shove him into the back of a blue Volkswagen with Bizkaia plates and drive off before anyone realized what had happened. They watched the men take José Antonio as they might watch a band of wild horses gallop down the street; there was a moment in which nobody moved at all, nobody said a word, until Miguel Becerra yelled to his wife in their bookstore to call the police. Goreti Zunzunegi described the scene to Joni before the kidnapping had even been reported to the news, and when the Ertzaintza arrived at the apartment a half hour later the old American was already there waiting with me.

They sent a single detective—young, prematurely bald, but with a confidence that was outside his years. He held a spiral notebook under the arm of a neatly pressed suit.

"She knows already?" I heard him say when Joni opened the door, not bothering with formalities. The old man nodded, holding the apartment door. I watched the young detective walk purposefully down the hallway to where I sat with Elena on the gray corduroy sofa, the same one where José Antonio had sat only four days before, where Robert and I had made love earlier that afternoon. His head swiveled as he walked, seeming to catalogue every detail in the apartment. A moment of panic came over me; would he find out about Robert Duarte? Did he know already? And just as quickly, the panic was replaced by the guilt of worrying about something so selfish. José Antonio was missing; he might already be dead.

"Mariana Zelaia, I am Detective Moreno Castro. I work with the Ertzaintza in Bilbao. You already know why I'm here?"

I nodded.

"Please," he said, pulling a sofa chair closer so that he faced me directly. Joni opened the window facing Calle de Atxiaga, then removed a cigarette from a pack in his pocket and held it to an old silver lighter. "Tell me what you know."

I told him what Joni had told me, about the men with the bandannas and dark glasses and the blue car. I told him about José Antonio's work for the Party, that he had announced his candidacy three months earlier. About the posters he'd been so proud of. That he worked at the Party headquarters in Bilbao three days a week, sometimes four. As I spoke, Castro nodded his bald head and scribbled notes in the black-and-white notebook that reminded me of the ones we used in *secundaria*. Elena was complaining next to me on the sofa, asking me to turn on the television for her; Joni had arrived just as I set her down for her afternoon nap. The phone rang several times, and each time, Joni perched his cigarette on the ledge of the window and answered without waiting for instructions from me or from Castro, each time shaking his head to indicate that the call had not been important. I remembered what Morgan had said about Joni in the refuge at Aizkorri, and I wondered for the first time why he had come that afternoon. The detective asked about José Antonio's work schedule, about the last time I had seen him, what we had spoken about the last time he called. By the time he finally sat back in his chair, flipped through a few pages of notes, then closed the notebook, Joni had gone through at least a half dozen cigarettes.

"Mariana, I know that it's difficult to believe, but there's really very little to worry about," he said. "These cases are more common than you realize, and the odds are that we'll have your husband safely home to you before you know it."

"Is that your attempt to reassure me?" I asked. Elena had come over to sit on my lap, and I bounced her gently, pressing her tightly against the crooked scar that held in my new organ.

He smiled, then stood to leave.

"I'm sorry," he said. "I can't imagine how difficult this must be." He took a business card from his pocket and placed it on the low wooden coffee table. "Call anytime. There are two officers down below, and one outside the door. There'll be another detective here within the hour. They may call to demand a ransom. We already have a monitor on your line from the external box. Keep them on the line as long as you can. Agree to anything they ask for."

He turned to Joni.

"Are you going to stay with her?"

"Yes, of course. Her mother is in Zarautz for the day but should be back soon. She knows."

It was strange how he said all this, as if giving the detective the idea that he might have been my uncle or my father.

"Good," Castro said. "Good. Just one other thing . . ."

He turned to Joni.

"Can I ask for a moment in private with Mariana?"

When Joni looked to me I nodded nervously, the panic suddenly rushing back.

"Sure," Joni said. He lifted Elena into his arms, and we watched the old man walk with the girl down the hallway toward the kitchen. When we heard the water running in the sink, Castro flipped his notebook open to a blank page.

"Is there anything that you haven't told me?" he said. "Anything at all?"

I felt it was a question that he already held the answer to. Was he asking if I was sure that I had ever loved my husband? If I had been violating my marriage vows three times a week for the past three months? If I was harboring a terrorist kidney just across the room from him?

"No," I said. I picked up the business card from the table and read it over, holding it by its edges. "Nothing that I can think of."

"The only reason I ask is—you understand—we're required to investigate all possibilities. To me, this clearly seems to be politically motivated. In fact, we've already identified several potential suspects here and in Bilbao and Mondragón. But we're required to investigate all possibilities."

"Of course," I said. I rubbed my palm unconsciously over the scar. "I would hope so."

"Great," Castro said, brushing his hands over the front of his dark slacks. "If something comes to mind—if you remember anything more—you'll let me know?"

"Of course," I said.

39. JONI (1953)

SHE DELIVERED IN FEBRUARY 1953, IN THE HOSPITAL DE Santa Marina. The child was two weeks early, slightly underweight but otherwise healthy. They required me to stay in the lobby for the seven hours that she was in labor, though it was unclear if this was because we weren't legally married or if Nerea had in fact asked the nurses to keep me out. After two hours of smoking the harsh Ducados that they sold at the hospital café, I asked again to be allowed into the delivery room and when I was denied I walked out through the hospital's heavy glass doors.

It was early still—the contractions had started after midnight, and we arrived at Santa Marina just after three. The streets of Bilbao were just beginning to stir; Franco's sanitation workers with their drab brown shirts and matching baggy pants angrily swept up crumpled papers and pieces of shattered cider glasses. The air was filled with the screeches and crashes of trucks unloading large spirals of sheet iron onto the massive ships in the harbor nearby. Closer, I heard the metal rattle of a restaurant's storm door rolling up, and I ducked under the half-open door into the dim bar.

The young man behind the counter was placing clean glasses in neat rows onto a head-high wooden shelf. He had the dark curls made popular that year by the goalkeeper for Athletic. When I pulled back a seat at the bar he started, then smiled.

"Early, eh?"

"Or late," I said. "Depends on how you look at it."

He nodded, as if waiting for further explanation.

"My wife," I said, nodding in the direction of the hospital. "She's having a baby."

"Right now?" he said, raising his eyebrows. He was a young guy, no older than twenty-five, but his temples were streaked through with early graying. "Shit . . ."

"Do you sell tobacco?" I asked.

"Of course. What do you smoke?"

I thought of Nerea alone in the hospital room with the stern nurses, and I wondered if the unborn ghost that we had refused to talk about for so many months was now the born ghost. If now at last we would be able to mention him or if we would be required to maintain our silence and to live out our existence with this new, living ghost. And then I thought of the November before last, the night of the rainstorm, and of just how much blood there had been on the sheets of the old doctor's bed and how when it came, the body of the boy was the dark purple of a bruise, as if he were gathering all his power to finally cry out, and how as I waited the doctor massaged the body of the boy and held the small chest to his ear, and the dark purple of his skin was slowly replaced with the waxy yellow of death and the cry never came.

"Anything besides Ducados," I said. "And a coffee with brandy."

He placed a pack of Chesterfields on the bar, then flipped on a radio before beginning to steam the milk for the coffee, the hiss of the steam mixing with the warm voice of Victoria de los Angeles singing "Hincarse de Rodillas."

40. JONI

MARIANA BEGAN TO DRESS DIFFERENTLY IN THE MONTHS before her husband was killed, before the three boys were arrested. She'd arrive at the Boliña in colorful summer skirts hiked up an inch higher than usual, or she'd be wearing a navy blouse with an extra button undone, the pale brown of her collarbone visible. Just the slightest bit of eye shadow, a gold band on her wrist.

It was the month that José Antonio's posters first appeared on the walls in the old part of town, "Torres, a New Vision for the Basque Country," and at first I wondered if this was the reason for these small touches of glamour. One Saturday afternoon not long after destroyed this idea, though.

I had left Muriga to see an American movie showing at the cinema in Bilbao, an indulgence I still allow myself once or twice a year. As I drove past the second bridge on the way out of town, I saw Duarte and Mariana sitting next to each other at the Bar Iruña—a roadside restaurant frequented only by passersby on the highway—halfway through a bottle of *txakoli*.

Before I realized what I was doing I had pulled over to the side of the highway, just down the road from the bar. I rolled down the window and lit a cigarette, watching the two with a hyperaware-ness that comes with jealousy; I read significance into the folds of their clothes, the closeness of their hands on the table, the exagger-ated way that Mariana laughed at one of Duarte's jokes. They had drawn their chairs near each other so that their knees touched under the table, and I saw Mariana's hand reach casually for Robert Duar-te's as if this had happened many times before.

I watched like this for several minutes before noticing that the girl was with them, playing among the empty tables. Elena was tug-ging at the American's sleeve, trying to get his attention, and if I hadn't known better I'd have thought they were just another young family enjoying an afternoon out.

✳ ✳ ✳

"YOU HAVEN'T asked about my shoelaces lately," she said one afternoon. We were sitting on the stone wall that surrounds the beach, and a few feet away Elena was sitting at the water's edge, the small harbor waves sending wet sand over her thick legs.

"Is she all right there, on the *orilla*?" I asked.

"She's fine," Mariana said, hardly bothering to check on the girl. "You used to ask. Or if not about the shoelaces, about the opera-tion."

"Well?" I said. "Was I right? Have the 'visions' gone away yet?"

"Just the opposite. My investigations are starting to pay off. I've discovered some details from my new friend's former life," she said, patting her stomach happily.

"What details are those?" I said sickly.

"Well," she said, putting a hand on my knee. "Now who's curi-ous?"

It was one of the sexless flirtations that I'd noticed more and more during those months, an affectation that reminded me that I was seen as only a harmless old man.

"He was from Aia," she said. "I read an interview with his sister. She mentioned a girlfriend in Zarautz—that explains the girl leaning up against the seawall. Remember how I told you about the girl?"

"Mariana, goddamn it, keep an eye on your daughter!" I said. A larger wave had come up the beach, spraying sea foam across Elena's legs and into her face. The surf lifted her briefly, floated her for just a moment out toward the sea before setting her back down onto the wet sand. The girl toppled over backward, her mouth readying to cry.

"Shit," Mariana said. She dropped down from the short stone wall where we were perched and ran the few feet across the beach, scooping the crying girl up against her. As she rubbed a hand under her daughter's wet cotton shirt, between the small edges of her shoulder blades, I was again carried back to that terrible morning when I had hidden all the knives in the house. I felt now that something both dreadful and inevitable had been set in motion.

A HALF hour later Mariana had changed Elena out of her wet clothes and given her a plastic container of sliced strawberries to snack on, and now the girl was sleeping soundly on the beach blanket. Mariana had been quiet since the incident, as if she were embarrassed.

"I'm sorry," she said. "I shouldn't have brought it up. About the kidney."

I didn't say anything. Elena's shoulders rose and fell as she slept, and I fought back an urge to put a hand on the girl's back, to touch the corn silk of the stray hairs behind her ears.

"It sounds crazy," she said. "I know how it sounds. I think I'm just looking for something new in my life."

"You don't have anything new in your life?" I said, thinking of the young American up in the old fortress of San Jorge, teaching my ninth-year grammar class. But if Mariana understood what I was suggesting, she didn't show it.

"It doesn't seem like it," she said, tracing her finger through the warm white sand.

"I've been meaning to talk to you," I said. I wasn't sure why I began like this or what I'd say next. But on some level, through some hidden desire, I'd been readying myself for this; it was part of a plan that led to José Antonio's kidnapping, to my late-night meeting with the young detective, to the day after José Antonio's funeral when Mariana cornered me against the wall in the plaza to demand that I never speak to her again. "I have a friend in Bilbao. A doctor."

The finger stopped its tracing in the sand. Mariana swept away the dark hair that had fallen over her face and looked at me closely.

"And?" she said.

"And I asked him about your . . . case," I said.

"Damn it, Joni. I must sound like an insane person," she said.

"No," I said. "Not about the memories. About the donor."

"It's confidential information," she said.

"Yes, for most people," I said, thinking quickly, trying to figure out the implications of the story as I told it. "But he's an emergency room doctor at Santa Marina. I asked if he could find the name of the donor."

"Why would you do that?" she asked. Her voice was shaking.

"I thought you'd want to know," I said. "I guess I wanted to know too."

She nodded. For a moment we both sat there in silence, the girl between us on the blanket. The wind blew voices over from down the beach, stirred the girl's hair.

"So?" she said finally. "What did he say?"

"Do you really want to know?" I asked.

"No," she said. "But it's too late now."

I like to think that at that moment I took a breath. That I paused, and in that pause I thought about what I was about to say—the lie

I was about to tell. That I considered the consequences, that I had Mariana's best interests at heart. I like to think that now.

"It was a boy," I said. "Fourteen years old. Hit by a work truck while he was riding a bicycle to his father's house."

"No," she said, shaking her head. "No, I don't believe that."

"It's true," I said. "I swear to you that it's true."

41. IKER

THE VISITING ROOM ISN'T LIKE WHAT YOU'D EXPECT FROM the movies. It isn't a wall of heavy glass divided by a bank of two-way telephones, and it isn't a large room cut in half by a row of rusted iron bars. It's a visitation room for offenders that have been deemed "nonviolent," a label I earned after my second year in the Salto. The prison administration has tried its best to make the visitation room comfortable for the families of the inmates. The room is filled with small tables, and the inescapably yellow concrete walls have been plastered with printing paper colored over by children's crayons and markers. The papers contain the shaky outlines of small hands, green and orange scribbles that seem completely meaningless but that are nonetheless dated by an adult and labeled with the young artist's name. There are art supplies in plastic boxes in a corner of the room, and there is a vending machine that sells Conguitos and Chupa Chups and sunflower seeds. The visitation room seems more like a primary school classroom than the south wing of Spain's most remote penitentiary.

Nere has remained faithful to me as much as I could expect or hope for her to be faithful. Which is to say, she remains faithful by faithfully telling me about her life in Muriga, which has carried on in my absence. On Easter Sunday last year, for the first time since my transfer to the Gran Canaria, she didn't come to the prison alone. I had been warned, of course, but when she entered the family visiting room carrying the boy, I held back tears for the first time since my transfer to the Salto, when I was only eighteen.

"Iker," she had said when she entered the visitation room, holding the colorful bundle close against her chest, "Iker, this is Julen."

We stood across from each other there in the visitation room, neither knowing how to proceed now that there was this new life held between the two of us. I tried to smile for her, but when I reached over to put a hand on her arm, she began to cry.

"He's very handsome," I said. She nodded weakly, looking down at the small face pressed against the thin ridge of her collarbone. "He has blue eyes."

"Yes," Nere said. She wiped her nose with the sleeve of her free arm. "Juan María has blue eyes. I thought he wouldn't get them, because mine are so dark. But yes . . ."

SHE HAD met Juan María during my second year. The sentence itself was a span of time entirely inconceivable—twenty-eight years before the first possibility of release—and I told her that I didn't expect her to wait. She had only nodded when I told her this. She had come to this long before. And yet it wasn't until that second year in the Salto—when Nere told me about the young doctor who had transferred to the hospital in Muriga from Pamplona—that I fully understood my life and plans with Nere had died with the Councilman.

We found ourselves trying to hold on to what we had first loved about each other—we tried to keep the openness that we had both valued so much in Muriga, the honesty that had set this relationship apart. But in the end she didn't want to know about the unpleasant realities of the Salto del Negro, and I didn't want to hear about her life without me in Muriga—the apartment that she and the doctor had paid a deposit on, Friday nights in the old part of town with a group of friends I didn't know. The spaces between our conversations in the Salto grew larger and larger. The letters became less frequent.

For the next two years I almost dreaded her annual visits. They seemed only to disturb the soothing monotony of life in the Salto. Her trips to the Canaries began to double as vacations—she would spend an afternoon with me in the visitation room, and then she and the doctor, Juan María, would spend three days drinking oversized cocktails on the beach of the Hotel Neptuno before returning to Muriga.

When the letter arrived in June of my fourth year in the Canaries, after almost five months without communication, I nearly threw it out without opening it.

"What's biting your ass?" Andreas finally asked after I had been carrying around the envelope for a week. He was shaving with the disposable razors that we are allowed to have in our cells once a week, and he stopped the blue razor halfway down his chin to point at the envelope. "Most of us are glad to get a letter every once in a while, but you've been in this mood ever since *that* arrived."

"I'm afraid of what's inside," I said.

"Well, that much is obvious," he said. "Manolito and I have a bet. He says that it has something to do with a woman, but I said that you have been in here for five years and that any harm a woman could do would have been done a long time ago."

He continued shaving, smiling at his own shaky logic.

"So what do you think it's about?" I asked.

"I think it's news that your mother is dead," he said, turning to study my expression, as if to verify his hunch.

"Well, thanks so much for the sympathy," I said.

He shrugged his shoulders, then continued to draw the razor across the hollows of his cheeks.

"You know how it is," he said. "You were here when my father passed last year. There's nothing for us to do—no funeral to attend, no one we have to console, no grave to tidy up. It's easier for us, in a way."

I sat down on the edge of my bunk and tore back the end of the envelope. I could feel Andreas watching as I slid the letter out and unfolded it. It was written in Nere's neat, slanted script—only a half-page long. I read the letter to the end, then looked at the black square photograph of the sonogram.

"So?" Andreas asked. "Was I right?"

I folded the letter and slid it back into the envelope, then placed the square photograph into the breast pocket of my shirt.

"Yes," I said. "You were right."

By now he had finished shaving and was rinsing his face in the small metal sink next to the toilet. As he splashed his freshly shaven face with cold water, he smiled with satisfaction.

"I knew it," he said. "I can't wait to tell the old man."

42. JONI

AFTER I LEFT MARIANA'S APARTMENT THE NIGHT OF JOSÉ Antonio's kidnapping I crossed the street to the Caledonian, an Irish-style pub that had recently been opened by two men from Orio. The place was nearly empty; a group in their early twenties, including Lulu Cortez's son Felix, was gathered around a dartboard toward the back of the room, and a couple of strays hovered over their pints of beer at the bar. The walls were overdecorated with Irish knickknacks—plaques with words that might have been Gaelic, photographs of John F. Kennedy and Gerry Adams, framed Guinness posters.

I nodded the bartender over to where I stood.

"You're the American, no?" he asked me in English. He put his cigarette out in a glass half-filled with water. "You teach at the academy?"

"Yes," I said, then ordered an Amstel and a Jameson in Spanish. As the bartender tipped the green whiskey bottle down from a shelf behind the bar, I tried to gather the nerve to call the detective. I had no actual proof that Mariana and Robert Duarte were having an affair, after all; she hadn't told me anything other than that they'd met a few times, that his wife had been unable to join them for one reason or another.

A better man might have been able to say that he was protecting Mariana from the dangers she seemed so oblivious to: not only Duarte's violent hatred of José Antonio and all that he stood for politically but also the way that Duarte had destabilized her, made her more reckless. I'd hoped that introducing her to the Americans would draw her out of herself, distract her from her crazy ruminations about ghosts and organs, but it had the opposite effect. She became more engrossed in her obsessions. She began to cancel our coffee dates at the Boliña, and on the rare occasions that she would now invite me up to her apartment, I noticed a new disorder that hadn't been present before. An empty biscuit wrapper left on the counter, burgundy rings left by a wineglass on the table. And her daughter, Elena, seemed to be lost entirely in Duarte's wake, a weight to be dragged along after her.

But even then, I knew that I wasn't just trying to save Mariana. I knew that I was about to betray the only real relationship I'd had in Muriga since Nerea; I was simply summoning up the courage to do it.

When the bartender placed the drinks in front of me, I sipped at the whiskey once, then tipped up the entire glass, chasing it down with half the beer. I drew a stool up to the bar and sat, then removed the detective's card from my jacket pocket. The whiskey was still warm in my mouth when I asked the bartender for the telephone.

CASTRO ARRIVED forty-five minutes later. It was nearly one in the morning, but he still wore his perfectly pressed dark suit, and his clear eyes moved with the quickness of a wild dog's.

"I'm sorry to call so late," I said.

He waved his hand.

"No, no," he said. "I was still at the station." He looked soberly at the three empty pint glasses in front of me. "So," he said. "What was it you wanted to speak to me about?"

I realized what this must look like—an old drunk alone at a bar. I wanted to explain, but every explanation seemed to begin with Mariana in a way that would sound wrong to the young detective.

"Earlier," I began. "When we were at the apartment. When you were alone with Mariana."

He looked at me closely.

"I could hear you. I was in the other room, but I could hear," I said.

"Fine," he said cautiously. "I was just trying to make her feel more comfortable in private. She didn't tell me anything."

"I know she didn't," I said. "Like I said, I could hear you perfectly."

"So then?"

"So I know what you were asking her," I said. "Or what I think you were asking her, at least."

"And what was that?"

The bartender came over and put his hands on the bar.

"Another Amstel?" he asked.

"Why not," I said, not looking at the young detective.

"And for you?" he said to Castro.

"Nothing," he said. "No. A *mosto*."

The bartender seemed annoyed by the order and reached under the bar for the bottle of nonalcoholic grape juice.

"So then," Castro said. "You were about to tell me what I was asking Mariana Zelaia."

"Yes," I said. "I think you were trying to ask if she was having a love affair."

Castro smiled.

"Crimes of passion are much more common than politically motivated crimes. I had to rule it out," he said. The bartender slid the two full glasses across the bar toward us, then went back to his cigarette.

"The reason I asked you here," I said, "is that I don't think Mariana was entirely truthful in her answer."

The detective sipped from the brim of his glass, looking at me with interest, if not surprise. He knew much more than he was letting on.

"Go ahead," he said in a way that you might speak to a young child trying to tell a story of no consequence.

"I think that there was a . . . a relationship. With another man."

"And who is this other man?" Castro asked. I took a long drink of the beer, then wiped my mouth with the back of my hand.

"There is another American," I said. "He works at the same school that I do. Duarte. Robert Duarte."

The detective removed from his jacket pocket the same notepad that he had earlier at the apartment and flipped to a blank page.

"Duarte," he said as he wrote. "A Basque name."

I nodded.

"His family is Basque," I said.

"So how does this Duarte know Mariana Zelaia?" Castro asked.

I dragged a finger through a bit of spilled beer on the bar, not knowing exactly how to answer.

"I introduced them," I said finally. "About three months ago. Maybe four."

The detective raised his eyebrows, as if this was the most interesting thing I had told him so far.

"And how did you become aware of this supposed affair?" he asked.

"Well," I stammered. I felt as if I had unexpectedly become a suspect myself in José Antonio's kidnapping. "I don't have any definite proof, I suppose. It's just a feeling I have. The way she talks about him. The way they act when I run into them having coffee on the street."

"I see," Castro said. "But you don't have any actual proof of this affair."

"I saw them once," I said. "At a bar on the way out of town."

I realized how stupid it must sound, wondered if I really had seen anything incriminating that afternoon. The detective flipped his notebook closed and pushed his half-full glass of *mosto* back across the bar.

"Well, it's certainly something that we'll follow up on," he said. "Is there anything else that you wanted to speak to me about?"

"No," I said. "That was it."

The detective stood up to leave, rubbing his bald head with the palm of his hand as if still in concentration. He told me that he'd be in contact if he had any further questions, but instead of turning toward the door he lingered, regarding me curiously.

"Can I ask you something?" he said finally.

"Yes," I said. "Of course."

"Why are you telling me all this?" he said.

"I'm sorry?" I asked.

"I mean, she's your friend," he said. "Mariana Zelaia."

"Yes," I said. "She is."

"So why are you telling me about this supposed affair?"

The bar seemed to fill with a momentary silence, only the high pipe of an Irish flute playing from a set of speakers behind the bar.

"José Antonio was a friend of mine too," I said finally. "I just wanted to do whatever I could to help."

The young detective closed his clear blue eyes, as if suddenly understanding. When he opened his eyes, he nodded and turned to leave. What surprised me was not that I had lied to the detective but that I had already begun to speak of Mariana's husband in the past tense.

43. MARIANA

THE NIGHT OF THE KIDNAPPING, AFTER THE POLICEMEN and Joni had left the apartment, there was a knock on the door just after midnight. Elena was asleep in her crib in the nursery, and the sudden noise clattered through the silence of the apartment, startling my mother and me as we sat numbly in the kitchen. The two of us rushed down the dark hallway, and when I peered through the peephole, I half-expected to find José Antonio standing in the blue light of the entryway, his dark suit sagging with the heavy rain that fell outside. Instead, I found the bald little detective waiting on the other side of the door, studying the black metal cage surrounding the elevator shaft as if it held some missing clue.

"I'm sorry to stop in this late," he said when I opened the door. He shuffled a bit where he stood, then held his hand open toward the apartment. "May I come in?"

"Of course," I said, standing aside. He nodded briefly to my mother, then led us back to the living room and gestured for us to sit down. He remained standing between where we sat on the sofa and the hallway where we had entered, as if to prevent us from escaping.

"I wanted to stop by before you heard from the news," he said, nodding to the muted television, where a photograph of José Antonio was being displayed on a news program from San Sebastián. A jagged pain arrived just under the scar from the operation, and for the first time, it occurred to me that José Antonio would never return home. Castro stepped across the room and turned the television off.

"We've received a message from the people who have your husband," he said. *Have your husband*, I thought. He was still alive.

"Who is it?" my mother said. "Do you know where he is? Is he all right?"

Castro held up a hand to slow her down.

"We think we know who it is," he said. "It appears to be politically motivated."

"ETA?" my mother said, putting a hand over her mouth.

"Shhhh . . . ," I said, gripping my mother's leg. "Let the detective speak."

Castro seemed to appreciate this gesture; he sat down on the edge of one of the chairs across from us, his hands on his knees.

"We believe it's a local group that has ties to the separatist cause. But no, we don't believe it's the ETA."

"Thank the Lord," my mother said, pushing closer on the sofa, taking my hand in hers.

Castro made the motion as if to slow her down again, then turned to me. I looked past the detective, to a bookshelf that was lined with small framed photographs. Elena's first week, swaddled in embroidered white cotton blankets that José Antonio's parents had sent us. I barely recognized myself as the woman in the next photograph, sipping at the hole cut into the top of a green coconut during our first vacation together.

I settled on a last photograph taken earlier that year. It had been the first warm day of summer, and José Antonio sat in the white wicker chairs of La Joya with Elena propped on his knee. Behind them, two old men batted a tennis ball back and forth on the beach with *paletas*, and José Antonio jokingly held his empty beer glass to Elena's mouth. I hadn't really thought about my husband for months—I had replaced him with the American, and with a dead man I had never met.

"Mariana," the detective said, as if preparing me for something. "This isn't necessarily a good thing."

He leaned closer from the edge of his chair. "If it had been the ETA, it would be more predictable. We've done this before with them—there's a ransom, or a demand. We have people with them. We know what they are going to do, more or less. With these people—the ones who have José Antonio—we don't know what they'll do."

"They're local," I said.

Castro nodded, and as if on cue, he reached into his pocket and retrieved a large white envelope. He placed it on the low table between us, then reached in and removed a series of photographs. He spread them out over the top of the old magazines on the table, seven photographs in all. Three of them had white borders, as if they were snapshots printed at a commercial photo shop. The other four were obviously from police records; these photographs were taken head-on, their subjects wearing somber, bleak expressions.

"We believe this is the person who organized your husband's kidnapping," he said, tapping a finger on one of the police photos. "Do you recognize him?"

I picked up the photo and held it on my lap. The photograph was of a young man, perhaps in his midtwenties. He had light-brown hair, sun-streaked to blond in places. He had the set jaw and thick neck of a natural athlete, dark eyes, a handsome face.

"No," I said. "I've never seen this man before."

"His name is Gorka Auzmendi," Castro said.

"Auzmendi," my mother said. "The name is familiar."

Castro nodded.

"You might recognize the name from the newspapers," he said. "His brother was arrested a few years ago for an attempted car bombing in Madrid. Xabi Auzmendi. And this is where your husband comes in, I'm afraid."

I put the photo facedown on the low table between us.

"Wasn't the bombing in Madrid—" my mother said.

"ETA," the detective interrupted. "Yes. The Auzmendis are associated with ETA-militar, without a doubt. But it seems that Gorka Auzmendi planned José Antonio's kidnapping without the knowledge of ETA's leadership."

"And these men?" my mother said, holding up the photographs remaining on the table.

"Mariana, do you recognize anyone here?" Castro asked.

The first photograph was of a boy who couldn't have been more than eighteen—he had black hair that was cut short except for a long churro hanging from behind his left ear. The photograph was taken at a bar that looked familiar, the boy leaning back against a white plaster wall holding a glass of *kalimotxo*. I shook my head.

"You're sure?" the detective said.

"Yes."

"He's a student at the public school here in Muriga," he said. "Dani Garamendi."

"He's a student?" my mother asked.

"Yes. We believe that at least three of them were recruited by Auzmendi for the kidnapping. Their parents tell us that they haven't been seen since early this morning."

I set the photograph facedown on top of the photo of Gorka Auzmendi, then looked down at the next photograph. It was of another young man, this time with neatly cut black hair parted on the side and dark, serious eyes. He wore the light-blue button-down and dark blazer of the private school on the hill, Colegio San Jorge. A jolt came through me, one of panic and of pain, as I realized it was the boy I had seen on the beach a week earlier. I had removed my swimsuit top for him. I touched myself for him. I lurched forward as if I were going to be sick.

"Do you recognize him?" the detective asked. I felt my mother watching me.

"No," I shook my head. "No. I've seen him before, around town. But I don't know who he is."

I picked up the remaining two photographs and flipped through them quickly.

"I don't know any of them," I said. I felt my voice raising. From the back bedroom, I heard Elena calling for me. "Why are you asking me about these people if you already know who they are? If you know they have my husband?"

44. JONI

TWO DAYS AFTER THE ARREST OF IKER ABARZUZA, ASIER Díaz, and Gorka Auzmendi, a shrimping boat spotted the body of José Antonio a half hour's walk north of Muriga. *El Diario Vasco*'s account stated only that the body had been recovered with gunshot wounds to the back of the head and the upper torso, but rumors began to circulate that the body had been picked apart by fish and scavenging birds, that his hands had been bound behind his back with electrical tape and laundry line, that his suit had been torn almost entirely from his body by the tide.

Small towns thrive on gossip, and Muriga is no different. In my fifty years here, I've continually been struck by the reserve with which gossip had been passed in Muriga, the strict privacy allotted to rumor. But in the immediate wake of José Antonio's kidnapping, Muriga seemed to collectively agree to unseal any information about anyone involved. Men like Santi Etxeberria, who had cursed at the campaign posters José Antonio had hung the week before his death, now remembered him as an ambitious young man— perhaps a little out of line with Muriga politically but hardworking and agreeable.

Conversely, Asier and Iker were remembered as more isolated, more mentally unstable, more radicalized than I knew they had really been. Over the course of a few days, they came to be known not as Asier and Iker but as Díaz and Abarzuza. Not as "the two boys" but as *bi gizonak*. The two men.

And in this way, almost simultaneous with the discovery of the body, Muriga began to construct its mythology. It began to tell, then revise and retell the story, each version spinning another protective layer around the town until any culpability on the part of its residents had been enveloped entirely by this narrative cocoon.

When I arrived at Mariana's apartment the afternoon after José Antonio's disappearance, her mother, Carmen, answered the door. She held Elena on her hip in an old and weary way that reminded me of the work-worn women in the smallest villages of the Basque Country. Two police officers sat on the sofa in the living room, reading José Antonio's sports magazines. I nodded to them, then followed Mariana's mother into the kitchen.

Mariana barely seemed to register my arrival. She sat hunched in a chair next to the tile counter, her right arm pulled tight across her stomach as if she had just been struck.

"This stress is too much for her," Carmen said quietly.

I sat at the small table in the corner of the room. The tabletop was covered with empty coffee cups, piles of papers from José Antonio's Party office in Bilbao, pencils with the imprints of teeth marks breaking through the yellow paint just below the erasers.

"Do you want anything, Joni?" Carmen asked. "Coffee? Tea?"

"Thanks," I said, shaking my head no.

At the sound of our voices Mariana straightened herself in her chair, pushed a hand through the dark thickness of her hair as if to try to make herself more presentable.

"You've heard the rumors, I suppose," she said. "About me and the American."

I looked uncomfortably at Carmen, who hiked the girl higher on her hip. The police had confirmed the affair between Mariana and the American that morning, I'd learned. Maite Tamayo, the neighbor across the hall, told the detective that she had seen Duarte enter the Torres apartment several times, and (not that she was listening, but . . .) she had heard what could only be described as obscene noises coming through the walls when he was there. The rumor spread quickly from there. Soon after, Goikoetxea called to tell me that the police had taken Robert to the station in Bilbao for questioning, two officers and a young balding detective escorting him out.

"It's all right," Mariana said, nodding toward her mother. "She was the one who told me the rumor was out."

"Yes," I said. I watched her carefully, trying to figure out if Castro had told her about our meeting the night before. "Goikoetxea told me that they are questioning him now. I think it's the same detective, Castro."

She didn't seem surprised by this, nor did she seem to suspect my involvement. She appeared resigned to the chaos that had swept into her life, the missing husband, the police officers waiting in her living room.

"It's true, of course," she said. "About the American. But he doesn't have anything to do with José Antonio."

Her confirmation of the affair wasn't surprising. But I began to wonder if it was possible that the American did have something to do with José Antonio's disappearance. It didn't seem likely that he would have the sort of connections required to carry out the kidnapping. But then again, he had mentioned family in Nabarniz, and I recalled the walk to the pelota match, when Robert had told me the story of his grandfather kept captive during the war.

"You're sure?" I asked. "How well do you know him?"

"It's true," Carmen said. "You don't even know this man. You know nothing about him."

The girl fussed in her grandmother's arms, and Mariana shook her head.

"Can you take her out for a bit?" she said. She took one of the yellow pencils and placed the eraser in her mouth, biting gently into the chipped wood. "It's time for her nap, anyway."

Carmen carried the girl down the hallway toward the bedroom, the afternoon sun flashing off a hanging mirror.

"You know it doesn't have anything to do with him," Mariana said.

"He hates José Antonio," I said. "Or at least, he hates what he stands for."

"To be honest, it was the first thing that occurred to me," she said. "When I heard the news, he was the first one I called. But even before I spoke to him, I knew that he wasn't involved."

"How could you be certain?" I asked.

She shrugged her shoulders, the corners of her mouth lifting into an odd smile. The pencil bobbed up and down like an unlit cigarette.

"Because he doesn't love me," she said simply.

45. IKER

AFTER GORKA AND I WERE ARRESTED AT THE FRENCH BOR-
der in Hendaye we were interrogated separately by the Spanish
police for two days. Within the first few hours I had told the young
detective, Castro, everything that had happened. They had arrested
Daniel and Asier at a roadblock the morning before—this much
Gorka had already told me. Dani had spilled everything to them,
Castro said. When Castro told me that Dani had admitted to burning the bus in Bermeo and that the rifle I had guarded the Councilman with had been taken from Asier's father's closet, I knew that
he had confessed, and so I began to talk. Gorka had been more
resilient; it wasn't until the second day of interrogation that he
admitted his role in shooting the Councilman.

During the fourth day of the trial the *fiscal* handed a transcript
of my interview with Detective Castro to the judge before asking a
judicial assistant to play the audiotape. There was static, followed
by Castro reading the date of the interview into the recorder, and
then the courtroom was filled with a voice both familiar and foreign. The courtroom watched me as my voice came through the
monitors.

We covered his eyes with an old beach towel, my voice said.

Who? asked the voice of the detective. *Who put the towel over his head?*

Gorka, my voice answered. *Gorka covered his head. He was squirming, trying to make noise. Gorka hit him once through the towel. I was the one who put the clothesline around his hands.*

In the recording, I recalled how Asier and I had spent the night with the Councilman in the bunker as Gorka and Dani drove to Bermeo and made calls to the Ertztainza headquarters in Bilbao as well as to the offices of the newspapers *El Diario Vasco, El País, Egunkaria,* and *El Mundo,* demanding the release of five political prisoners, including Gorka's brother, Xabi Auzmendi. The recording ended with my voice telling the courtroom about the morning when I had been left alone to guard the Councilman—how after he was dead, we had pushed the body over the edge of the cliffs and down into the sea. But the recording captured just a series of facts, of events. It was incomplete. Everything important had happened in between.

✳ ✳ ✳

THE MIGRAINE had just begun to pass when I heard my name being shouted from the trail. I had pulled my shirt over my head to escape the sunlight, the rifle on the ground next to me. I pushed my head through the shirt and squinted against the landscape; there was a scraping noise coming from behind me in the bunker, and I struggled up to my feet.

"There he is!" I heard Gorka yell across the pasture, and when I turned I could make out the Councilman's dark silhouette running from the bunker, his hands still bound behind his back, taking off toward the cliffs. I picked up the rifle and stumbled after him, closing my eyes against the whiteness of the morning sun, running blind for a few steps.

Gorka overtook me in less than a hundred meters, cutting powerfully through the grass like a shark through the dark waters of the harbor below. As he passed to my left, he reached behind his back to pull a revolver from the waistband of his pants. There was only forty meters separating Gorka from the Councilman when I saw the Councilman trip over the eroded wall of another bunker. His body pitched awkwardly into the grass beyond, unable to catch himself with his hands still bound behind his back.

I knew the chase was over. I held on to the rifle as a crutch and closed my eyes tight again. The pain radiated around the left side of my head, into my neck and jaw. I listened, waiting for Gorka to drag the Councilman back to the bunker, waiting to hear Asier approaching from the trail.

When I forced my eyes open Gorka was standing behind the Councilman, who was trying to get to his feet. Gorka yelled something at him that I couldn't make out. The Councilman's head moved as if he were saying something in return. Behind the two men the sun glared off the surface of the harbor, and gulls circled in the empty air. I turned back toward the bunker, wondering where Asier and Dani were, what we would do now. But I saw only the gray, crumbling walls of the bunker, the green stretch of pasture leading into the dark rows of ash and birch, and, somewhere beyond, the tall fortress walls of San Jorge.

Even now, six years away from that morning, this picture of the empty bunker and the trees comes as a flash, as I wash out the green plastic cup in the sink of our cell or as I lie awake in bed listening to the rise and fall of Andreas's breathing in the bunk above mine. In this flash I don't just see the abandoned building and the blowing grass but also the smoothness of Nere's shoulder half-covered by the blanket we had carried to the beach from her father's house. I breathe in the burnt-coffee smell of the old American professor, feel the sting of my father's aftershave as he holds my head tight against his shoulder after the verdict is read. I hear the cries of the gulls and shorebirds and feel the salt air and watch the empty spot in the cold green water of the harbor where the Councilman disappeared, a trail of white air surfacing in his place. All of this in an instant, and then Gorka lifts the pistol to the head of the Councilman. The pistol jumps in his hand, and a moment later the sound of the shot arrives. In the seconds that follow the world seems to stop, as if to take a breath; the wind stops blowing and the sea no longer pitches against the cliffs below us. The gulls pause in midair to watch, and then the pistol jumps once more in Gorka's hand and the world begins again.

46. JONI (1955)

IT WAS THREE WEEKS AFTER THE GIRL'S SECOND BIRTHDAY when the car went off the road.

We had settled into a routine that, to an outsider, might have even seemed normal. The bedroom light that came on several times a night as a pale young man or his wife woke to attend to a crying child, the plume of exhaust spitting from the battered Peugeot as the young man drove from the house each morning, the slow walk the wife took each day at noon along the trail leading to the river's edge, carrying the girl against her breast.

Our dysfunction wasn't visible. On the drive back to Muriga from the hospital, when I suggested that we stop at her mother's house to show her the child, Nerea looked at me incredulously.

"Why would I do that?" she said, holding the small bundle that was our daughter close against her. "That woman threw me out of the house at thirteen and has never done a thing for me since."

"I'm sorry," I said. "It's just—"

"Why would you ever say that?" she interrupted.

For two years we carried on this way, as we had in the nine months before our daughter's birth in Bilbao. Nerea's dark periods lasted days, and then weeks, during which we would hardly speak. Soon after we returned from Bilbao, without explanation, Nerea began to sleep in the girl's room. Our friends asked to come see the girl, and each time I turned them down, finding some excuse or another, until finally they stopped asking. She hardly trusted me to even hold the child.

"Not like that," she would say, stepping over to take the girl from me.

"Not like what?" I'd ask. "I hold her the same way that you do."

But she would only shake her head and carry the girl into the next room.

"Just go to your work," she'd say. "Drive up that goddamned hill to work with all of the other fascists. Tell my father I say 'hello.'"

A TRUCK driver had been following behind the Peugeot on the way to Bermeo and saw the car go off the road. The highway runs along the coastline for the last twenty kilometers, and a light mist had just begun, which might have accounted for the missed turn. But the truck driver, in his report to the police, stated that the car didn't seem to turn at all, that he didn't remember the brake lights coming on before the car went off the road.

A police investigator came to the house five days later. It was early afternoon, and Juantxo Goikoetxea and I had already been drunk for several hours. The investigator ignored our gloomy drunkenness, as if he understood that he would do the same. He asked if he might have a cup of coffee, and when Juantxo went to the kitchen to put water on the stove, he told me that the deaths had been ruled an accident due to inclement weather and poor road conditions.

"Can I see the police report?" I said.

He looked down at the folder he held in his lap; it was obvious that he had brought it in only as a prop, as a way of giving his visit an air of authority.

"Yes," he said finally. "Of course."

The officer sat nervously in his chair, occasionally glancing out the window toward the rain blowing across the river. With one hand I held the glass of brandy that I had been drinking before he arrived, and with the other I flipped over the pages. There were black-and-white photocopies of the accident scene: a police officer holding a tape measure to indicate how far the tires had traveled, another of the same officer at the wreckage, the Peugeot wrapped among the rocks and marram grass, his tape measure indicating that the car had traveled thirty-eight meters from the highway before coming to a stop. The front end of the car was destroyed, the driver's-side door twisted awkwardly out as if peeled open.

A police report included the statements of the truck driver who had been following Nerea and the girl, as well as the accounts of several other drivers who saw the car leave the road. I paused on a field report by the investigating officer, a short narrative describing the various eyewitness accounts and the physical evidence collected at the scene, ending with three short sentences: *No mechanical failure found or suspected. Family members and acquaintances of adult victim report history of depression and mental illness. Preliminary conclusion is that adult victim drove vehicle from roadway with intent to inflict injury and/or death upon herself and upon infant victim.*

As I reread the paragraph I heard the investigator shuffle in his seat across from me.

"There was some dispute over the cause of death," he said. I emptied the brandy glass into my mouth and turned to the next page of the report.

A few minutes later, when Juantxo came back into the living room with a cup of coffee, I closed the folder and slid it across the table to the investigator. He stood.

"I'm sorry," he told Juantxo quickly. "I don't think I'll have that coffee after all."

47. IKER

"MY FATHER USED TO SKI," NERE SAID, READING IN ENGLISH from a note card. Even I could tell that her pronunciation was terrible.

"*Mi padre esquiaba,*" I said.

"Very good," she said, flipping over the card to check the answer. We had just arrived at the beach, and Nere was still wearing her baggy green hospital clothes. The hospital was only a couple of blocks up from the harbor, and when the weather was nice we liked to pick up sandwiches and carry them down to the beach for siesta. She seemed happier with her own English than she was with my correct answer. She leaned over on the beach towel to bite me lightly on the shoulder, then switched back into Basque. "You're getting better already, you know? Keep studying like this and your test will be no problem."

At first I had worried about what Nere would think of the weekend English classes. I thought she'd react like Asier had. That she'd think I was selling out or going against our cuadrilla. But she saw the exam as our ticket out of Muriga. We were both getting tired of the meetings in the old bunker, the weekend nights throwing firecrackers and spray-painting the same used-up political slogans on back alley walls. Instead, we talked more about our new lives in San Sebastián, about the concerts on the beach, about what part of town we would look for an apartment in.

She began to help with my English like this—quizzing me from note cards or vocabulary sheets over *kalimotxos* in the Scanner Bar or while we ate sandwiches at the beach. It never really helped as much as she thought it did, but I liked the idea of the two of us working at something together.

"These cards the old man makes are so boring," she said. She straightened the pile of note cards against her knee. "Let's make some better ones."

"Sure," I said.

"I'll tell you in Spanish and you translate."

"Go ahead," I said.

She pulled at the small hairs on the back of her neck, the way she did when she was thinking. "OK," she said, smiling. "*Hace demasiado calor para llevar tanta ropa.*"

It was her lunch break, and she was still wearing the plain blue shirt she always wore under her nurse's scrubs. She took a drink from the Coke can between us, then stretched her shoulders back in the way that made her tits look bigger.

"Well?" she said. "Are you going to translate?"

"It's too hot . . . ," I said. "It's too hot to wear so much clothes."

"Very good," she said. She reached back, pulling the blue T-shirt over her head. She rolled the blue shirt up and set it on my backpack to keep it out of the sand. She liked to sun herself during her lunch breaks and after work, and her shoulders were still brown from the summer. She was wearing a black bra, and when she lay on her back next to me she undid the strap so that she wouldn't get a tan line. Her eyes were closed and I could see the soft blond hairs on her lip, the small holes on either side of her eyebrow where she had worn a piercing the year before.

"See?" she said. "Isn't this more fun?"

I ran my fingers across her brown stomach, and I remembered the Councilman's wife a few days earlier on the beach. I thought of the red scar that ran from her belly button halfway to her side, how it looked hot and infected. It stood out from the pale skin of her belly and her breasts.

"Yes," I said. I lay down next to her, then kissed the smooth of her stomach. I put my hand on the inside of her legs, over the baggy hospital pants. She squeezed her legs together against my hand, and I felt her move just a little. "These are a lot more fun."

"Next sentence?"

"*Bai.*"

✳ ✳ ✳

SOMETIMES GARRETT and I would meet at a café, at Bar Zabaleta or the Boliña, but most often we met in his stuffy little office in San Jorge. It didn't make sense to start going to class now, he said. I'd missed too much, and I was better off writing out sample essays and studying vocabulary on my own until I was up to speed. I don't know whether he really believed this or if he just saw it as a way of figuring out how committed I was to passing my exams in the spring, instead of continuing to screw around with Asier and Dani. But while the rest of my class was repeating the different forms of the imperfect tense or giving group book reports in English, and while Asier and Dani were off attending an anarchist rally in Bilbao, I was studying in the public library in the basement of the city hall.

Even after a month without a missed appointment, the old man always seemed surprised to see me show up. He marked up my papers with handwriting that was so jittery it looked like it was written in the backseat of a car. While I was waiting for him I'd flip through a stack of vocabulary cards that Nere had written out for me, or I'd just smoke a cigarette and stare out the tiny window that looked down on Muriga below.

"You're going to have to do better than this on the exam," he said on one of these afternoons after we had gone over a reading comprehension sample. An answer sheet I had spent nearly two hours on was covered with his blue ink. "You're getting better, but we only have a couple of months left."

"I know," I said. But it surprised me, actually. I thought that the hard work of the previous month was guaranteed to pay off, and for the first time I wondered what would happen if I didn't do well on the exam. We both reached for the packs of cigarettes we had left out on a corner of the old man's desk. I lit my Lucky, and when I was done I handed the lighter to the old man. We smoked in silence for several minutes, Garrett reading over another practice exam while I read from the next chapter in my lesson book.

"How're your friends these days?" he said after a few minutes, taking off his reading glasses to rub his eyes with the palms of his hands.

"My friends?" I said.

"Sure," he said. "Díaz. Who are the kids from the public school? Daniel Garamendi? Umberto Rodriguez's kid?"

"Joseba. Fine, I guess," I said. "I don't see them as much, since . . ."

"Since what?"

"Nothing," I said, thinking of the fat bus driver in Bermeo clutching the aluminum fare box while his bus melted onto the street.

"The Young Nationalists," the old man said.

"Eh?"

"That's what the new English teacher calls your group," he said. "Duarte—do you know him?"

"I've seen him around," I said.

"He's . . . how can I say this? He's an admirer of the cause," he said. I didn't like the way he said it; his tone made clear that he didn't think much of Duarte or his beliefs.

"There are a lot of people that believe in 'the Cause,' if that's what you want to call it," I said.

He looked at the tip of his cigarette like he was thinking about something else.

"Sure, sure," he said, flicking his ash into an empty coffee cup. "I was around during the worst of the Franco years. I can understand why *some* people believe in the cause."

"But not others," I said. I wanted him to come out and say it.

"No," he admitted. But he stopped short of calling my friends and me fakers, posers. He rolled the tip of the Chesterfield slowly in the bottom of the coffee cup, rubbing the gray ash off. I couldn't figure the old man out—what he was after. But I felt that he had crossed a boundary, talking about the new American teacher this way. I took a chance.

"Is it true what they say about you?" I asked.

He kept rolling the cigarette, and for a minute I thought that he hadn't heard the question. He stubbed the yellow filter out in the cup, then brushed off a little ash that had fallen on his dark-gray sweater. He reached again for the pack of cigarettes and shook another out into his bony fingers.

"What do they say about me?" he finally said. He smiled at me in a cold way that I hadn't seen before.

"Never mind," I began to say. He pushed my pack of Luckys toward me, then lit his own.

"No," he said. "It's all right. I've been telling you what I think of everyone else. I can listen to what they say about me."

The room was hot and stuffy with the cigarette smoke, and I began to feel claustrophobic and nauseous. Garrett's face softened a little, and he leaned back in his chair to blow out a long cloud of smoke.

"Besides," he said, "I'm kind of curious."

"Well," I said. And then I thought, Fuck it. He was the one who started this whole thing, wasn't he? If the old man wanted to hear the straight story, I'd give it to him. "Well, my dad says you're a—that you're a faggot. That's his word. He says that's why you haven't been with a woman that he can remember. He told me to watch myself around you when we meet like this."

The old man nodded a little bit, then looked at me through the cigarette smoke.

"And did you believe him?" he asked.

"Not really," I said. "He's an asshole anyway. I try not to listen to anything he says. Besides, you used to be married."

"That's true," he said. He seemed far away, like he knew the next question I was going to ask and he was already thinking of the answer.

"Did she kill herself?" I asked. "My mother says that the paper wrote it was a car accident, but that everyone knows she did it on purpose."

"I'm not really sure, Iker," he said. He brushed again at his sweater. "Does it really matter?"

I didn't say anything, but I thought to myself that of course it must matter. It was silent for a minute in the small office, and then I turned the page of my notebook and pushed a vocabulary exercise over to be graded. Garrett picked the notebook up, looked at it for a second, then put the notebook back on his desk.

"If it's all right with you, let's leave this for Thursday, OK?" he said.

"I'm sorry," I said. "I shouldn't have asked about your wife."

"No," he said. "That was a long time ago."

"Does it still bother you that much?" I asked.

"As if I lost her yesterday," he said.

Another of the old man's warnings that I only deciphered in the Salto del Negro.

48. MARIANA

THE NIGHT OF THE KIDNAPPING, AFTER DETECTIVE CAS-
tro had come back and left the apartment a second time, I told my
mother about the affair with Robert Duarte.

As I spoke I felt my secret escape the safety of the apartment,
sliding out the cracks around the windows and under the frame of
the door, seeping out into the streets below. If the detective discovered the affair, Duarte would become an automatic suspect. They
would question him, perhaps even arrest him. I'd gone to *secundaria* with the clerk at the police station; his wife cut my hair at the
salon near the post office. I could already see the story of the affair
traveling into the corners of beauty salons and through doctors'
waiting rooms, across the rims of glasses in bars and restaurants,
through the bleachers of the pelota court.

My mother listened quietly, and when I was through, she merely
patted my knee.

"It's all right," she said. "We're all only human, Mariana."

I sat rocking on the sofa and stared at the muted television.
Across the screen came a series of images: police officers at the
Muriga train station, marking with white tape the places on the
asphalt where the kidnappers' car had stopped. Jokin Palacio

opening the front door of our apartment building earlier in the evening, a sack of groceries tucked under an arm.

My mother tended to Elena in the girl's bedroom as I rocked in the silence of the living room. The glowing screen of the television lit up now with the photos of José Antonio supplied by the Partido Popular office in Bilbao, then the word *secuestro* in bold letters below the female newscaster, and finally the silent volleyball game of a sunscreen commercial. My mother sat down on the sofa, both of us watching the weatherman, until she nudged me gently with an elbow.

"Here," she said, holding a small white pill out in her palm. After the conversation in Spanish with Castro, the soft familiarity of my mother's Euskera seemed to take an edge out of the room. In her other hand she held a glass of water. "To help you sleep. Just for a bit."

When I began to protest, she held up a hand.

"I promise to wake you if anything happens," she said. "But you need a little rest."

In the months since the surgery, swallowing pills had become just another of those things we do during the day, like scratching your head or stretching a shoulder. I took the pill and placed it on my tongue, then swallowed it down. I lay back on the couch and pulled up the wool blanket that José Antonio's mother had knit a few weeks after we had announced that I was pregnant. My mother stood to turn off the television, then sat next to me on the sofa. She ran a hand slowly through my hair.

"It will be fine," she whispered, as if this were already something whose outcome she understood. I was surprised to find that I was crying. "This is the worst of it, Mariana. Tonight will be the worst."

"Are you ashamed, *Ama*?" I asked.

"What do I have to be ashamed of?" she said, still pulling her fingers through my tangle of curls.

"Of me, of course," I said. "The American . . ."

Her hand stopped its movement.

"These things happen, my love," she said.

"But if they find out," I said. "You know how it will be. People will talk."

The fingertips again began their slow walk across along my hairline, and I closed my eyes. The pill had begun to settle in, and I felt my breathing begin to slow.

"Oh Mariana," she said. "Don't you know by now? In a town like this, people will always talk. What else would we do?"

THAT NIGHT, for the first time in weeks, I dreamed.

After the pill took hold, my mother turned off the lights in the living room and went to our bedroom to sleep herself. But fifteen minutes later I was still awake on the sofa, the living room swimming unnaturally in a mix of exhaustion, desperation, and the intoxication of the medication. Light crept out oddly from behind the dark shapes of the drawn curtains, throwing unsettling images onto the glassy black of the television and the shadowy corners of the room, and then the smell arrived.

It was a thick smell, heavy with diced vegetables and chicken stock and the dark weight of a hambone simmering in an invisible, impossibly full pot. The living room seemed to fill with the smell, as if it had been prepared just there, on the low table that was covered with José Antonio's old sports magazines. I threw back José Antonio's mother's blanket and sat upright on the sofa, searching the room for the source of the smell. A heat began to radiate just below me, and I felt the familiar sensation of steam rising up to touch the underside of my arms.

"Hello?" I said quietly. "Have you come back?"

There was no answer, only the dark shadows dancing on the wall across the room, forming twisting shapes and faces that disappeared with the rustling of the curtains. I closed my eyes and waited for it all to pass.

It's the pill, I told myself. *You're asleep right now, and when you wake it will be morning and your husband will be back and you will not hear again from the kidney.*

But it *had* returned; I was sure of it when a moment later the heat of the stew trailed off and was replaced with the unmistakable smell of cigarette smoke and sea air. A cold came over me as if the living room window had been left open, and I pulled the blanket up tight as if to protect not only against the cold but also against the smell of smoke and the warmth that had pressed against the underside of my arms. I knew for certain that he was in the room. I felt him there, sitting across from me. The room seemed larger than I remembered it; malevolent black pools grew out from the corners, and the smell of smoke continued to build.

"Please," I said into the dark, my eyes still squeezed shut. "What is it that you want? Why are you here for me?"

There was silence on the other side of the darkness, but for the first time I saw him, Iñaki, his dark hair cropped short, his muted laugh revealing the crooked lower row of teeth. He was in the chair that the detective had sat in just an hour before, slapping a knee, throwing his head back. *He is here for me*, I thought, and then *No, he is here for Elena.* Dark stains seeped through his shirt, dripped from his ears. I felt the weight of the sleeping pill fill my head and knew that I was in that impossible place between sleep and reality. I leaned into a corner of the couch and waited for this to pass, but still the image came across the dark, passed through the woolen loops of the blanket: Iñaki, as I had imagined him, sitting in the detective's chair, but now flanked by two other fig-ures. I didn't recognize the man who stood to his left, a short man with a hooked nose, dressed in a rough work shirt. He was look-ing at Iñaki, as if trying to understand the cause of the young man's laughter. To his right, still dressed in his dark suit, was José Antonio.

When I woke, it was to Elena's cries coming down the hall in the early morning light.

49. MARIANA

"WHO TOLD YOU?" I ASKED THE DETECTIVE.

"It's not important," Castro said. "What's important is that you trust me, Mariana. If I'm going to find your husband, I'll need your complete honesty."

I shook my head, feeling the power of the affair escaping my control, just as I had feared the night before.

"How can I trust you, if you won't even tell me how you learned about Robert Duarte?" I asked.

He smiled, as if he appreciated this turn.

"An excellent point," he said. "But I think you already know, don't you?"

I'd been careful in my few months with Robert; we never spoke by phone, were never seen together in public after those first two innocent meetings. The only person I'd disclosed the affair to was my mother, the night before, and she'd been with me ever since. But that aside, I knew she would never betray my confidence.

And then suddenly I thought back to afternoons with Joni Garrett over the last few months. I remembered the old man delivering the news of José Antonio's kidnapping only a day earlier, how he held me close to him as the news began to register, as the first surge of incomprehension hit. I felt sick, as if the floor had become rolling waves under my feet.

He knew, I realized. He'd known since the beginning.

50. JONI (1955)

I LEFT MURIGA THREE DAYS BEFORE THE FUNERALS. Juantxo would later tell me that there was no public ceremony, that the priest made only an oblique reference to Nerea and the girl during Sunday mass, when he asked the congregants to pray for the souls of the departed.

I had taken the train to Bilbao the Friday before, wandering the streets of the industrial town until I found the small bar where I had taken refuge the morning that our daughter was born. It was early afternoon, and the bar was nearly unrecognizable, the tables filled with regulars gathering for *pintxos* or a drink before heading back to work. I looked around for the curly-haired bartender, but the only people working were a couple in their midfifties who moved in a synchronicity that only comes from decades of coexistence.

"Are you looking for someone?" the woman asked, catching me peering past the bar into the kitchen where the man scraped furiously at a hot steel grill.

I shook my head. She watched me standing there dumbly for a moment.

"Well, is there something I can get you?"

"A *caña*," I said. "And a whiskey."

She poured a small glass full of Ballantine's, then quickly moved down the bar toward the tap; a short man shouted an order as she passed, and she nodded to show that she'd heard. When she returned, she placed the glass of beer in front of me, as well as a plate of golden *croquetas.*

"I'm sorry," I said. "I didn't order these."

She waved a hand at me.

"They were an extra order," she said, already moving to another customer at the end of the bar. "On the house."

✳ ✳ ✳

I HAD planned to take the evening train back to Muriga, but when I arrived at the ticket window the specter of the empty house loomed darkly. Instead, I bought a ticket to Bakio, a tourist town on the beach just outside of Bilbao. I checked into a room I couldn't afford and spent the next four hours at the hotel bar with a German man on vacation.

My mother wired money for the plane ticket after I called her drunk from the hotel's front desk at two in the morning. It was the first time we'd spoken in nearly two years, when she learned that she'd had a grandchild and also that this grandchild was dead. The next day I took the overnight train to Madrid, lighting one cigarette after the other.

"On vacation?" the desk agent said at the airport, reading the name on my ticket.

"Something like that," I said.

"Your Spanish is very good," he said. "You've been here before?"

"It's my first trip, actually," I said. It was true—the last time I had been in Madrid was seven years earlier, when I arrived from San Francisco with a few hundred dollars in traveler's checks, a Fodor's guidebook that I'd bought at the airport, and a suitcase of slacks and shirts that I'd taken from a box of my brother's old clothes in storage.

But even so, this didn't feel like a return, like my life in Muriga was coming to an end. Rather, I was in full retreat; I already knew that I would be trying to escape Nerea for the rest of my life.

My father dealt with my return—and with the story of my dead wife and daughter—as he'd dealt with the death of his own son. Which is to say, in silence. When my mother returned with me from the airport in San Francisco he barely looked up from the television set, as if he'd been expecting this moment since I'd left. And as much as I knew I had needed to flee Muriga, I soon came to understand that my life was there now, or away from the United States, at least. The house had already been consumed with mourning; there was no place for my own here.

I rode with my father to the train yard the next morning, and the foreman agreed to give me the night shift starting that same day. But when I returned to the signal booth that night I was overcome with loneliness, despite the familiarity of my surroundings. The same screeching of the rails, the same gasoline smell of the booth. The strangeness of my name spoken in English.

A few days later I wired Juantxo to see if I might be able to have my job back at San Jorge. When he wrote back the next day, I realized how ridiculous it had been to ask. As if anyone else would have swooped in to take the job in my absence. In his cable, Juantxo told me that there had been a collection taken among the teachers at San Jorge, and among some of the parents as well. Enough for a ticket back. Muriga didn't *need* me, I understood then, but I had a place there. It was more than I could say about the house I'd grown up in.

51. MARIANA

WHEN I WAS VISITED BY IÑAKI THE NIGHT OF JOSÉ ANTO-
nio's kidnapping—or dreamed or imagined him, as Joni might have
put it—it was for the last time. By the next night they had caught
two of the kidnappers and were conducting house-to-house searches
and roadblocks in the hope of finding my husband alive with the
other two fugitives, who by now had been identified as Iker Abarzuza and Gorka Auzmendi. Our apartment on Calle Atxiaga had
been occupied nearly all day with police officers and officials from
the Party office in Bilbao; I was questioned several times by Detective Castro, about any identifying marks or scars that José Antonio
had, about any suspicious people I had noticed over the last several
weeks, about the affair with Robert Duarte.

When my mother ushered out the last of the police that second
night, I swallowed down another of the chalky white pills and waited
for Iñaki to arrive again. But when I woke the next morning after
nearly ten hours of unbroken sleep, it was with the certainty that
Joni had been right, that these visits were over for good.

It wasn't until Beatriz Martínez's wedding six years later, long
after the reporters had stopped calling to ask for interviews and after
the women at my mother's beauty salon stopped staring each time

I passed the shop, that I spoke with Joni again. We talked that night until the deejay cut the music and the staff finished clearing the empty coffee cups, until I had finished telling him my theory. When I stood to leave, the old man reached a hand out to hold on to my sleeve.

"It's been how long now?" he asked. "Since the surgery, I mean."

It seemed like the first time since the kidnapping that someone had asked me about anything other than José Antonio's death.

"Let's see," I said. "Elena was born in October. It was the year after that that I got sick. I guess that makes it seven years now."

"That's good," he said slowly, as if considering what to say. "That's good."

He leaned in.

"Do you still get the . . . sensations?"

My right hand went to the scar.

"From the kidney, you mean?" I asked.

"Yes," he said. He placed his empty wineglass onto the blue-tiled table. "From the kidney."

As I shook my head, I was filled with a great sense of loneliness.

"No," I said. "I think you were right. That it was something that I was imposing on my own memories. A mixed-up sense of déjà vu."

"You know, I'd been meaning to talk to you about this," the old man said. "Before José Antonio's death."

The last of the guests had left, and the hotel staff was lingering impatiently at the doors.

"I think I was too quick to judge, when you first told me about these sensations," he said. "I thought it was just loneliness. Or boredom, maybe. That you were looking for something to do, something to investigate."

"I think that was true, to a large degree," I said. "That's pretty obvious now, isn't it?"

He shook his head.

"No," he continued. "I think I had confused you with someone else, someone from a long time before. Maybe you were right after all."

"Why are you telling me this now?" I asked.

He didn't answer immediately. Instead, he touched a finger to the smudged rim of his empty wineglass.

"I think I'm saying this now more for my own benefit than for yours," he said finally. "I used to think that our meetings were about me helping you, but more and more I realize they were about something else. Something I'm ashamed to admit."

I didn't say anything.

"I didn't think I was capable of surviving in a world that allowed for ghosts of that kind," he continued. "But now, after these last few years, I'm starting to think that these ghosts just might be real. I'm starting to think they might be necessary to our survival."

52. IKER

"HOW DO YOU SAY, 'TODAY IS TUESDAY'?" ANDREAS ASKS.
It's early again, before sunup, though the shorebirds have already started their morning racket. But I have been awake for an hour already, so when Andreas asks this question, I am quick to respond.

"*Gaur asteartea da*," I say. There has been talk over the last two weeks that they will be transferring two *etarras* to the Salto del Negro after their trial in Madrid last month. When the rumor began, Andreas asked that I teach him a few words of Euskera so that he could properly greet the celebrity prisoners. "But it's not Tuesday," I tell him.

"Wednesday?" he asks.

"Wednesday."

"Well then, how do you say, 'Today is Wednesday'?" he asks.

"*Gaur asteazkena da*," I say. "*Asteazkena.*"

He tries to repeat the word, but it comes out in a tumble, doubly mixed up with his Argentine accent.

"Good," I say. "By the time they arrive you'll be an honorary Basque."

I am also looking forward to next week, but not because of the arrival of the *etarras*. Next week is the second week of April, the beginning of the Holy Week even here in the Salto, where it doesn't seem like anything could be holy, even for a week. (I can't take credit for this line—it's one I've stolen from Fernando, a young mulatto from Cádiz who spent a few seasons at the Salto after he burned his mother's home to the ground.) But it's not the week of extra rations that we are given in the cafeteria that I look forward to, or the small box of candies that each prisoner receives from the children at Colegio Arenas, one of the local Catholic schools. I'm looking forward to the arrival of Nere and the boy.

In the photograph she included with her last letter, Nere is kneeling on the beach in Muriga. Behind her are the tall cliffs that lead up to the crumbling old bunkers where I had stayed the night with Asier and the Councilman. It is a clear summer day, the kind that turns the water in the bay a translucent green. The boy stands next to her, gripping her finger to steady his chubby legs. His feet leave small impressions in the sand, and his blue eyes look seriously at the camera. I know that the cameraman is Juan María, Nere's husband. But I don't feel the anger, or jealously, or hate that I might have felt a year ago. Instead, I experience something more like a sense of friendship. As if I am allowed to live his life, inhabit his body, for even the moment that it takes for the shutter to blink open.

THE LETTERS from the Councilman's wife had begun to arrive two months earlier. I didn't recognize the handwriting or the return address and assumed it was just more of the perverse "fan mail" I get from time to time from kids in the Basque Country, thanking me for my "contribution." When I finally realized who it was, my hands began to tremble.

They start very formally. *Dear Mr. Abarzuza.* She introduces herself as you might introduce yourself to a distant cousin, mentioning people we have in common. *I am the wife of José Antonio Torres. I think that we may have crossed paths once or twice in Muriga before your arrest.* The letter seems to stumble here, as if, after mentioning these small commonalities—our town, the death of her husband—she's run out of things to say.

She tells me that she has done some research on the computer, that she has seen photographs of the Salto del Negro and she hopes it isn't as bad as it seems. The Councilman's wife tells me that she thinks it is a shame how the Spanish government transferred Basque prisoners to the most remote prisons in Spain. *Your mother introduced herself after the last day of the trial, before the sentencing,* she writes. *It's obvious how much she cares for you.* The letter stumbles along like this for a while—half a page, maybe—and then something happens.

She begins to tell me about Elena, her daughter.

It's at this place that I hold my breath when I reread the letter even now, as if the words will have changed and she will use her daughter as a weapon against me. The daughter without a father. But instead of this attack that I'm waiting for, maybe hoping for, I find only this: *Elena has just started her first year in primaria at San Jorge. This was your school, wasn't it? The teacher tells me that she already has two boyfriends, and to watch out, she'll be trouble by the time she reaches secundaria.*

The letter seems to gather steam after this. She tells me about her childhood in Muriga and about how she fell in love with the Councilman. She tells me about the funeral, and the way that the Party in Bilbao tried to get her to speak out against political violence. In a single paragraph that takes up an entire sheet of paper she tells me about her in-laws in Sevilla, about a surgery she had the year before the trial, and about a wedding that she recently attended. And in none of it is the accusation that I wait and wait for.

I had already drafted several responses when two more letters from Mariana Zelaia arrived just four days later. Finally, I think, she's gathered the nerve to accuse me, to condemn. But the first letter is conversational, again, like she's just catching up with an old friend. She describes a dinner with her mother. She tells me that she is considering looking for a job, just a little something on the side. She wishes me well, tells me I should feel free to write her back.

She starts the second letter by apologizing for writing twice in a single day, but there is something she wants to tell me.

When Elena came home from school today she asked about José Antonio, she begins. *This isn't the first time she's asked about her father, of course. But it was different this afternoon. Today she didn't ask what happened to her father—we've talked about the fact that he died a long time ago—but instead she wanted to know* why *he was killed. She wants a reason for why her friends are all allowed fathers, but she is not.*

I can tell that she knows something more than she's letting on. You know how Muriga can be, and the kids at San Jorge talk (like you must have talked, right?). But she won't tell me what she's heard— she wants my version of it. I don't tell you all this because I want you to feel guilty. You'll have to take my word for it when I say that I feel just as guilty as you must. I told her that it was a good question, why her father had died, and that there probably wasn't just one answer. Can you think of a better response for her?

She was watching television when I began this letter tonight. When she asked what I was doing I told her that I was writing a letter to an old friend of her father's who lives in the Canarias. I hope this is all right with you.

I'm EAGER to show the letters—five in total now—to Nere when she comes with the boy next week—as eager as if they are something that I've created myself. I want to show her the news about the girl at San Jorge and tell her the story of the Councilman waiting for two months before he asked to come up to the apartment of his future wife. But this part—this last letter—I've decided to keep for myself.

"How do you introduce yourself?" Andreas asks from the bunk above. "How do I tell someone my name?"

I refold the first letter and slide it back into its envelope. I think back to the day that I followed the Councilman's wife to the beach, the week before Gorka Auzmendi's pistol jumped in his hand. How she was looking at me when she reached behind her thin neck to undo the swimsuit top.

"*Ni Iker Abarzuza naiz*," I said.

53. MARIANA

THE ABSENCES CAME IN WAVES IN THE YEARS AFTER JOSÉ
Antonio's death. First, the most tangible: José Antonio himself.

He'd only lived in the apartment half-time during the final year
of his life, when he was commuting to and from Bilbao, but after
his death his absence seemed disproportionately large. The weekend after the funeral I gathered all of his clothes and threw them
into the dumpster next to Etxeberria's hardware shop, as if I were
throwing my husband out of the house. But his side of the closet,
his dresser drawers, stayed empty. Each time I tried to fill them with
a shirt, a pair of underwear, one of his daughter's small jackets, they
stood awkwardly alone, out of place, trespassing, until finally I would
remove them and leave the space empty.

The second absence was the one left by Robert Duarte. News of
my affair with the American was the talk of Muriga for months after
José Antonio's killing. After Joni revealed the affair to Castro, the
rumor spread quickly from the police station, as I had feared it
would, traveling the usual circuits that gossip followed in town. The
last to hear, of course, is always the shamed woman herself.

"Are they talking about it?" I asked my mother, a few weeks after
José Antonio's murder. "About the American?"

"Yes," she said. She shrugged. "You know how it is, Mariana. They'll talk for a while, and then they'll forget about it."

But she was wrong about that; she knew, just as well as I did, that even if they stopped talking they wouldn't forget. That it was now a part of me, as much as the scar across my abdomen: adulterer. Betrayer of a dead husband. *Sinvergüenza.*

Just when interest in the affair began to fade later that year, it was revived again by reports from the trial of the three young men charged with the murder. Each day, the newspaper's headline reminded me—and Muriga—of my guilt.

It wasn't until a month or so after the trial that I began to miss the affair with Robert Duarte, the imagined life that I had allowed myself. I'd told myself from the outset that the American hadn't loved me, but I never truly believed that our afternoons together weren't significant to him as well. I'd told myself that he didn't love me, that he'd never leave Morgan Duarte, but I'd also allowed myself to imagine that one day he might. Robert was my escape, I realized— from José Antonio, and from Elena, and from Muriga—one I could never make myself.

I obsessed over the end of the affair even as I began to mourn my husband's death. I'd been told only that Robert had been held at the police station in Bilbao for two days after José Antonio's kidnapping—until the four young men had been arrested—and that both he and Morgan Duarte had left Muriga soon after.

It was the last I heard of Robert Duarte. In the weeks after he left I waited for a phone call, a letter—any sort of communication, but it never came. I couldn't make sense of it any more than I could make sense of José Antonio's death; one day, I had both a husband and a lover. The next, I had neither.

THE NEXT absence was the hardest to admit. Eventually, I realized how much I missed Joni Garrett, despite his betrayal. He was the closest thing to a friend I'd had in a long while, and he'd become almost a grandfather to Elena. I had trusted him completely. With my friendship, with my daughter. With secrets I could barely admit to myself.

After the chaos surrounding José Antonio's death began to settle—after Robert Duarte disappeared back to the United States and after the four young men were sent off to prisons far away from Muriga—I was confronted with long empty spaces each afternoon that had previously been occupied by Joni. I wandered the streets with Elena, stopping alone for coffee or aimlessly walking the aisles of the Todo Todo.

It was in these empty midday hours that I understood exactly how much I had lost the moment José Antonio was pulled into that car.

I FOUND myself fixating on Elena to fill these empty spaces. I began to take her everywhere with me. Not just to the grocery store or to the hair salon but to the insurance agent for a meeting to discuss the life insurance policy José Antonio had taken out when Elena was born. To doctor's appointments in Bilbao, where the nephrologist who performed my transplant discussed hormone levels and dietary restrictions and life expectancies for transplanted organ recipients. To the funeral home, where I was informed that the Party office in Bilbao had paid for my husband's burial through member contributions. Elena was with me at all of these places.

I spoke to her as I would speak to an adult, a peer. In the late hours of the night as she slept in front of the blinking television set, I would tell her about the way her father used to complain about Muriga, about her mother's afternoon hike to the *refugio* at Aizkorri with her friend Morgan Duarte, about the three men that had come to me in a dream the night her father was kidnapped.

It wasn't until this last year, six years after José Antonio's kidnapping, that I discovered the final absence, which had in fact preceded the other two: the loss of my terrorist kidney when Joni

Garrett revealed the identity of my organ donor. Not Iñaki Libano, the young man with the crooked nose who had killed a Spanish intelligence officer in Madrid in 1995. Not the militant nationalist who had been shot to death in his sister's apartment in Mondragón but, rather, a fourteen-year-old boy who had been killed in a senseless accident.

The next morning after waking to this realization, I registered Elena at San Jorge, where several of the women from my mother's *mus* group had grandchildren attending. When I returned home without her—the first time since her father's death—I set a pot of coffee on the stove and began to draft a letter to the Abarzuza boy.

54. JONI

WITH THE BOMBING OF THE TRAINS IN ATOCHA YESTERDAY morning, Muriga has again begun its old rituals of self-preservation. Just as it turned on the Abarzuza boy in the weeks after José Antonio's murder six years ago—dehumanizing him, scrambling to manufacture evidence that he wasn't one of us, that he was an outsider all along—the town has changed its dialogue to set itself apart from the Basque terrorists that are purported to have detonated the explosives that tore apart four trains in Madrid. In the bars last night, I listened to Aznar's speech and watched Estefana Torretxe and Santi Etxeverria nodding in agreement as he condemned the Basque independence movement. They spoke of the unidentified terrorists as "monstrous," the bombing as "cowardly" or "shameless." They spoke as if it were impossible to consider that this monstrous act might have been carried out by their sons, their nieces, their neighbors. Anything to distance themselves.

The reports began to come in this afternoon, just ahead of the general elections in two days. The Basque news anchors are now happily reporting that the attacks in Atocha are most likely the work of al-Qaeda in northern Africa, that four suspects have already been identified. I've tried to go about my day as usual, though even the students in my ninth-year English class have been whispering about them. After the final class of the day, I sequester myself in the small office that has been my second home for fifty years. A half hour later, there is a familiar knock on the pebbled glass of my office door, and then Juantxo's toadlike face peeks anxiously into view.

"You've heard?" he asks.

"No," I say, looking up from a stack of student essays about their approaching Easter vacations. "About the bombings?"

"Yes," he says eagerly. "They've decided that it was the Arabs—that the ETA was not involved."

I nod, not knowing what to say. Juantxo stands awkwardly in the open doorway, shifting his weight from one foot to the other.

"This is wonderful news, isn't it?" he says.

I guess that it is, though I think of the photographs I'd seen in the paper this morning, of the trains ripped open from the inside and of the woman's shoe scattered in among the debris on the train platform, and wonder how anything about this could be considered wonderful news.

"We're going out for a drink," he said. "Lucinda and a couple of the secretaries. You'll come?"

"No," I say, and I tap a finger on the pile of papers on my desk. "Not tonight."

"Sure," he says, "of course," and then he is gone.

When I close the door to my office an hour later, the sun has just begun to dip over the foothills of the Pyrenees to the west. I start toward the entryway, past the old broom closet that had been the American Robert Duarte's office in the year of José Antonio's death. The office is empty, as it has been since the day José Antonio's body was recovered.

In a way I envied his ability to simply abandon Muriga. Morgan had left as soon as she had learned why her husband was taken into questioning by the police; while Robert was trying to deny the affair to Detective Castro at the Ertzaintza headquarters, she was packing three suitcases. She drove the Renault to the airport in Biarritz and was back at her parents' house in Boise by the time Robert was let out of custody.

I visited the American the day before he was to leave. The apartment, which had never been tidy, now looked as if it had been ransacked—kitchen drawers were flung open, dishcloths and silverware spilling from their edges.

"So you're leaving," I said. "Just like that?"

Robert looked at me incredulously. He was folding winter jackets and stuffing them into the bottom of a cardboard box. For the first time he looked lost, bewildered.

"As opposed to what?" he said, in a way that seemed to hope I might have another answer for him.

"To staying, I suppose."

"She's my *wife*, Joni," he said. "Or at least she was, anyway. I have to follow her. You of all people must understand that."

THE AMERICAN continued filling the cardboard box, unpinning the charcoal sketches that Morgan had left tacked to the wall of the living room, folding them hastily and stacking them on top of the winter jackets.

"Do you think I might keep this one?" I said. It was a roughly sketched portrait of a young girl, about three. She had dark curls that fell over her eyes, and in her hand she held a melting ice cream bar.

"It's Mariana's daughter, you know," he said awkwardly.

"Yes, I know. Her name is Elena."

"Anyway, sure. You can have it."

I unpinned the paper from the wall, then carefully folded the portrait lengthwise and slid it into my briefcase.

"Do you think you can get her back?" I asked.

"Morgan? I don't know," he said, shaking his head. "I think so, but I don't know."

He paused for a moment, stood up from the box he had been packing as if he just now fully realized that I was in the room with him.

"And what about you, Joni?" he said. "Why are you staying here? Juantxo is going to replace you the next chance he gets."

I looked down at my empty hands. They were pale and thin and broken down. In the brief time that I had known him, I had secretly admired the Euskaldun—his ability to drop in and be so accepted, then to just as easily leave it behind.

"It's my home, I think. All my old ghosts are still here with me, keeping me company. They'll never believe that," I said, gesturing out the window toward the street below. "They'll never believe that but it's the truth."

THE HALLS of the old fortress are empty now—it's my favorite time to be in San Jorge. I lock the heavy exterior door behind me, but instead of walking along the sidewalk that leads out to the faculty parking lot I follow one of the small paths the children have worn into the grass, dropping down into the empty moat that surrounds the ramparts of the fortress. I circle around the north side to where the gymnasium door has been cut into the thick limestone walls. The area around the doorway is littered with broken sunflower shells and snubbed-out cigarette butts, the wall scratched over with nationalist slogans. I retrieve a plastic lighter wedged between two blocks in the fortress wall, flick it a few times to warm my fingertips in its flame, and then return it to its hiding place. I've been noticing the group that huddles here during recesses. They're a tough bunch, friends since *primaria* that are often being reprimanded for ditching class or for drinking beers in the lavatories, and I wonder if this lighter will be used to light cigarettes or to ignite bottles filled with gasoline.

I can remember Iker sitting in this same place with the Díaz boy in the autumn before José Antonio's death. It is hard to recall them as they existed in that empty doorway, in the blue oxfords of the San Jorge uniform, laughing and conspiring as all young men do. Instead, it's easier to remember them as Muriga does: as the flat, uncomprehending faces that were shown over and over on the news during their trial. I tap a cigarette from the pack and sit down on the cold stone of the threshold. There is still a bite to the spring air, but the sky is unnaturally clear.

I remember the story Nerea told me that afternoon as we lay in bed in the apartment above Martín's grocery store, about hearing her father taken out this same door in 1937, about how the Falangist captain had fired a shot through her father's forehead without warning, without ceremony.

I remember the saying I heard once, how the Basque Country's history can be divided in half by the Civil War, and it occurs to me that perhaps that bullet has never stopped moving through our town. That it is still traveling through Muriga, striking one of us down every now and again.

Inevitably, I think about Nerea and our girl. I come back to the picture in the investigator's report, of the police officer holding a tape measure out from the edge of the road to the place where the Peugeot had come to rest in the rocks at the sea's edge. *Thirty-eight meters*, it had read.

I smoke the cigarette down to the filter and watch the lights begin to appear below as the sky darkens. In between drags my lips move silently, and it isn't until I have finished the cigarette that I realize the word that they have been saying.

Txirimiri, they say.

Tsk . . . tsk . . . she had said, touching her lips to my fingertips so I could feel how little air escaped her mouth. The sound of a drop of water on a hot skillet, of a cup sliding from a saucer. *Tsk. Tsk.*

ACKNOWLEDGMENTS

This book is the product of much hard work by many people. I particularly would like to express my appreciation to the following:

To my agent, Katherine Fausset, as well as Stuart Waterman and the rest of the good folks at Curtis Brown, Ltd. Special thanks also belong to my editor, Sarah Bowlin, whose patience and vision taught me so much about writing and editing, and to the staff at Holt.

Thank you to the friends who saw and read early chapters and drafts, and who I hope will see their contributions in this book. Ben Rogers, Curtis Vickers, Bill Riley, Alex Streiff, Clayton Clark, Daniel Carter, Molly Patterson, Adam Carter, David Torch, Matt Herz, and website designer extraordinaire Ilsa Brink.

This book would not exist if I had never met my friend and mentor Christopher Coake at the University of Nevada, Reno.

This book was born from workshops at the Ohio State University, and I would like to thank the following people for their guidance and friendship: Michelle Herman, Erin McGraw and Andrew Hudgins, Lee K. Abbott, Lee Martin.

Thanks to my sparring partner, Derek Palacio, who always

pushed and believed in this book, and regularly hit me upside the head. And, of course, to Claire Vaye Watkins, Nevada royalty.

I hope this book accurately reflects the expertise, wisdom, and patience afforded me by Dr. William Douglass and Asun Garikano, as well as Zoe Bray with the Center for Basque Studies at the University of Nevada, Reno, who gave vital feedback on later drafts and were especially helpful with the Euskera that appears in this book.

Thanks to Professor Geoffrey Bennett of the University of the Notre Dame London Law Programme and to the Kellogg Institute for International Studies.

To the attorneys and staff of the Washoe County Public Defender's and Alternate Public Defender's Offices, in particular Joe Goodnight, Tobin Fuss, and Sean Sullivan, for showing me that a good lawyer is most often a good man.

Thanks to my friends in the Basque Country, especially Katrin Diaz and Ager Insunza, Nerea Sorauren and Gorčin Stanojlović, Alain Gonfaus, Dani and Christine Rueda, Pedro Ibarra and Carmen Oriol, Gregorio Monreal, and Bernardo Atxaga.

A special thanks to Raija Bushnell, who not only put up with me through all of this, but did so with kindness, patience, and encouragement.

And finally, to my family, who are in every page: Carmelo Urza, Monique Laxalt, and Alexandra Urza; Kris Laxalt, Don Nomura, Amy Solaro, Kevin Nomura; Bruce Laxalt and Pam Sutton; Henry and Conchita Urza; Kristi Fons and Susan Estes. My grandparents Robert and Joyce Laxalt, Maria Luisa Larrauri Goicoechea, and Anastasio Urzaa Aboitiz.

GABRIEL URZA received his MFA from The Ohio State University. His family is from the Basque region of Spain, where he has lived. He is a grant recipient from the Kellogg Institute for International Studies and his short fiction and essays have been published in *River Teeth*, *Hobart*, *Erlea*, *The Kenyon Review*, *West Branch*, *Slate*, and other publications. He also has a degree in law from the University of Notre Dame and has spent several years as a public defender in Reno, Nevada.